Birds of Passage

Anthology

Copyright © 2015 EdgyChristianFiction.com

All rights reserved.

ISBN-10: 0-9763126-5-4
ISBN-13: 978-0-9763126-5-9

Dedication

This book is dedicated to those living in poverty and to those who work tirelessly to help others overcome poverty's grip.

BIRDS OF PASSAGE

Table of Contents

Dedication iii

Table of Contents v

Foreword..i

A Psalm for Morning –Fr. Steve Kluge O.F.M 3

A Reflection - Fr. David McBriar, OFM 5

Gumdrop Alley - Kim Bond 9

The Light - Ken Kuhlken 17

My Big Faith Marriage - Helena Kamerra.....................23

Hell of an Opportunity - John M.Shaver.......................39

Little Black Dress - Wendy Stenzel Oleston 57

The Pure in Heart - Peggy Payne 73

Garment of Praise - Danyele Read 89

According to John - Jeff Hendricks 103

A Psalm for Mid-Day – Fr. Steve Kluge O.F.M. 113

He Knew - Kristine Kohut 115

It's About Choices – R.S. Crow 123

Until He Was Gone - Kelsey Gillespy 133

Safe Passage – Jarrod L. Edge 141

April and Mr. Grim - Parker J. Cole.............................159

Letters From Damascus - Greg M. Dodd 173

The Children Who Lay Down – Deb Palmer....................183

Naomi – Bobbie Ann Cole 193

Ordination Day – Diogenes Ruiz 205

A Psalm for Evening –Fr. Steve Kluge O.F.M. 221

Acknowledgements 223

About the Authors...225

Foreword

Passage Home appreciates the stories written in this Anthology in support of our work to help break the cycle for those who are homeless and living in poverty. When we began in 1991, we shared a vision and a mission that was built on the Matthew 25:35-40 scripture. We hope that those who have worked alongside us would say that we are achieving our purpose. We would also like to say "thank you" to all those who have helped along this journey. And to those whose lives have been touched, thank you for the courage and humility to allow us to help. With and through Passage Home, many lives have changed.

Jeanne Tedrow – Chief Executive Office, Passage Home

Matthew 25:35-40New International Version (NIV)
35 For I was hungry and you gave me something to eat, I was thirsty and you gave me something to drink, I was a stranger and you invited me in, 36 I needed clothes and you clothed me, I was sick and you looked after me, I was in prison and you came to visit me.'
37 "Then the righteous will answer him, 'Lord, when did we see you hungry and feed you, or thirsty and give you something to drink? 38 When did we see you a stranger and invite you in, or needing clothes and clothe you? 39 When did we see you sick or in prison and go to visit you?'
40 "The King will reply, 'Truly I tell you, whatever you did for one of the least of these brothers and sisters of mine, you did for me.'

BIRDS OF PASSAGE

A Psalm for Morning *–Fr. Steve Kluge O.F.M*

Let my first thoughts be of thanks O Lord,
For You have led me safely through the night.
Let my next thoughts be of thanks O Lord,
For all You will give me throughout this day.
Let my speech be salted with thanks O Lord,
As I recognize Your abiding presence within all.
Let my actions be signs of thanks O Lord,
As without words I preach Your presence.
Let my last thoughts be of thanks O Lord,
And that will be enough.

A Reflection - *Fr. David McBriar, OFM*

Let me begin this reflection with a legend from "The Little Flowers of Saint Francis of Assisi." It's the legend of *"How St. Francis taught the people of Gubbio to feed their wolf."* It is a strangely humorous story with layer upon layer of meaning. In a nutshell, the people of a little Italian town named Gubbio have a problem. The bloody remains of some of their townsfolk start showing up on the streets of their beautiful city when people awake in the morning. Since the people of Gubbio are very proud people, they are convinced that a stranger passing through must be responsible for the terrible crime. Nevertheless, they begin to lock their doors at night. When more deaths follow, the same denial: no one in Gubbio could be responsible for such a thing. And then, someone sees a wolf wandering the streets of Gubbio one night after everyone has retired; and the people of Gubbio realize that there is a wolf living in the dark woods on one side of Gubbio.

Of course, this could not be their wolf; because they never asked this wolf to come to Gubbio. Immediately, they begin to find ways to dispatch this wolf. After a number of futile attempts, the people get desperate enough to approach the holy man of Assisi who has a reputation for being able "to talk to animals". St. Francis "speaks" to the wolf and gives the people what appears to be some strange and, not entirely, welcome advice. He tells the people of Gubbio that they must "feed" their wolf. At the first, the people are not impressed with this suggestion and begin to wonder why they ever approached the holy man in the first place. And, then, something miraculous happens. Bit by bit, people begin to leave food out for the wolf as he prowls the streets of Gubbio. The violent deaths cease and it is not long before every man, woman and child has learned how to "feed their wolf." As a result, the people of Gubbio are transformed. They become more easy-going, less arrogant human beings.

Is this just a sweet legend that makes you smile, made more for Disney than for real life? Or is the story a life mirroring parable? Are the people of Gubbio haughty folk who blame their troubles on strangers, refusing to acknowledge that the problem is theirs? Is the wolf their way of life? Does everyone have a hungry wolf inside? What's yours? What needs to be changed, healed, and tamed in your life? What's ours? What needs to be healed in our nation's life? What's its wolf? What about your community? Your city? Is the invitation of St. Francis the invitation to everyone with a wolf inside? Is his invitation to first of all acknowledge what you fear? Is this the way that you come to a new and healthier understanding of yourself, of your country, of your church, of your community? When you acknowledge your enemy, even feed him or her is it then that you tame the enemy?

Today war is raging in Afghanistan, Iraq, Pakistan, Lebanon, Israel, and the Occupied Territories. There continues to be killing in the Congo and in the Sudan. The United States and Europe are on heightened alert for a terrorist attack. We are living in a society which believes that our safety can only be achieved through domination, or others will seek to dominate us first. The "world" is not at peace. Moreover, on the home front our cities continue to be torn by racial and economic discrimination. Is a living wage possible? Is health care for all possible? When will be have a just immigration policy? These are human issues and as such they claim our individual and our communal response. If we are to fulfill our vocation as believers, as faith filled people, our churches and synagogues and mosques must ask: "What does the city need? How can we help?" We can't be paralyzed by the magnitude of the task. One example of response is given by Tikkun. Tikkun means "reconciliation." The Tikkun community of Christians, Jews and Muslims ask, "Where is our strategy of generosity? Don't people have an enormous capacity for goodness and generosity? Can't we recognize the humanity of the other? Can't we repent and atone for the long history of insensitivity and cruelty to the other side?" What has proved unrealistic time and again – whether we are talking about the U.S. policy in Afghanistan and Iraq, or Israel and Arab policies in the Middle East – is the fantasy that one more war will put an end to wars. The path to peace must be a path of peace. This is the belief, the hope, the challenge of Tikkun. Our well-being depends on the well-being of everyone else. This is not only the peace for which Jesus prayed, it is at the same time the path to that peace. There is within every man and woman the power for good. We Christians call this the Holy Spirit. This Spirit was poured out upon us at the creation of the world when the Creator breathed into us a soul, making us in the very image of the Creator. Jesus calls this "breath of God-life" the Holy Spirit. It is given to us, each of us and all of us. The Holy Spirit, the Spirit of Jesus, is our Consoler, our Advocate for peace. The world does not give us this peace, if by the "world" we mean the spirit of domination and power, the spirit of aggression and control.

Are we the new people of Gubbio, haughty folk who blame our troubles on strangers, refusing to acknowledge that the problem is ours? Has the wolf become our way of life? What needs to be changed, healed, and tamed in our life? In our nation's life? In our congregation's life? Is the invitation of St. Francis the invitation to everyone with a wolf inside? Is his invitation to first of all acknowledge what it is we fear? Is this the beginning of claiming that Holy Spirit which is Jesus' spirit of peace and reconciliation?

Gumdrop Alley - *Kim Bond*

We lived on the east side of Peru. Mother would send me to the market on account of her sick leg. I went frequently and became friendly with a man named Pedunk. He seemed genuinely interested in me—asking all kinds of questions. Later, I understood he was only calculating how much I would be missed, if my family would search for me, and with whom he must contend if he was caught.

I guess my answers made me a good kidnapping candidate. He offered me a piece of gum; I do not remember much after that. When I awoke, my body was being lifted by unfamiliar arms from an old pickup truck

to a hut in Gumdrop Alley. I never knew the exact location. I only knew it was where a mountain curved into a slope. We were hidden away in thatched huts shaped like gumdrops.

Pedunk and the Missus kept a close eye on us from the windows of their stone house. The Missus concerned herself with our cleanliness, food, and clothing. At times, I got the impression she viewed the twelve of us girls as her children in some twisted way. Pedunk considered only our behavior toward the clients to be of any weighty significance.

The clients were part of an underground ring. Men from all over Peru came to see us. They saw us greet them at the doorway with long black hair cascaded over one shoulder. They saw us remove bright colored skirts and lay down with them on mattresses.

The guard sat in a chair outside of Pedunk's home day and night. The machine gun's strap was draped around his neck, his hand always on the trigger. He paid little attention to us. He was paid to watch over the clients—not to protect us girls. They did not fear us leaving either. We were too scared to flee, and the village was too isolated for us to travel to any town on foot.

All the girls lined up every morning to be inspected by his wife. We held out our hands for inspection—palms down. The Missus walked down the line, scrunching her freckled nose now and then. At the end, she turned around. We flipped our hands in unison—palms up. She inspected them again. If we had clean hands and nails, she gave us a small ration of rice and fruit, usually a pawpaw. If a girl's hands appeared dirty to her, she denied that girl's daily food ration. She approved my hands daily—almost smiling as she handed me the food.

That is every day until March. It started when I laid in bed half asleep and heard the crunching of leaves underfoot. I assumed one of Pedunk's clients had come to receive my service, but it was Pedunk himself. His familiar silhouette stood in my doorway, lit up by the moon like a ghost.

At first, I felt relieved to see him. Maybe he wanted to ask me to fetch an extra jar of water from the well by the road because Mara was sick again. But the way he leaned against the wall and stared for so long gave me an uneasy feeling. He said nothing as he began unbuckling his belt and unbuttoning his jeans.

I treated him as I would any client, laying still and spacing out. My thoughts drifted away from my usual hope of returning home and turned to a new, more desperate hope: one of the clients might haggle with Pedunk to take me away and make me his wife. Together, we would have children, and I would never let them out of my sight. Ever. I envisioned this so fully that I only snapped back to reality as Pedunk walked out the doorway of my hut.

The following morning, I scrubbed my hands same as always. However, the Missus shook her head as she walked past for inspection. As she walked past the second time (palms up), she smacked them down and said, "Put those filthy things away. No food today."

It was then I realized the girls who failed inspection in the past did not fail because their hands were literally dirty. And I had not passed inspection prior to this moment because I scrubbed my hands so adequately. All this time, she had been punishing us for Pedunk's wandering.

Still, her cruelty was kindness compared to that of Pedunk's behavior, especially in the company of his guard. Together, the two men behaved inhumane. I discovered just how humane the following night.

I laid in bed and listened to my stomach growl after not having eaten all day. I clutched the handmade doll I had stitched together. Salwa's face was shaped like a pancake with black thread stitched in the shape of X's for the eyes, and the shape of a minus sign for a nose, and a smiling mouth. She was made of old material—dull brown coffee color for the face and a floral print for her undersized torso, floppy arms, and understuffed legs. I had been careful to stitch a belly button right where a belly button would go. It made her more lifelike. I needed Salwa to be lifelike and sweet. The girls seemed too coarse for my liking, too callous for a best friend anyway.

Mara's hut was beside mine, so I heard everything perfectly. Pedunk yelled something about how long she had known she was pregnant and kept it secret. I considered how well she had hidden it under baggy dresses because I never noticed. Pedunk said his customer requested a new girl since he had accidentally chosen the pregnant one.

I hugged Salwa tighter and slid further under my cover as the first smack echoed in my ears. Pedunk demanded to see her belly.

"Oh man, oh man. What have you done? Six months. You have to be six months pregnant, Mara. I might have been able to fix this for you. I could have made it disappear painlessly, but now...."

The next sound was more thuddish like a punch. Though my whole body trembled, I commanded myself to get out of bed. I stood there wanting to go next door and defend Mara but either out of cowardice or honest prediction, I convinced myself I would only make things worse for her.

Pedunk's voice started again. "The baby's too strong now to go easily. Might as well shoot her."

Another voice cackled. That is when I realized the guard

was in there with them. I imagined him taking aim at that moment. I jumped back in bed and covered my head completely with blankets. Under there, Salwa and I hid and listened to Mara try to explain.

"I just wanted to keep my baby. I want someone for my very own, someone to love. You do not understand how it is to feel the baby grow inside you."

Afterwards I heard a loud crack as if the gun had slammed against her head or something else. I did not hear Mara's voice any more that night.

For the next two weeks, I thought she was dead. Then one morning Mara appeared at lineup. The Missus said her hands looked extra clean and gave her more food than usual.

That is when we heard a baby's cries from Pedunk's house. The Missus set down the pail of rice and rushed away.

I leaned forward in line and strained to see Mara's face, about three girls down. Her face was stone. She dropped her jar of rice on the dirt and walked back toward her hut. I chased after her, careful not to spill one grain of my own rice. By the time I reached her doorway, her face was buried in her mattress. She sobbed without pride; her tears absorbed in her blanket.

I returned to my hut next door and set down the rice. Salwa smiled from where she sat in the middle of my mattress. I wrapped my two hands around her torso and lifted her up to my face. I stared into her little X'd eyes.

"I am sorry, my dear friend, but it is time we part ways. I do love you. It is just Mara needs you more right now."

Dragging her by the hand, I marched over to Mara's hut. The sobbing mound did not acknowledge my presence. I placed Salwa by Mara's arm. At that, Mara seemed to have been startled. She grabbed my arm and pulled me close. She embraced me though my arms hung lifelessly at my sides.

In my soul, I knew I could never understand what she had gone through. A chasm of maturity had been formed in such a short period of time. She had become a mother and become childless all in one day. I had nothing to offer her—no advice or words of comfort. No bridge ever built could close the gap between us at that moment in time.

Mara did not seem to notice the chasm. I doubt it mattered

who I was, only that I was a living being— warm and near. She eventually stopped squeezing me so tightly and simply let go. She looked down at Salwa, who was still laying on her mattress, then back at me again. "Thank you." After that, she laid on her mattress, face first as she had been when I entered, except now she wrapped one arm around Salwa.

I backed out of her doorway and into the morning light, once again hearing the baby fuss. My hut seemed the right place for me to go even though Salwa would not be waiting on the mattress for me.

I retrieved my hidden sewing kit from a stack of clothes. With the sewing shears, I cut a shirt into the size of a pancake head. The rest of the afternoon, I threw my focus into making a new Salwa, a better Salwa—a Ximena.

After that day, we saw less and less of the Missus and of Pedunk. The guard was there, same as always, and the clients came and went as usual.

That was until an unusual client entered my hut. He looked like the medical missionaries I used to see in the marketplace. He spoke better Spanish though. His first words were, "Do you like it here?"

I pondered the question as I unbuttoned my shirt. It seemed an absurd question. He placed his hand on mine to prevent me from unbuttoning my shirt.

I dropped my hands to my sides. "It is alright." I did not want to say the wrong thing.

"What if I told you that you could be free?"

My heart skipped a beat. I thought, "Could it be my dream come true? Has this man come to buy me, rescue me, and marry me?" I said aloud, "Oh yes, I want to be free!" I wrapped my arms around him as he stood like a statue. The moment had a strange resemblance to the embrace I endured from Mara. The man's seriousness quieted my heart about the hope of becoming his bride.

I scratched my arm. "Are you a medical missionary?"

The man sat on the mattress. "I am a missionary of Jesus Christ."

Suddenly, it occurred to me he was not speaking about a literal freedom from Gumdrop Alley but a spiritual freedom from something or other.

"Oh." I could think of nothing more to say, so we sat in an uncomfortable silence for a few moments.

"So why do they call this Gumdrop Alley?" I inhaled deeply, much relieved to discuss something definite. "I think it started with the huts shaped like gumdrops."

The man leaned forward and put the tips of his fingers together as though he pondered his whole life's burdens in that one instant.

"Look, the man who took my money to sleep with you..."

"Pedunk."

"Yes, Pedunk. He says I have thirty minutes with you. We need to get to business."

"Right," I said, unbuttoning my shirt again.

"No, not that kind of business." This time he put his fingertips on his forehead and then through his full head of hair. "I mean getting you out of here. Today is the fifth of April. On the twentieth, I will have a car waiting at the road alongside the well. Can you be there just after dark?"

My heart started beating right out of my chest. "I cannot. The guard..."

"We will take care of the guard. Will you be there?"

"We? We who?" I felt my eyes squinting.

Everything seemed so confusing all of a sudden.

"I know people that can help us. First, I want to talk to some more of the girls. You might see me around in the next few nights. Just act natural. Most of all, be there." He stood and walked out, leaving me with so many unanswered questions and the doubt I could make it outside of Gumdrop Alley alive.

Time moved slowly until the twentieth of April, but it arrived nonetheless. I stood in my doorway scanning the landscape. Just as the man had said, the guard was not in his normal spot.

Just then, Pedunk came around the side of my hut. "Where are you goin'?" He smelled of liquor and pushed me back in the hut into my stack of clothes. My heart hammered in my chest so wildly, I wondered if he could see it beating through my shirt.

Still looking into his eyes, I reached my hand under the clothing stack behind me to feel for my sewing supplies. I felt a needle, a spool of thread, and shears! I pulled the shears out of the pile. I jumped to my feet. In one swift movement, I jabbed him in the left eye with the scissors.

Pedunk pulled out the scissors from his eye and covered it with his hands. As I backed out of the hut, I said, "When a girl has hope in her heart, she has already been set free. Nothing can stop someone who is free!" I burst into a sprint to the well. I heard others around me, but I did not look back. One of the girls darted past me.

When we arrived at the well, there was five of us. Mara was not one of them. I thought, "Why didn't she come? Of all people, she must hate Pedunk the most. The baby! She wants to see her baby grow up."

A large black car, larger than any I had ever seen, coasted slowly up the road without any lights on. The back door opened. Two girls crawled inside. I was the third. As I stepped inside, I glanced at the well. I had to pause when I saw Mara starting over the hill.

"Wait, here she comes. Mara," I whispered.

Just then, I saw she was not alone. First, I saw Pedunk's short figure through the darkness, and then the guard's huge frame. Mara stopped and pointed in our direction.

The girl behind shoved me in the car and dove in next to me. Shots rang out. The fifth girl cried out and fell. We reached out and dragged her in the car and slammed the door shut as the car sped off.

In the backseat was the man who visited my hut. "Are you alright?" he asked the girl bleeding from her leg. She made no reply.

"You are safe now. This limousine is bulletproof." Turning his eyes to me, he said, "I told you I know people." He smiled contented with himself and began dressing her with supplies from the car's compartment.

It seemed so strange that a ride with a stranger was how I got in this mess to begin with. My heart sank as I allowed skeptical thoughts to entertain my mind. I thought, "What if he is only kidnapping us to take us to his own Gumdrop Alley? Or worse."

"Man of Jesus Christ, where are you taking us?"

The man continued to bandage the wound with a certain gentleness that suppressed my apprehension about the future.

"There is a safe house for victims of sex trafficking. They will give you a bed and hot food until you feel ready to return to your families."

I wondered if my family would recognize me. I felt like a different person than the girl who was kidnapped a year ago. I relaxed in the velvety soft seat and closed my eyes until thick warm tears welled up in them.

The man of Jesus Christ probably assumed they were tears of joy. I might have cried from joy if my heart allowed it, but the feeling seemed too strange and unnatural. Honestly, I cried from sorrow because I realized I had forgotten Ximena—my sweet half-made doll.

Gumdrop Alley is based on true-life rescues by the International Crisis Aid organization. Learn more at www.crisisaid.org.

The Light - *Ken Kuhlken*

Skip and I worked at a coffee shop a dozen miles northeast of where the Pacific meets the Mexican border.

The waitresses called us boys, though we considered ourselves men, since we had lately returned from some months rambling around. Before the journey, we tried out college. One semester convinced us it wasn't the place to learn who we wanted to be. So we hitchhiked and found brief jobs in New Orleans and Chicago. As summer neared, in Fort Lauderdale, we bought an old Chevy and drove it home, coast to coast.

At the coffee shop, Skip bussed and I washed dishes. On breaks we consorted with the waitresses. Tina, a truck stop veteran, had eyes for Skip, though she was twice his age. She was toying with his hair when sweet Heidi came in and gasped. She fetched a Bible from her cubby and read aloud, "Her lips drip honey, but in the end she is a bitter *fruit*. Her steps lead straight to the *grave*."

Tina laughed and sat in the chair between Skip and me. She arched her back so her breasts rose up. "Heidi, last night I took your advice. I said, 'God, help me out here. Don't let temptation lure me down to the Inn Spot again.'"

Heidi beamed, and leaned across the table. "You stayed home? Honest, you stayed home?"

"Well, I stayed home all right, but that's not the whole story. You see, the devil came for me."

"No." Heidi covered her face with both hands and peeked out.

"Yes ma'am. He came right up and knocked on my door."

"But you didn't let him in?"

"Well, I wasn't going to, but one look at that man, and he got me in his spell. I hardly remember what happened. All I can tell you is, when I woke up in his arms this morning, I jumped out of his clutches and ran straight to here. You want to go home with me after the shift? If he's still hanging around, maybe you can chase him off."

By now, Heidi was shaking her head and wringing her hands. Her eyes had misted over. She was about as bright as the girls in blonde jokes. But she was a darling, generous and kind. So when she invited us to a Billy Graham crusade, to keep from disappointing her, I said "Why not?"

We didn't plan to attend, only to read a newspaper account and tell Heidi we'd gone and found plenty to think about. But by the evening of the crusade, something like conscience bit us. Besides, we reasoned, we had dropped out of college to go rambling and experience the real world, and here was another experience.

The crusade was at a downtown football stadium. It seated about 20,000. Since we were among the last to straggle in, we climbed to the top. From our seats, by glancing over our shoulders, we saw the harbor crowded with battleships and carriers. In front of us sat a trio of babes, probably still in high school. They looked wholesome, with cheeks made rosy from the chill and breeze, and curls that adorned their tender necks and shoulders.

Way down on the stage stood three big men. Even from afar, they looked like giants. The one in the middle gave announcements in a deep and strong yet cordial voice. He introduced the man on the right, who stepped to the mike and silenced the crowd with a hymn.

Billy Graham followed and began to speak with such gentle authority, it stopped my eyes from wandering to the neck of the babe with auburn curls.

Mister Graham quoted from a Bible prophet. "Learn to do well," he commanded. "Relieve the oppressed and the fatherless, plead for the widow. Come now and let us reason together. Though our sins are as scarlet, they can be as white as snow. If only we're willing and obedient, we can reap and share the good of the land."

He warned us that the hydrogen bomb had cast its shadowy

threat of annihilation over the whole earth. Sooner than we imagined, the basic power of the universe would be given into the hands of madmen. Then, how could our planet avoid destruction?

While he told us about a Chicago judge who claimed our generation's teenaged criminals made Al Capone's gang look like a Sunday school class, a flutter of auburn hair caught my eye. I looked down and noticed goose bumps on the babe's shoulders.

Mister Graham told us that, after traveling the world and witnessing racial tensions rising all around, he felt evermore certain that the only solution was at the foot of the cross. The foot of the cross, he said, was the only place where in every sense all of us are equals.

"We're all sinners," he said, "and we're sinners by choice. We choose to break God's moral laws. We become drunkards or fornicators, selfish, consumed with pride and prejudice and intolerance. But the sinful heart can't find happiness."

And God wants his creatures to get happy, he assured us, which is why Christ said we must be born again so he could give us new moral natures, new affections, new objectives, and new directions.

What planted the hook in me was: according to Billy Graham, when you make your decision for Christ, you do it for the sake of the nation. Without God, any nation will perish. And a nation is only as strong as its people. A better world requires better people. Christ can make us into those people.

Mister Graham had given me the answer. Now I knew who I wanted to be. So when he asked for all who would surrender to Christ to come to the altar, I stood and followed the auburn haired babe.

About halfway down, I heard Skip behind me. He said, "Are we sure about this?"

I didn't answer, only kept descending. Dark had fallen. Hundreds of us crowded in front of the portable stage somewhere around the goal line. I suspected the others, like me, wanted to get near Mister Graham and his companions, for comfort and to borrow some of their power.

The singing giant led a few thousand folks in a hymn. "Softly and tenderly Jesus is calling, calling oh sinner come home, come home, come home, ye who are weary come home…"

I mumbled the surrender words I heard someone else say, and waited. Skip had stayed beside me. He mumbled too. I looked for the girl with auburn hair and wondered if she had bolted, too proud or afraid to surrender.

Then a kid tapped me on the shoulder. I tapped Skip and we followed the kid. He looked about sixteen. His haircut might've come from a Marine base. He wore glasses and a practiced smile.

He passed out a Bible tract, a directory of churches, and a card with his name and phone number. I thought, Call you for what? This kid, I believed, had spent more time in church than outside. He hadn't gotten beat up in Chicago for no reason, or escaped from thugs who invited him to join a Miami gang of smugglers. He wasn't yet about to get drafted and sent to war. Most of all, he wasn't Billy Graham.

Besides, I glanced to the right of the kid and saw the babe with auburn curls. She stood with hands folded at her waist and creamy white legs quivering below the hem of her flowered sundress.

And I knew for certain that if I smiled and she smiled back and I asked her name and number and picked her up later at her churchgoing folks' house and promised to bring her home by midnight, I would drive to a lookout at the sea cliffs and invite her into the back seat. And if she complied, I would do exactly what I would've done yesterday, before I surrendered.

Luckily for her, we lost her in the crowd.

In the car, Skip and I didn't mention surrendering. We drove to a party, and told nobody about Billy Graham. We stayed in the kitchen, drank a couple beers and talked baseball with a couple lonely guys. A card game started, but poker's no fun if you don't care who wins. The only girls were hanging on their boyfriends. So we left.

In the Chevy, Skip said, "Tijuana?"

"Sure," I said. "Why not?"

Before our rambling days, we used to visit Tijuana regularly, mostly for the experience. On Avenida Revolución, even when nothing was happening, you knew any second most anything could. Police could falsely charge you with some offense so you would pay them to let you go. One drug dealer could shoot another, right beside you on the sidewalk. A gang of gringo sailors might pick a brawl with a gang of locals. A drunken homecoming queen could fall into your lap and coo about how much cuter you are than her boyfriend who's gone to puke in the alley.

We chose one of the quieter nightclubs. Still, it was crowded, so we shared a table with some friendly Marines.

Skip had resigned himself to getting drafted. Neither of us were anxious to shoot anybody or die as heroes. But Skip's dad fought in Korea and wasted no respect on those who let other boys go to war while they attended college. Even before our tequila arrived, the Marines were telling us about a training film. It showed photos of camouflaged pits where guys fell onto sharpened and poisoned poles, and tunnels through which soldiers had to crawl chasing invisible warriors.

Maybe thoughts of death by poison or stabs in the dark made my stomach roil. Or maybe the cause was the sight of a dancer on the stage beside the bar. She was naked except for the panties that sagged around her knees. I thought, she could be the babe with auburn hair. The beauty in her flowered sundress could be here on stage, if she had gotten born where I imagined this stoned, lost and weepy dancer had, as the fifteenth child of folks who lived in a hut beside a brown river.

When a fellow vacated his bar stool, I excused myself from the table and moved there. I ordered another shot of tequila, and stared at the mirror behind the liquor shelf, wondering if I looked any different than before I surrendered. I couldn't spot any feature that appeared more saintly or pure. I felt no more likely to turn my other cheek if somebody slugged me or to hand over my jacket to whomever asked. The only change I recognized, I felt more confounded than before, less certain I wanted to return to college and study philosophy. I thought of suggesting to Skip that we could go rambling again.

Then I remembered Jack Kerouac. The guy in Florida who sold us the Chevy claimed the past summer he'd tended bar in Long Island, at a dive Kerouac frequented. Most every night, he said, Mister Kerouac stayed until closing then left with whatever sorry old gal had stayed upright that long. Not the kind of report you want to get about a hero of yours, the writer who convinced us to go rambling.

Someone had told me, when you drink tequila, make sure

you count the shots. So I kept count. I was on seven, and still waiting for the buzz, when I felt my stool tipping backward.

If I had asked, once I recovered, Skip would've told me what else happened between the time I started tipping and the morning after. But I preferred not to know.

The way I recall, I tipped backward and landed in the shotgun seat of our Chevy, where I woke up shivering. Dawn had commenced. The sky was cornflower blue. We were parked on dirt near a bridge across the Tia Juana River, about fifty yards downstream from a squatter village of tin-roofed stick and cardboard shacks. The river was low and mossy green below a film tinted with shimmering rainbows. A few women in rebosos of vivid reds and oranges waded and filled clay pots and coffee cans with water. The niños who crawled on the muddy bank had implausibly shiny hair and wide eyes of gleaming obsidian.

Beyond the shanties, across the river and the road, a building invaded the sky. Shaped like a Hershey bar but high as mountains and made of chrome and glass. A thousand beams from the rising sun ricocheted off it.

I felt Skip staring at me. He was in the back seat. When I glanced his way, he asked, "How's your head?"

In truth my head felt big and heavy. Even my eyes ached. "Okay," I said. "But check this out, everything looks weird. I mean, *awfully* weird."

"How so?"

"Well, awfully bright, way more beautiful than I remember anything every being, only scarier. Something like that."

"Probably tequila," he said.

"Maybe."

But it wasn't. Tequila doesn't last.

Read plenty more of where *The Light* comes from in *CARS: CALIFORNIA STORIES* and *GET THE SCOOP*, in which Ken admits to his latest escapades, reflects upon the art and craft of writing, the highs, lows and in-betweens of living as a writer, and other thorny topics. Go to: kenkuhlken.net.

My Big Faith Marriage - *Helena Kamerra*

"Where's that blasted IRS bill?"

Thirty-six-year-old Dr. Michael Leycester scrambled through a pile of papers on the desk in the bedroom.

"Calm down, dear," Janet Leycester replied from the adjacent bathroom. "If you're paying bills, don't forget we owe tithes this Sunday."

He snorted and flung his hands in the air.

"Did you check the kitchen drawer?" she asked.

He cut his gaze toward the bathroom, his jaw tensed. "It's not in the kitchen. I put it in here."

Janet walked out of the bathroom, her hands to her ear as she placed an earring. She wore a pink blouse that complemented her gray dress pants and her petite figure. Her brunette hair was in a bun.

"I'm supposed to counsel a couple at four this afternoon, so I might be a little late." She put her hands to her hips and watched as he plundered through the desk. "You didn't come to bed again last night."

"I was out on that cow call till three." He let a small book fall out of his hand and plop down onto the desk with a thud. "It's not in here."

Children's voices filled the hallway outside the bedroom door. "Matthew. Give it to me!" A mischievous giggle followed the demand as a six-year-old girl with long, dark hair stomped into the bedroom. "Momma, he's got my lip gloss."

Michael walked into the hall with his three-year-old son and snatched the small cylinder of lip gloss from his hand. He held it out toward Tia. She grabbed it. He stepped out of sight toward the living room. "I'm gone."

"Wait, Jasper and Neely are coming tonight," Janet said over Matthew's screams. She hopped around on one foot trying to get her shoe on.

"Gotta go see a horse."

"But it's Friday. It's my day to open the clinic. Can't you get the kids to school? Michael?" She lost her balance and fell onto the king-sized bed. "Michael?"

"Hey, Doc, everyone's gone." The young strawberry-blond woman sashayed closer to Michael as he steadied a Sheltie on the treatment table. "Did you hear me?"

"Just help me get blood on this girl, will ya? We've got company coming to the house any minute."

Samantha frowned and slid her arms around the dog. He took a syringe and tore it from the packaging when a sharp aroma filled his nostrils. *Whoa.* Perfume. Funny, he hadn't smelled it all day, until now. He swallowed and let out a controlled breath. *If she thinks I'm falling for this again...*

"So who's coming?" she asked.

"Jasper and Neely."

She watched as he collected the sample. "Oh, they're back in town. So, he'll be working next week?"

"Yep, after class."

Michael laid the blood tubes on the counter, picked up the dog, and carried her through the door to the kennel room. He stooped down and placed her in a large cage with food and water.

He stood, his eyes trained on the closed treatment room door. A tingling sensation crept up his spine. What was going to happen when he walked back through that door? *Not tonight, Sam. Not ever again.*

He charged forward into the treatment room. No one was there. *Thank goodness.* The blood machine buzzed next to him. The timer showed nine minutes left.

Thankful she had initiated the blood work for him, he walked toward his office with a tired swagger. The woman's work ethic was never an issue. It was her persistence. Inappropriate persistence. But he had allowed it. He would take the blame, whatever came of it. Yet it was obvious. Samantha had to go. Somehow, someway.

He pushed his office door open. He stopped in the doorway, his jaw dropped. There was Samantha, stretched out across his desk. Her bare skin glistened from head to toe. He grabbed the door facing with one hand and glanced both ways up and down the hall. "Have you lost your mind?"

She rolled over onto her stomach and bent her knees, lifting her feet in the air. Her eyes locked on to his. "I want my paycheck, but I've been a very bad girl."

"The hell you say." The words slipped out rushed and heated. Fire coursed through his blood. He could still walk back out that door, but the girl wanted him. No one else did. Not even his own wife. Just one more time. The last time. He stepped inside the office and shut the door, his hand on his belt buckle. "In that case, you need a good spanking."

$$+ + +$$

"Kids, settle down. I can't hear the radio." Janet reached down and turned the volume louder.

"This is My Big Faith Marriage Minute with Steven Oslow. Have you ever experienced a lull in your marriage?"

"Mom, Matt is staring at me."

"Tia, shush," Janet said.

"Worries and clutter of this life can be distracting. As a result, lack of communication and intimacy can begin to snowball. Ephesians chapter 5, verses 24 and 25 says, 'Just as the church is subject to Christ, so let the wives be to their own husbands in everything. And husbands, love your wives, just as Christ also loved the church and gave Himself for her.' Now, this isn't permission to abuse authority. It's simply an instruction to make each other a priority second only to God."

Matthew screamed. Janet turned, glaring at Tia. "What did you do to him?"

Tia's eyes grew big. "I just stuck my tongue out at him."

"That's it. The computer is off limits for two days."

"Mom!"

"—unhealthy marriage. So take the time to nurture your relationship. These times together will soon become an anticipated—"

"I want to see Mrs. Neely," Tia muttered.

"We're going to help Daddy get finished first."

Janet pulled into the Leycester Veterinary Services parking lot and drove around to the back of the building. She saw his blue full-size mobile clinic pickup parked next to an older, smaller SUV.

Samantha. Janet smiled. *Such a sweet girl. Always willing to stay late and help.*

She got out and helped Matthew from his car seat as Tia bounded toward the back door. Steven Oslow was right. It was high time for her and Michael to have a serious talk about their own marriage. Later that night would be the perfect time.

Matthew pulled Janet through the treatment room. Tia ran back down the hall toward them with a frown.

"Mom, I think Daddy's mad. He said a bad word."

"What?" Janet said with a smile. "Oh, honey, he's probably just—" A high-pitched moan echoed down the hall. Janet stood motionless. That wasn't Michael. "Uh, Tia... take your brother into the feed room and stay there."

"But Mom—"

"Just do it."

She watched Tia take Matthew's hand and walk back toward the treatment room. She turned and looked up the hall. *Okay, this is a joke. It has to be.* She shook her head and walked toward his office. A faint smile turned up the corners of her lips. *Of course it's a joke. He would never...* She turned the corner in the hallway when the sound of his voice stopped her in her tracks. She gasped. Was that the F-word?

"Don't stop," a female voice said. "Please, don't stop."

Samantha? Janet fell against the wall as the blood drained from her face. Michael cried out. The raw ecstasy in his voice forced her to her knees. She put her hands to her head, her body trembling. Michael would never say those things. Never. *It can't be.*

Seconds passed. The office door flew open. She flinched

and jerked her head up. *No.* There he was, staring down at her. His short, dark hair pointed in all directions. *No!* She felt the air squeeze from her lungs.

"Well, girl, we're busted."

Janet let out a whimper. *That's it? That's all he has to say?* "Michael?"

A shrill scream came from inside the office. "Mrs. Janet? I'm so sorry!"

Michael glanced over his shoulder. "Shut up, Sam."

"Michael…" Janet gripped a handful of her blouse over her chest.

He stepped over her. "Don't you worry. I'll be out of the house before you get there." He stormed around the corner in the hall.

What? He's what? "Michael?"

Samantha stepped in the doorway in her panties, holding her shirt over her chest. "Mrs. Janet, please."

Janet glared up at her with flushed cheeks. "Shut up, Sam!"

A tall man with sandy blond hair ran around the corner in the hall. The twenty-year-old stopped in his tracks and turned his back to Janet and Samantha. "Holy…" He looked down the hall to his right. "Neely, baby, get those kids to the car now."

"Okay," a female voice said from down the hall out of sight.

He turned halfway, his eyes on Janet. "What in tarnation is going on around here?"

"Jasper, sweetie I don't—"

"I'm so sorry!" Samantha stumbled over Janet in the hall. She had managed to get her scrub shirt and jeans on, but she was barefoot. She ran toward Jasper. He grabbed her by the arm as she tried to pass.

"You're not going anywhere till you calm down." He stomped toward the office door with Samantha in tow. She ran back inside.

Jasper knelt and took Janet's trembling hand in his. His gaze searched her face. "We saw your vehicles out back and thought we'd surprise… Aw, man."

"Surprise." The word came out soft. Not quite how she would describe her present state, but it was all she could muster.

Her eyes grew wider. "The kids?"

"They're with Neely."

She couldn't take her eyes off him. She trusted him like a son. The only sane thing in her sight at the moment. She grabbed on to him and fell into his chest. Gut-wrenching sobs shook her body as his arms enveloped her.

"Mrs. Janet?"

+ + +

"Wha... Janet, why aren't you at work? What's going on?"

Janet stared at the blond woman in her front doorway. She hated to call her with such troubling news, but she had to talk to someone. She couldn't stay at work. Not after signing for that parcel. She hoped her clients scheduled for that afternoon would understand. Not that there were many. Thursday afternoons were usually slow. She held up some papers stapled together.

Sharon Warren looked at the papers. The widow of Michael's best friend, she was no stranger to chaos. "A divorce?"

Janet swiped her hand across her forehead. "I thought we would talk, you know? I thought he'd come around after a few days, but I haven't heard from him all week. He won't answer his phone. Jasper said he's staying with Edward Bloomberg."

"That's what he told me," Sharon said.

"Tia and Matt talked to Michael yesterday on Neely's phone while she was keeping them after school..." Janet lowered the papers to her side.

Sharon wrapped her arms around her. "We're praying for you."

Janet closed her eyes. "I didn't go to church last Sunday. If I go this week without him... you know it's gonna get out."

They let go of each other. Sharon put her hand on Janet's back and led her to the couch. "Honey, it's already out. You've got to be strong for those kids. They need you."

"How could he do this?" Janet spun around and threw the papers into the air. The pages opened as they fluttered to the floor in the middle of the living room. "Fifteen years of marriage... no excuses, no explanation. Nothing. He just wants out." She turned back to Sharon, tears brimming in her eyes. "Am I not worth it? I know we've neglected each other… but am I not worth fighting for?

Jasper Warren rinsed out the stainless steel bucket beside Michael's clinic truck. Michael stepped up behind him. "Hey, don't forget to grab the twitch. It's in the barn by the stall. I've got to make a phone call."

"Yes, sir." Jasper didn't bother to look up. He cut off the water, slung the bucket with some force into the open compartment, and slammed it shut.

Michael put his hands on his hips. "All right, Warren, we've been dancing around this all week. Just spill it."

Jasper tensed his jaw and brushed past Michael as he walked toward the front of the truck. Michael turned around.

"This is what Janet wants."

Jasper stopped and turned to him. "Really?"

"Trust me. It's for the better."

"For who?"

"For both of us. She doesn't have time for me. She's better off without me." Jasper stared at him, motionless. Michael expected a nod, some sign of agreement, but there was none. "You saw the look on her face when she caught me with Sam."

Jasper held his hand out to his side. "What kind of look did you expect? And what if Tia had walked in on you?"

"Tia heard it!" Michael grimaced and both men glanced toward the horse owner's house behind them. No one was in sight. Thankful his outburst went unnoticed, Michael turned back to him. "She told me on the phone yesterday, Warren. My little girl heard it." He leaned back against the truck and lowered his head. "I'm not fit to be a father."

"You are, and screwing around with Sam doesn't change that. Come on, a divorce?"

Michael looked at him. "Tell me, son, If Neely had a headache for a year, would you get the idea that maybe she wasn't interested anymore?" Jasper stared at him, his mouth agape. "It's been a year. Before that, it was five months."

"Why did you let it go that far?"

"I didn't. I tried to talk to her." Michael turned his head toward the brown brick house. "But she just turns it back on me.

Like when I didn't make it to Tia's birthday party because of an emergency. Oh, and the Easter musical two weeks ago. You know Matt was in that one too." He turned his gaze back to Jasper. "I guess that was the last straw. Never mind that I was trying to get some bills paid. Of course, now she can tell everyone I've been screwing around behind her back this whole time."

Jasper raised his eyebrows. "Have you?"

He sighed and stood up straight. "Look, I've been with Sam three times in the last month. That's the extent of it."

"Then tell her that."

Michael shook his head as he pushed the last open compartment shut. "I blew it, okay? Just drop it."

+ + +

Janet squinted against the setting sun as she drove down her driveway. Was that a truck in front of the garage? *Michael's truck.* Her heart skipped a beat.

"Daddy!" Tia shouted.

"Now, sweetie, don't—"

Tia opened the door as they came to a stop and bounded toward the white farmhouse. Janet got out and took Matthew from his car seat. She led him to the front door. What would she say? No, he'd better have something to say. Oh, did he have some explaining to do.

She drew in a deep breath. *He's here now.* A faint smile crossed her lips. *Should have known he didn't mean all this divorce talk.* She stepped inside the door.

"Michael?"

She heard voices in her bedroom. She and Matthew walked past the staircase to the doorway of the master bedroom. She peeked inside to find Michael sitting on the bed with Tia in his lap. He whispered to her. Janet knocked on the door facing to get his attention. They looked her way. Tia's eyes were wet with tears.

"Honey?" Janet said.

Tia slid off his lap and he stood. "I stopped by to get the rest of my things."

Janet was motionless. "What?" There was no reply as he stepped inside the closet. She put her hand to her chest when she noticed Tia in the corner. "Sweetie, you and Matt go to your room." Tia ran from the room. Janet turned around, her heart pounding. "Michael, what's going on?" He stepped out of the closet, a stack of shirts on hangers hung over his arm.

"What does it look like?"

She let out a quick breath. "Michael, this is cruel."

He slammed the clothes down onto the bed and spun around to face her. "Cruel? You think this is cruel?" He stepped closer, towering over her. "You think this is worse than scraping, trying to please you for the last five years? Worse than walking on eggshells, all the while wondering which Janet will walk through the door? The easygoing one, or the snappy, insatiable witch?"

"Wha—" She covered her mouth with her hand.

"I'm failing at everything. We're behind on taxes and the truck payment. We're one month late on the clinic mortgage and I consider myself lucky if you give me a pat on the back and spread your legs twice a year."

"Why you..." Janet lost her breath. *Who is this man?* She put her hands to her head, tears streaming down her cheeks as he walked past her with the suitcase. Seconds later, the front door slammed.

"Daddy?" Matthew's cries filled the living room from upstairs.

The kids. It was bad enough their dad was leaving. They couldn't see her like that. She wiped her face with her hands and stood up. It seemed to be what he wanted. *Fine. Not sure I'd ever trust him again anyway... Why would I want to?*

"Mrs. Janet, is there anything Jasper and I can do?"

"Just pray."

Neely Warren tossed her long black hair over her shoulder and walked toward Janet across the living room. "Do you need me to pick up the kids this afternoon?"

"Yeah." Janet nodded. "That would be great. Thanks." She crossed her arms over her chest and looked toward the window. "You know, I called in sick this morning. After getting those papers yesterday, and then Michael..."

Neely touched her on the arm. "You know, we can keep the kids until Sunday night. That would give you the weekend to try to figure things out."

"How could he just stop loving me? After all these years?"

Neely shook her head. "Dr. Michael still loves you."

Janet glared at Neely through narrowed eyes. "Oh, and I suppose it's easy for you to see that, being you have the most devoted husband in the world." Neely lowered her head as Janet put her hand to her mouth. "Oh, sweetie... I'm sorry."

"No, it's just... I don't know what to say. But I know that." Janet tilted her head and pressed her lips together as Neely walked toward the front door.

"Thank you."

Neely turned with a smile before she walked out and shut the door. Janet looked back at the window and pulled the curtain back. Billowy gray clouds covered the sky. She closed her eyes. "Dear God, where do I go from here? How do I do this by myself? Please turn Michael's heart back to me and help me to be the wife he wants... that he needs. Help me want to be."

Jasper released the last heifer from the chute. Michael and the older cattle farmer next to him climbed down from the side of the chute. A clap of thunder turned their heads. Dark clouds stretched across the sky from the southwest.

"That looks pretty bad," the farmer said.

Michael nodded as he walked to the truck. "We don't need to be caught in this, for sure."

Jasper gathered their equipment as Michael washed off his boots at the back of the truck. After putting everything away in the mobile clinic, the men climbed into the cab of the full-sized pickup. Jasper tuned the radio to a nearby station.

"I shouldn't have said those things yesterday," Michael muttered as he pulled the truck out onto the highway.

Jasper looked at him. "Huh?"

"She's not used to being talked to like that."

"Then make it right."

Michael glanced at him. "You make that sound real simple, boy."

"It is." Jasper shook his head and looked out the window.

Michael gazed back out at the road. *Make it right. Sure.* A few seconds passed. He let out a sigh and keyed up his phone.

"Call Janet."

A frail, cracked voice answered. "Michael?" He stared out at the road in front of them, his mouth agape. The pain in her voice had caught him off guard. "Michael are you there?"

"Yeah, yeah, I'm here."

"Where are you?"

"I'm with Warren. We're on the way back to the clinic now. Listen, I—"

"I'm at home. I, uh, didn't get to tell you yesterday, but I got your papers."

He let out a long sigh and shifted his hand on the steering wheel. "Well? Are you satisfied with the terms?" Silence ensued over the line. Michael glanced at Jasper and did a double take when he saw the look on his face.

"Are you kidding me, Michael Lee?" Janet said. "I'm not satisfied with any of it."

"What do you mean? It's fair and you know it."

"What's fair about any of this? Gosh darn it, Michael. One day we're a family and the next, you're playing slap and tickle with the help."

"And this is precisely why I haven't called you. It's always my fault. I knew you'd fight me on this."

"I'm not trying to fight you, I just want a chance to make it work."

"We've had years to make it work. Just forget it." He shifted in his seat.

"Yeah, forget it," she said. "I guess that's just what we need to do."

The line clicked before Michael could respond. He hit the steering wheel with the palm of his hand.

"You were right. She sounds real excited about this divorce," Jasper muttered.

Michael glanced at him. "Yeah, and I can do without the sarcasm."

A lightning bolt webbed across the sky. The radio began to blare out an alarm. Jasper turned the volume up as they waited for an announcement. "The National Weather Service has issued a tornado warning for the following counties: Eastern Geneva and Houston in southeast Alabama, effective until 4:00 p.m. central time. At 3:20 p.m., Doppler radar indicated a developing tornado three miles west of Taylor moving northeast at forty-five miles per hour."

"That might be headed to my house," Michael said. His countenance dropped. "Wait, did Janet say she was at home?"

Jasper nodded. Michael began making another call as Jasper took his own cell phone from his pocket. Michael waited for Janet to pick up, but there was no answer. Jasper began talking to Neely. Michael tried the call again. He hung up as Jasper got off his phone.

"Warren, she won't answer."

"Neely's gonna try to call her."

The alert message had finished when the radio announcer's voice came across the speakers. "Okay, folks, this is a serious situation. A tornado has been spotted by law enforcement north of Taylor and is headed in the general direction of county road 34 just west of Dothan."

Michael felt the blood drain from his face as the announcer continued. "Warren?"

"Where's the kids?"

"Tia should be at daycare by now with Matt. They're out of the way, but—"

"Keep trying to call," Jasper said.

Michael dialed Janet's number again. There was no answer. "It's no use. She's mad and I know she's not paying attention."

"I'm sure she can hear the sirens."

Michael's heart pounded. Something just wasn't... "I'm going to the house."

Jasper jerked his head toward him. "Say what?"

+ + +

Janet touched her forehead against the shower wall. Warm water and tears trickled down her slender body. How could he take it as a personal attack every time she opened her mouth? If he hated her that much, what was the point in trying?

A loud clap of thunder startled her. She turned the water off and stepped out onto the bath mat, grabbing her towel. Where did that come from? She'd begun to dry off in front of the mirror when an eerie howling noise echoed in the glass block window over the bathtub. Was that storm sirens? A loud bang made her jump, and she jerked her head toward the window. Something had hit the side of the house. She ran from the bathroom into the closet. Her towel fell to the floor as she fumbled for her robe.

The bedroom door flew open. Startled, she grabbed the shoe rack next to her.

A male voice screamed, "Let's go!"

Michael? She spun around to see the bed comforter coming at her. She put her hands up, caught off guard. He wrapped her in the cover and scooped her up in his arms. Howling winds rattled the house as he ran from the bedroom with her.

"The half-bath, hurry!" Jasper said, holding the door open. A loud crashing sound filled the air as the three of them piled into the tiny bathroom. Jasper shut the door as Michael and Janet fell to the floor. Janet tried to pull her legs underneath her, still wrapped in the comforter, but the weight of the two men on top of her forced her flat to the floor. A deafening sound, much like an explosion, roared through the house. She screamed.

Jasper's voice was faint in the chaos. "Jesus, don't let us die."

Wind rushed through the house. The floor shook and she was sure she heard someone yell something about the roof. She felt the blood rushing to her head in the darkness of the comforter, and her teeth clenched, as if waiting for some big, final blow. "Oh God, please save us from this storm!"

It got quiet. Raindrops fell around them. The smell of fresh, moist air whipped through the tiny room.

"Warren? Son?" Michael's voice called out from above her. There was no answer.

Janet began to move. "Michael?"

"Sweetheart, you hurt?" He unraveled the comforter and gazed up and down her naked body.

"The kids? Are they—"

"They're okay." He covered her again, forcing his eyes back to hers. "They weren't in the path."

"Help." Jasper's voice sounded far away.

"Warren?" Michael scrambled to his feet and began stepping over broken boards. Janet sat up and watched him meander in the debris. A hand emerged in front of him. He reached down and pulled Jasper to his feet.

"Oww," Jasper said, holding his shoulder. Blood trickled down his face.

"Take it easy," Michael said. "Come on."

The two men walked back toward Janet. Michael knelt down beside her as Jasper made his way out of the wrecked house. "Come on, baby."

She gazed up at him, motionless. "You came for me."

Michael raised his eyebrows. "Of course I did. You're my wife."

His wife? A quick breath blew past her lips. "But you..."

He blinked and opened his mouth. He lowered his head. "I know."

"You came for me." She put her hand on his rough, unshaven cheek. "You ran into the path of the storm for me. For heaven's sakes, Michael, you could've been killed."

He lifted his head, and his blue eyes met hers. Tears streamed down her cheeks. He reached out and pulled her close to his chest. Despite the blood on his hand, he stroked her dark, wet hair.

"Baby, I'm so sorry." His voice was cracked as his body shook. "Oh God, help me to know where to even start to make this right."

"You already have." She pulled away from his chest and lifted her eyes to his. "I know that you love me. You were willing to die for me."

He rested his forehead against hers and closed his eyes. "I do love you." She closed her eyes, savoring his warm breath on her face.

"Hey, you two," Jasper said from behind them, his hand still resting on his injured shoulder. "In case you haven't noticed, half your house is gone."

They looked around at the sea of shattered wood, insulation, and sheet rock. Michael stood up and held his hand out to her. Still wrapped in the comforter, she grabbed his hand and stood.

He gazed down at her. "Yeah, it is."

Janet stared at the rubble that used to be her home as people meandered about. Both of her kids stood at her feet as Neely walked closer.

"Good thing you're close to my size."

Janet glanced down at the mint-green t-shirt and sweatpants. "Thanks for the clothes, sweetie." She put her hand to her head and scanned the wreckage before them. "I might be a while catching up on my laundry."

Neely nodded. "I can imagine…"

"You know, I should be upset right now. Absolutely devastated. But I'm not." Janet looked at her with a furrowed brow. "Is that weird?"

A corner of Neely's mouth turned up as Michael walked toward them with a wet envelope. "Well, sweetheart, half our house is gone, my truck's gone, but not that friggin' IRS bill."

Janet eyed the soggy envelope in his hand. "I told you it was in the kitchen drawer." He narrowed his eyes at her and tapped the top of her head with the envelope.

"You were right… as always."

"Not always." She looked up at him, the corners of her mouth turned down. "But I have no idea where the divorce papers are."

He stepped closer. Her heart picked up pace. There was so much to work out. Would it be possible amid so much pain? Did he even want to?

He placed a bent index finger under her chin and lifted her gaze to his. "What divorce papers?"

Thank you for your interest in my short story, *My Big Faith Marriage*. It is a spin-off from the 'Christina's Purpose Series' which begins with the novel, *The Party Gift*. More books are in the works for this series. For updates, visit www.helenakamerra.com and sign up to follow. I can be reached by email at helena@helenakamerra.com. I love to hear from my readers!

Hell of an Opportunity - *John M.Shaver*

After three hours in the internet café browsing scanned archives of *The Psychology Review* in hopes of stumbling across a suitable thesis topic, Donald Dobson decided he could afford a break. He signed onto AOL and noticed an email from Dr. Irene Estherhouse, the chair of Berkeley's psychiatric department. The subject heading read "helluva opportunity."

He clicked on it, and was pleasantly startled to find that Dr. Estherhouse was notifying him of an available internship at the American military base in South Korea, a job that entailed performing psych evaluations on servicemen stationed there. Dr. Estherhouse was offering him first dibs on applying for the position, partly because of his academic record and partly because he didn't have any strong familial ties binding him to the United States.

Dobson wasted no time thinking it over. After all, what did he have to lose? Life on the base couldn't be any worse than living on a dry, smoke-free campus with a roommate who ate in the bathroom and wore the same shirt for weeks on end. There were also other benefits to working for Uncle Sam, such as a nifty signing bonus and the fact that he couldn't be sued for malpractice if he screwed up someone's medication. Best of all, he'd gain exposure to a broader range of psych disorders than if he interned at a private practice. It wasn't every day you treated someone with PTSD.

Besides, this way, he'd have more time to work on his

thesis. He could stay in touch with his professors via email.

While still at the café, he did some research on Korean culture and considered maybe doing his thesis on Korean superstitions. From what he read on the internet, there were certainly plenty to go around.

He sent a message to Dr. Estherhouse expressing interest in the position.

+ + +

Receiving his U.S. government contract took a week. He then wasted a day faxing it back to Washington DC with his signature. Work visa approval took an additional six weeks. At this rate, he thought, he wouldn't see his signing bonus before turning fifty. After a total of two months preparation time and an awkward interview at the Korean consulate, he finally drove down to San Francisco International Airport and boarded a jetliner for Busan, the coastal city where Douglas Macarthur once repelled a beach invasion during the Korean War. From there, he caught a train for Seoul, where he was met by a pair of official escorts.

He didn't take long settling into his new life on Youngsan military base, entertaining neither homesickness nor second thoughts. His work was interesting without being demanding. Mostly, he helped soldiers cope with the stress of being deployed overseas, and he provided a sympathetic ear whenever they needed to vent their frustrations. The fact that his job mostly boiled down to being a good listener did nothing to diminish the pride he took in it. He figured he was performing an invaluable service if he prevented but one American serviceman from taking out his pent-up aggression on the local citizenry. The U.S. military already had more than enough public relations disasters on its hands.

With more free time on his hands than any soldier ever got, Dobson ventured out into the surrounding areas of Seoul, taking frequent hikes into the nearby mountains (mere foothills, by American standards) the tranquility of which was usually obliterated by crowds of hollering schoolchildren out on field trips. Many of these children had never seen an honest-to-God Westerner, and their curious stares were both wearisome and strangely endearing.

Because he was the newest member of the base's psychiatric staff, his caseload was relatively light. Furthermore, the various Korean military liaisons, in return for a chance to hone their English skills, did everything in their power to make him feel at home. Sure, Dobson still had trouble communicating with the outside community, but he almost preferred it that way. He considered himself a lone wolf, and he enjoyed intimidating the locals with his exoticism. People stared as he walked by, and Dobson reflected on how strange it felt to achieve a degree of instant celebrity after going unnoticed for so much of his life.

The first thing he fell in love with about Korea was the cuisine. The smells wafting off street-corner food carts were as mouth-watering as anything offered at a five-star restaurant. Everything was spicy and sizzled on his tongue, but without being soaked in grease, lathered in sugar and salt, or laced with MSG. Dobson found himself finally shedding his gut, resulting in a better self-image than he'd had since childhood.

When he met Min-Hee, it was as though the whole world got pulled out from under him. She was a Korean army liaison who had learned English while studying in the Philippines. The fact that she giggled at every stupid thing he said gave him the courage to ask her out. To his great surprise, she accepted.

After the success of their first date, they met with increased regularity, sometimes at a local theater that showed recent American films with Korean subtitles, and other times at a quiet café where they often conversed late into the evening. Occasionally (once they had grown comfortable with each other), they would get sauced on plumb wine and rent a private room for karaoke. Dobson had a singing voice like a wood-chipper, and his squawking rendition of Queen's "Somebody to Love" made Min-Hee laugh so hard that beer spurted out her nose. Which only made her laugh even harder. It was the most Dobson had ever enjoyed the company of another human being.

+ + +

One rainy afternoon, while drinking ginseng tea at a traditional Korean café, Dobson explained to Min-Hee his intention to write his thesis on Korean superstition.

"But how is that psychiatry?" Min-Hee asked, her cheeks dimpling as she smiled. Her charcoal-colored hair was tied in a bun, and her eyebrows were arched in puzzlement. She certainly knew how to massage his ego: namely, by looking at him as though he possessed the secrets of the ages. Most university professors would give their eye teeth for students like her who hung on their every word.

"Oh, it's all closely related," Dobson explained, failing to keep the haughtiness out of his voice. Her apparent fascination in him made it difficult not to show off. "Religion is, after all, just a sociological construct, a tool for controlling the masses by promoting a moral and cultural hierarchy that benefits those in power. It is a non-scientific rationalization of anything we lack the capacity to understand, or the willingness to accept. Furthermore, religion serves a psychological function by shielding us from our own insignificance in relation to the universe as a whole. Understand?"

Min-Hee fanned her fingers in front of her mouth and giggled. "Not at all! Is this how psychiatry people talk? So many big words…"

Dobson smiled and made a dismissive gesture. "Sorry. I got carried away."

"So," Min-Hee said, "does what you say mean you don't think supernatural things exist?" Her English wasn't perfect, but, to Dobson, such imperfection made her even more adorable.

"Of course they don't exist. Modern science has proven all that hocus-pocus stuff to be total bullshit."

"It's not *bullshit*," Min-Hee said. "You Americans don't know everything." She winked to show she was partially teasing. "I've seen hocus-pocus stuff with my own eyes."

Dobson gazed at her, a hint of mockery on his lips. "Oh, really? What exactly?"

Min-Hee leaned forward and whispered, her voice barely audible over the *ga-ya-gum* music drifting from the overhead sound system. "I met a woman who talks to invisibility things…things that give her secret knowledges."

"Stop pulling my leg," Dobson groaned playfully.

"But, I don't touch your leg…" Min-Hee said, confused.

"I mean, stop joking around."

Min-Hee's mouth inverted into a wounded frown. "No joke. Korean shaman is very powerful. Everyone in Korea know this."

"'Shamaness.' You said the fortune-teller was a woman."

Min-Hee's brow furrowed as she committed the word to memory.

Dobson cleared his throat. "And you say you visited one of these so-called shamanesses?"

"Yes, of course."

"What on earth for?"

"Because I wanted to know about my future. You know, will I find a good job? What university major should I choose? Will I marry with a good man, and when? Things like that. The shamaness told me I will marry with a foreigner. I thought she meant a businessman from maybe China or the Philippines. But now I wonder if maybe she was talking about an American."

"Yeah?" Dobson said, floored by the sudden twist in their conversation. Was he hallucinating, or had Min-Hee just hinted at something?

Min-Hee. Her very name was like ambrosia on his tongue. Might the two of them actually end up together? She was so far out of his league, the idea seemed laughable.

"I think I'm starting to like this shamaness."

Min-Hee beamed at him, eyes sparkling in the ambient light. "Oh, she's definitely your style."

"What else did she tell you?"

"She said I will someday become a professor at a Korean university. She said I will be very successful there."

Dobson *harrumph*ed into his teacup. "Sounds like she was just telling you what you wanted to hear."

"Not true," Min-Hee said solemnly. "She told me I would have trouble…what is the expression?...conceiving children."

"I'm sorry to hear that," Dobson said. But on the inside, he thought: *Sounds perfect!* Dobson looked forward to having kids about as much as he anticipated his first colonoscopy.

Min-Hee sipped her tea thoughtfully. "Actually, it was a little scary. I felt…dirty…being in the room with her. Afterwards, I wanted to get a shower. Many Koreans feel that way when they meet a shamaness. No one would go if life wasn't so stressfulness and uncertain."

"Why? What exactly bothered you about her?"

"Well, many things, actually. Her...uh, ritual...included a disgusting thing like killing a pig and dancing with it. She knew a lot of secret information about me: where I was born, how many brothers and sisters I have, my star sign, and so on. I went without an appointment, so she couldn't have researched these informations beforehand."

Min-Hee rushed on. "Then she summoned her...I don't know what it's called in English...spirit guide?"

"Uh-huh."

"She said it was the spirit of Soon-Sheen Lee, a famous and powerful general during the Chosun Dynasty."

"Hmmm."

"And when she...called? summoned?...the spirit, the atmosphere of the room was changed. It got colder. Very colder. I could feel a negative energy. As she talked to me, she watched past my shoulder, like Soon-Sheen Lee's ghost was standing there behind me. It was...oh, what is that word... Unnerving."

"Sounds it."

Min-Hee tilted up her nose at him. "That was sarcasm, yes?"

Dobson raised his hands in mock surrender. "No, no, not at all. But you don't realize the sort of tricks a woman like that has up her sleeve. In America, we have shamans who do the same kind of thing, but they don't live in caves or in Buddhist temples; they live in Las Vegas and perform for full-capacity crowds at seventy bucks a head. We call them illusionists. And the only difference between them and this shamaness of yours is that they freely admit their magic is bullshit."

"In Korea, it's not bullshit," Min-Hee said, punctuating her statement by stamping her foot.

"OK, prove it," Dobson said.

"What?"

"You heard me. Introduce me to this shamaness, and let's see if I have a similar experience. I reckon she'll have a harder time pulling the wool over my eyes, seeing as how I'll be on the lookout for any tricks."

"I don't think that's a good idea, Dobs."

Dobson signaled the hostess to remove their empty teacups and table trays. "Oh, come now. It's perfectly fine. You don't even need to accompany me if you'd rather not. Someone else can translate for me. Just tell me where this shamaness lives."

Min-Hee stared at him in obvious displeasure. "If you go, I go also. But I don't want us to go. I don't know how she will react to meeting a foreigner."

Dobson chuckled. "She'll probably be more intimidated of me than you are of her."

"I doubt it."

"Look at it this way. A good fortune teller would already know I'm coming, right?"

Min-Hee wasn't in a joking mood. "You should take this more seriously."

"I *am*! Very seriously. This kind of thing could be the heart of my thesis paper, the reason I came to South Korea in the first place. I'd be an idiot not to look into it."

+ + +

A week later, they took a railway train out of Seoul Station and headed straight for the coast, toward the ramshackle cabin where Shamaness Woon-Su was said to live.

During the long ride, Dobson asked Min-Hee why she'd chosen that particular shamaness, rather than someone closer to home.

"Shamaness Woon-Su is one of the best respected shamanesses in all Korea," she explained. "She felt the sickness very early, when she was only a baby."

"What do you mean, the sickness?" Dobson asked.

"All true shamans feel it. It's the spirits of the unseen world trying to communicate with them. I don't know why they wish to communicate with some people and not others."

"What is it like, this sickness?"

Min-Hee mulled it over for several moments, her nose crinkling in thought. "People who feel the sickness—in Korea, usually women—experience lots of dizzy feelings and...how do you say, painting?"

"Fainting?"

"Yes, fainting. There are other symptoms, but I don't know well."

Dobson leaned back in his adjustable chair and closed his eyes. He could feel Min-Hee's forearm brush against his on the armrest.

Ten minutes later, he was asleep. In his dream, he saw Min-Hee. Only now, she was naked, and they were engaged in the sort of erotic activities she'd certainly disapprove of in real life. At least before marriage, anyway.

When they reached the train station in Busan, they exited the station and transferred to a bus that would shuttle them to the foot of Mt. Jiri, nearby where the shamaness lived.

The bus was far less comfortable than the train had been. The driver alternated between flooring the gas and slamming the brakes rather than finding a happy medium. Dobson was grateful his seat was back far enough to prevent him from seeing out the windshield; he didn't wish to keep track of how many near-misses they had. Min-Hee, on the other hand, immediately dropped off to sleep, as though the lurching of the bus was but the rocking of a porch swing.

Dobson decided he might as well take in the scenery as best he could. How different the country felt once you ventured away from the big cities! Seoul was a thoroughly modern metropolis, comparable to Tokyo, Hong Kong, or Shanghai. But the region through which the bus now traveled was like glimpsing back into ancient history. Rice paddies blazed past Dobson's side window, tended by haggard old women with bent spines from a lifetime spent rooting in the soil. Children meandered along the highway shoulder, looking for plants to add to their evening stew.

It was obvious what made these people so vulnerable to superstition. Apart from the stream of traffic along the highway, Dobson felt as though he had traveled back to the Dark Ages, like the main character in Mark Twain's *A Connecticut Yankee in King Arthur's Court*.

The bus arrived at its destination: a small, rustic village scattered like an afterthought beneath the towering silhouette of Mt. Jiri. Hiking had recently become a popular pastime in Korea, and the local villagers made their living off trekkers who treated the area like a base camp. Dobson gazed at all the houses—shacks, really—renovated into makeshift restaurants and convenience stores selling bottled water and wide-brimmed straw hats. The permeating odor of boiled fish and seasoned chicken made his stomach growl.

Disembarking from the bus, Min-Hee grabbed his hand and led him to a half-assed rental car agency catering to people who preferred to drive up the mountain rather than hike. The owner showed them to a gravel lot where a handful of late-model Hyundais and Samsungs were parked. Dobson hadn't realized Samsung even made cars. He quickly opted for a Hyundai.

Min-Hee drove with the self-assurance of a born navigator. Their car plowed steadily up the mountain along a two-lane road bendy enough to make anyone car sick. Houses here were composed not of wood, but stone. Meadows were littered with small mounds like ski moguls. Min-Hee explained that they were graves.

They didn't talk much during the drive. Min-Hee seemed nervous, her hands pale from clenching the steering wheel. Dobson reminded her there was nothing to worry about. She favored him with a wan smile and then returned to staring blank-eyed out the windshield.

Sooner than he expected, the shamaness' house came into view. It was a rickety wooden affair, its windows papered over with strips of cardboard. From the porch roof hung a series of paper Mache lamps shaped like upside-down raspberries. Both sides of the entryway were painted with Chinese and Korean characters, and Dobson noticed several numerical amounts which he presumed were the shamaness's service fees. The front door was left open, as though welcoming them inside.

Min-Hee pulled onto a tiny dirt lot, killed the engine, and motioned for Dobson to hop out. They made their way slowly toward the house, neither of them speaking.

When they reached the porch, Min-Hee dropped to her knees and folded her hands in her lap, waiting. Dobson, not knowing what else to do, followed suit.

"What are we doing?" he whispered.

"Waiting to be invited in," Min-Hee replied.

"How will she know we're here?"

"The spirits will tell her."

R-i-i-ght, Dobson thought. *And the sound of us parking the car would have nothing to do with it.*

They knelt there for less than a minute before a serious-faced girl of about fourteen stepped outside, bowed, and beckoned them to accompany her. She wore brightly-colored dress robes, and her cheeks were painted red and blue, the colors of the Korean flag.

Dobson stood and followed the two women inside. The girl led them into a small sitting chamber with Western-style furniture. Min-Hee reclined daintily on a faded Barka Lounger, and Dobson plopped down beside her. The young girl—Min-Hee identified her as the shamaness' apprentice—poured hot liquid into elegant china teacups and continued to bow subserviently. Dobson sipped politely at the foul concoction, finding it disgusting but determined not to show it.

Several minutes later, the shamaness herself entered, and more bowing ensued. She briefly chatted with Min-Hee while Dobson looked on uncomprehendingly, then she gestured for them to follow her deeper into the house.

They walked down a short hallway with a room branching off to either side. On the right was what appeared to be the old woman's sleeping quarters. The shamaness stepped through the doorway on the left, and Dobson found himself in some sort of altar room.

The walls were covered with pictures, photos, and drawings, many of which were garden-variety depictions of animals. Of greater interest to Dobson were the images of holy deities from a wide assortment of world religions. Hindu gods like Shiva—unmistakably blue-skinned and effeminate—and Ganesh, a human/elephant hybrid; Korean gods like the Spirit of the Mountain, usually depicted as an old man with blue robes and a flowing white beard riding on a tiger. Dobson recognized several others. The Chinese Supreme Divinity, the Japanese Yama, Vishnu... Obviously, the shamaness was a woman who had all her bases covered.

There were also illustrations and photos of various historical figureheads, mostly Korean patriarchs. A hand-painted portrait of King Sejeong, the creator of the Korean language system, had been lovingly hung above the altar itself.

Many of the paintings, portraits, and statues had plates of food set in front of them. Rice cakes, sweets, steamed fish, sesame seeds, dried fruit, roasted pork, kimchi, Miso soup—Dobson even spotted a tiny bowl of what looked suspiciously like M&M's. Apparently, the spirits worked up quite an appetite.

The shamaness collapsed cross-legged in front of the altar as Min-Hee and Dobson sat side-by-side on the other side of the room. They waited in silence until the apprentice finally entered, now wearing a bright pink *hanbok* and carrying a flute-looking instrument that Dobson thought looked straight out of a David Carradine movie. She sat on the bare wooden floor next to the shamaness and then—after receiving the go-ahead nod from her mistress—put the instrument to her lips and began to play. The shamaness, twisting at the waist, snatched up a ceramic mixing bowl and two antique flint knives from beneath the altar shroud. Turning to face Dobson and Min-Hee, the shamaness set the bowl upside-down in her lap and beat the knives against it as though it were a drum. She chanted in a high, sing-song voice, her eyes lifted to the ceiling in glorious rapture.

Min-Hee leaned over and whispered into Dobson's ear. "She's asking the spirits to honor us with their presence."

The chanting continued for several minutes before the shamaness suddenly stood and picked a plate of raw fish heads from off the floor. The apprentice ceased her flute playing. The old woman shuffled to the doorway and flung the plate's contents out into the hallway. Then she bent down and studied the mess carefully.

"What's she doing now?" Dobson whispered out the corner of his mouth.

"Checking the spirits' answer. If the fish heads point away from this room, it means they accept our invitation to join us. If they point toward the room, the answer is no."

Charming, Dobson thought.

The old woman smiled and raised a bony fist in the air.

"Success," Min-Hee said. Satisfied, the shamaness returned to sit in front of the altar, motioning for the apprentice to resume her playing. The crone's chanting began in greater earnest now, and she occasionally punctuated her words by slashing at her own forearms with the flint knives she'd been using for drumsticks.

However, the knives were dull, and the only wounds she inflicted on herself were scratches. The old woman gave no indication she even felt them. Her chanting segued into a piercing wail.

With the shamaness seemingly beyond all distraction, Min-Hee translated portions of her chant for Dobson's benefit.

"Spirit of the morning star…the spirit of the tiger is in its jaws…the spirit of man is in his groin…gather the spirits and enter the clay…the spirit of the clay is in the seed…"

Dobson didn't pay much attention. Typical heebie-jeebie nonsense—although, perhaps something was lost in translation.

The shamaness ended her chanting mid-word. Her eyes rolled back until only the whites were visible. She expelled a deep breath, lowered her eyes back to their proper position, and regarded them in a manner that was strangely serpentine.

"Thou dost not belong here," the shamaness said, her voice now lower by a full octave. "Why hast thou come?"

Dobson was nonplussed. Not due to the change in the woman's voice—such things were part and parcel of this sort of performance art—but by her English fluency and manner of speaking. Not only was her grammar flawless, he couldn't detect any traces of a typical Korean accent.

And Dobson had never met a Korean who spoke with King James diction.

This woman is a true maestro, Dobson thought. Based on the simplicity of her lifestyle, he'd assumed she hadn't received any foreign language training. He mentally applauded the old hag for brilliantly concealing her English ability and thereby lending credibility to her supposed spirit possession. Were Dobson some ignorant rice farmer and not a university-educated sophisticate, he would've bought her act in a heartbeat. No wonder so many people fell for this woman! His thesis paper was practically writing itself…

He wondered what other languages she could speak.

"Mother," Min-Hee said, sticking with English for Dobson's sake. "We're here to ask for your blessings on our future. We wou—"

"Liar!" the shamaness snarled, though her interest seemed entirely focused on Dobson. "And thou. Tell me from whence thou dost hail."

Dobson resisted the urge to applaud the woman's performance. God, she was convincing! He wished he could introduce her to a Las Vegas talent scout.

"I hail from the United States of America, m'lady."

The old woman squinted in the candlelight. "I've oft heard of it. A land of great wealth and opportunity, yes?"

"Sure, if you believe the hype." Dobson couldn't resist a smile. He was enjoying himself. He saw what Min-Hee meant about the temperature, though. The room was freezing now—more special effects, no doubt. Probably a Frigidaire set up in the other room.

The shamaness was not amused. "Thou art an unbeliever, come to feed off your own arrogance."

Dobson wiped away his grin. "We're here to gather knowledge. To research. Not to insult you."

"And yet, insult me thou hast."

Min-Hee chimed in. "We are deeply regretting of any offense we may have given. Please...we will go now."

The old woman ignored her. "What wouldst it take to convince you, unbeliever?"

Dobson shrugged. "Convince me of what? That you're really possessed by a spirit? I'm afraid I'm going to need proof."

"Then proof shalt thou have."

"What do you propose?" Dobson said.

The shamaness regarded Min-Hee for the first time since the ritual began. "This woman...she is not an unbeliever like you. I shall call the spirits to enter into her, and thusly shalt thou be convinced."

"Fine," Dobson said coolly. "Go for it."

"Dobs!" Min-Hee gasped. "You mustn't let her do that!"

"What could it hurt?" he asked.

Min-Hee's face slackened.

Dobson stroked his jaw thoughtfully before addressing the old woman. "Why don't you call the spirits into me instead? After all, I'm the willing candidate. That way, everyone's happy."

The crone shook her head. "With unbelievers, the task is made more difficult. More time is required."

Oh, Dobson thought. *Surprise, surprise. Your magic only works on people who are susceptible to your bullshit.*

Min-Hee remained silent, her eyes pleading.

"Oh, why the hell not?" Dobson said and squeezed Min-Hee's shoulder reassuringly. "As I said, the whole thing's a scam anyway. Nothing to fear but fear itself. Besides, it'll only take a minute."

"But I don't think it's a good idea…"

"Listen, Min-Hee," Dobson said, whispering in her ear. "If you to do this for me, my thesis is as good as written. This situation…it's perfect! I couldn't ask for a better setup. I'm begging you, please. I swear nothing bad will happen."

"And if she really does summon a spirit? What then?"

Dobson gave her a hug. "Believe me, she won't. It's not possible. All you have to do to prove her a fraud is keep a tight rein on yourself."

Min-Hee made no reply.

"Please?" Dobson begged. "For me?"

A deep sigh. "All right. For you, Dobs. Only for you."

+ + +

The shamaness's apprentice sat in the corner of the altar room playing an antique *so-go*. He watched in fascination as the hag instructed Min-Hee to lay on the floor, then lifted her shirt to expose her taught belly and perfect navel. It was an inviting sight, one that Dobson admired with relish as he contemplated what further enticements lay concealed beneath her clothing. The eyeful of creamy, caramel-colored skin was enough to make the whole trip worthwhile all by itself.

The shamaness reached out a leathery hand, fingers extended, so that her wrinkled palm hovered over Min-Hee's belly-button. He watched as the old crone closed her eyes and mumbled incantations under her breath, occasionally patting Min-Hee's bare stomach for emphasis. Min-Hee's breathing was rapid and shallow, a sign of her nervousness. Dobson stroked her hair in reassurance.

The shamaness spoke. "Relax, child. This cannot be done against thy will. Thou must fashion thy heart into a place of invitation and welcome."

Min-Hee's response was hardly more than a whimper. "I don't know if I can, Mother. I'm too frightened."

"Thou hast nothing to fear, child," the old woman soothed.

Min-Hee nodded bravely and tried to swallow her misgivings.

The shamaness sank deeper into meditation, the movement of her hand the sole indication she hadn't drifted off to sleep. Eventually, she said, "The spirits hath prepared to merge. Repeat these words of invocation."

Dobson squeezed Min-Hee's hand in an attempt to bolster her confidence. Bullshit or not, this was turning out to be quite an experience!

"Spirit of the Netherworld, I welcome thee into the hearth of my bosom. I bequeath you the use of my body, for thou art lacking in flesh and blood."

Min-Hee, resigned now to playing the guinea pig, repeated the mantra, stumbling over the words but getting the general gist.

The old woman continued. "I subjugate myself to thy will. Through me, thou art loosed upon the world."

Again, Min-Hee repeated the words…

…and a moment later every candle in the room flickered and died.

+ + +

One year later...

Dr. Estherhouse moved behind the podium and leaned into the microphone. "Ladies and gentleman, we will now begin the public portion of Donald Dobson's defense for his PhD thesis, 'Authenticity in Korean Shamanism.'"

The people milling about the back of the classroom tore themselves away from the free cookies, donuts, and punch, and made their way to their seats. The tables directly in front of the podium were reserved for members of the Psych department faculty, as it was their job to ask the questions. Behind them, seats were available for any of the general public interested enough to attend (of which there were few), as well as for any of Dobson's family who might be present (of which there were none).

Dobson waited until he and the faculty panel had been properly introduced, then made his way behind the podium. After adjusting the mike to match his height, he said, with just a twinge of sarcasm, "Thank you, Dr. Estherhouse, for that warm lead-in."

The truth was, her introduction had been entirely perfunctory. This, from the very same woman who not-so-long-ago gave him first dibs on an amazing opportunity. It was the first real indication that his former instructors intended to crucify him on this podium—not that he hadn't seen it coming.

Dobson spent the next ten minutes summarizing his dissertation, then gave the floor to his questioners.

The first faculty member to speak up was Don Bentley, an owlish man in a tweed jacket who had been Dobson's favorite professor prior to Korea. Now, he regarded Dobson with barely concealed disgust. "As I'm sure you are aware, this dissertation flies in the face of everything taught by modern science. Too many people as it is already consider the fields of psychology and psychiatry questionable without you lending credence to tales of soothsaying and spiritcraft. My only query for you is this: How do you expect to hand in such drivel without getting laughed out of the room?"

Dobson gripped the sides of the podium and leaned forward like a Southern Baptist preacher. "I fully anticipated your hostility to what I'm suggesting. I also realize it'll take more than well-worded arguments to change your minds. The reason I expect you to accept my dissertation is because I'm prepared to initiate, here in this very room, contact with the spirit world. Perhaps seeing such evidence with your own eyes will put my words in a different light."

Before he could continue, a large, ebony-skinned man stood up in the third row and coughed to get everyone's attention. He then addressed the audience in a deep, booming voice. "Name's Harvey Dunn. Been teaching higher math here for the past fifteen years." He cleared his throat before continuing. "I believe there are times a man ought to speak, and others he ought to keep silent. Mostly, I practice the latter. Sure, there's a lot about modern education I think is bunk, but I make a point not to interfere with how other teachers go about their business." He sighed. "I'm a Christian—and not just a professing one, but a practicing one— which pretty much makes me *persona non grata* in today's academic world. But I don't get all bent out of shape about it. Wasn't so long ago, the shoe was on the other foot, so I reckon turnabout is fair play."

Dr. Dunn's voice steadily rose. "But I cannot sit quietly by and watch you meddle with spiritual forces you don't comprehend. Especially on the off-chance you make contact." He reached down to retrieve his coat from where it hung off the back of his chair. "There's no protection against the devil for those who believe he doesn't exist. Take my advice and approve Mr. Dobson's dissertation—the accuracy of which I have no reason to doubt—and send him on his way. Good day."

The audience murmured as Dr. Dunn moved down the aisle and toward the exit. Dr. Estherhouse stood, her expression sour. "Sorry about that, ladies and gentlemen. Sometimes even in academic institutions we get people who are not completely rational." She bowed apologetically, saying "Mr. Dobson, you have the floor."

Dobson forced himself to smile as he motioned toward the back of the room where Min-hee sat apart from the rest of the group, as though abhorrent of human contact. She wore a simple cotton-print dress that was incongruous with the storm-cloud expression on her face. Standing, she pulled the dress over her head, displaying her perfect naked form in all its glory.

The room erupted in gasps as the men struggled not to leer while female academics like Dr. Estherhouse mentally debated whether this constituted an act of self-debasement or female empowerment.

Dobson was determined not to show how heartsick he felt. He wondered if, somewhere deep down, Min-Hee realized that the spirit that once haunted shamaness Woon-Su was now parading her body around in such a wanton fashion. *Spirit...*, he thought. *Or was the Bible-thumper right to suggest it was a demon?*

He had been forced to keep her tied up anytime they weren't together. Otherwise, who knows what might've happened? The airplane ride from Korea to the U.S. had been a nightmare, with Min-hee reaching into the lap of the man sitting next to her and stroking him through his jeans. Dobson had nearly gotten himself punched in the face when he prevented the man from hauling her off to the toilet for induction into the Mile High Club. Only the fear of being denied entry to the U.S. kept her from acting out even further.

Once in the U.S., Dobson and the spirit found themselves at a stalemate. The only way to resolve the situation was for the spirit to find a new host—something Dobson was all too willing to assist with.

Out among the audience, Min-Hee was parading naked up and down the aisles, searching for just the right victim. Finally, she settled on a young couple seated in the second row. The man was obviously enjoying himself tremendously, but the woman next to him had reservations over the whole affair.

Min-Hee pointed at the woman, who drew herself closer to her husband.

"I don't want any part of this," the woman said, almost pleadingly.

Her husband offered her a patronizing stare. His voice was smug. "Oh, come now, dear. This is what we came for. Don't let what that math teacher said creep you out. There's no such thing as "the spirit world," for Chrissake. Go ahead and volunteer. What's it going to hurt?"

Little Black Dress - *Wendy Stenzel Oleston*

TWENTY-THREE YEARS OLD

Bree never felt more alive than in that very moment. A soft breeze was swaying the trees as summer was obviously making its way to town. The college commencement ceremony was now over and the weather had remained perfect, despite the meteorologist's prediction of rain.

She saw her older sister in the sea of people out on the college main square and headed straight for her only guest. First a hug, then the question she knew was coming, "Where are your friends, Bree?"

Shrugging the sadness away quickly, she replied, "I don't know... it doesn't matter." With the return of her smile, Bree beamed. "Can you believe I did it, Bianca? I finally graduated from college and it only took me five years!"

Bianca grinned, releasing her from the tight squeeze. "Stop your bragging... yes, we all know it took me seven to get out of college. Congrats on your speedy escape." Leaning in with a whisper, Bianca taunted, "Of course, if I had managed to stay pure all the way through college, I may have graduated in five years as well. Heck, maybe even four."

Bree's eyes narrowed. "You say that like my purity is something to be embarrassed about."

Bianca looked around the college grounds, perusing the crowd. "You might be the only virgin standing on this lawn right now."

Bree pointed at a five-year-old. "Really… you think so?"

Bianca shook her head. "You know what I mean."

"What's in the gift bag? Is it for me?" Bree asked, already knowing the answer.

"Of course it's for you… go ahead… open it."

Bree took the medium-sized gift bag from her sister and slowly poked her fingers through the white tissue inside. After digging for a moment, she felt something… cotton. Her fingers grasped the material and soon she knew exactly what it was. Eyes filling with tears, the realization she was receiving something she always wanted washed through her. "Oh, Bianca! You didn't have to give this to me. Mom left this dress to you."

Tearing up as well, Bianca shrugged slightly. "Yeah, but it's not really my style so it would just hang in my closet until the moths had their way with it. Mom… well, she gave it to me because I'm the oldest, not because she expected I would wear it." She took the little black dress from Bree, allowing it to drop down the length of Bree's body. Holding it up to Bree's slender, shapely torso, she finished, "It will look perfect on you. Mom… would be so proud of you, Bree. I hope you know that."

Another hug squished the dress right where it hung.

"Oh my goodness! I was hoping you would wear it tonight!" Bianca shouted loudly, seeing Bree walk through the crowd of The Jar Bar. She removed her purse from the barstool next to her. "I saved you a seat… they won't have a table for us for another thirty minutes so… I got you a margarita! Are you ready to celebrate your official induction into adulthood?"

Bree proudly struck a runway pose, showing off the simple black dress that once belonged to her mother. Smooth, fitted, and cinched at the waist, the hem fell right below the knee. The U shaped neckline showed off her neck perfectly and the cap sleeves revealed almost all of her arm. The patterned over-lay just below the bust, ending at the waist, showed off her small waist while also accentuating her bust. She paired the perfectly, fitting dress with simple black heels, leaving one word to describe her overall fashion statement… elegant.

"Gorgeous!" Bianca said after a whistle. "You better watch out, that dress might put your cherry in danger."

Bree laughed as she slid her rear onto the edge of the bar stool. "Leave my cherry out of this!" Her fingers wrapped the chilled margarita glass and she lifted it towards her sister. "To adulthood... may it be more gratifying and less terrifying than expected."

Clink. Sip.

"Oh my, that is strong... but I like it!" Bree's eyes scanned the bar and full restaurant. "Looks like we aren't the only ones celebrating tonight."

"There are some hot guys looking at us."

"Where?" Bree's neck snapped, wanting a peek.

"Play it cool..." Bianca's voice went to a whisper, "To the left... at the end of the bar. Don't be so obvious."

Bree tried to be nonchalant as she turned to see if the guys were really looking at them... and if they were hot. *Damn... they are hot... and they ARE looking at us.* Her eyes met the eyes of the handsome... no, sexy, guy who was definitely checking them out. He had short brown hair gelled in a faux hawk style with blue eyes and just a touch of facial hair. Her heart palpitated as she smiled at him and he returned the gesture. He raised his glass slightly, as if to say hello. Bree looked at Bianca and said, "I call faux-hawk."

Bianca glared. "Bitch."

"Hey, it's my night, I get first choice."

"Fine... I'll take..." she leaned to see what faux hawk's friend looked like. "I'll take Bieber boy... I don't mind."

"Agreed... now we wait and act like we could care less."

They clinked glasses again with a chuckle.

The flirty game of peek-and-ignore went on for ten minutes before faux-hawk finally got off his butt and headed down the bar towards the girls.

"Oh my goodness! He is coming this way, Bianca. Crap. What am I gonna..."

"Excuse me..." his look wasn't the only thing that was sexy; his voice paired quite nicely. " I'm sorry to bother you ladies, but... I couldn't help but notice you are both quite beautiful... and I don't like to see beauties like you alone on a night like tonight. Are you waiting on someone or may my friend and I accompany you?"

Bree and Bianca looked at each other, knowing exactly what the other was thinking… *thick… this guy was laying it on THICK.* They giggled quietly in unison before turning their bodies slightly towards the strangers.

One side of Bianca's eyebrow dipped. "How well does that line usually work for you, faux- hawk?" She took a sip from her straw, which hung sideways out of her mouth.

His face puckered slightly, his confidence not wavering whatsoever. "Lines are for losers. But the truth… well, that is what win's a heart's desire." His eyes pierced Bree's. "If I had thought a line would work on you… I wouldn't have wasted my time walking over here."

Oh, he is smooth.

"My name is Adam and this is Eric. You never answered my question… are you waiting for someone or shall we keep you company?"

The sisters glared at each other for a moment before speaking at the exact same time with very different sentiments.

Bianca said, "We are waiting for our boyfriends."

While Bree spoke the truth, "No, it's just us tonight."

A glare resumed between them.

Adam took a breath and sighed with a sexy smirk. "So, which is it? Boyfriends or solo?"

Neither girl spoke.

Adam pointed at Bianca. "I'm good at reading people, and I'm going to call bullshit on you, blondie."

Bree laughed, knowing just how much her sister hated being called blondie… and to be called a liar.

Bianca squinted tightly. "Just so you know, Adam… you are not winning any points with me as of yet."

"Well, that's good. I want all of my points to be counted up by your friend here, not you… no offense." Adam stared into Bree's eyes again, holding his hand out to her. "And what is your name, beautiful?"

Bree was mesmerized. No one this good-looking and charming had ever paid attention to her before. And right next to her sister, too. Bianca wasn't just the older one… she was also the pretty one. "Bree. My name is Bree." She placed her hand in his, tingling all over at his touch. The warmth of his palm set her heart on fire as she watched him slowly draw her hand up to his mouth and place a tender kiss to it.

"Well, I am quite pleased to make your acquaintance, Bree. Will you allow me to buy your next drink?"

Bree removed her hand from his grasp, "Uh… yeah. Sure. I guess."

They kissed feverishly, her hands searching desperately for the right place to touch him. Each part of him she felt just didn't seem right, so she pawed at him all the more as he did the same. After several moments of grasping, he separated their lips and spoke softly, "I can't take it… I need to touch you… I mean, really touch you."

Eyes connected, she thought. *Oh I like him… I've never liked anyone more. I've never felt this way, ever. It's everything I have ever wanted in a man and he is right here, holding me in his arms. He wants me… and damn, I want him.* She bit her lip seductively. "I… I've…"

"What?" he asked as he began kissing her neck.

Oh, my gosh… I don't know if it's the alcohol or if it's just my time… but I think I'm going to… "I've never had… sex before."

His lips and hands paused abruptly. He slowly leaned back so he could look her in the eyes. "Really?"

Sure of her rosy exterior, she cringed. "Is that bad? Is that a huge turn off?"

Slowly he shook his head. "No, it's just… really? Never?"

His tone made her feel completely insecure so she instinctively pushed him away. "Never mind… maybe you should just go."

He grabbed hold of her quickly. "No… I didn't mean it that way. Really."

She checked him over for the truth. "Really?"

He nodded slowly, leaning in as if to kiss her again. Hand to her cheek, he whispered, "It's nice. It's different, but it's nice."

"Well, I am different."

He grinned, "Yes, you are."

EDGY CHRISTIAN FICTION ANTHOLOGY

She smiled too. "So, you don't mind?"

He shook his head. "Nuh uh. But you should know something."

"What's that?"

His hand smoothed down the side of her face. "The first time isn't very... fun... for girls I mean."

She swallowed hard, with seriousness in her eyes. "I know... I mean I don't know, but I've heard."

He played with her hair for a moment then looked back to her face. "You know what I think?"

Oh no, he is going to try and talk me out of it. He is going to leave and I will never see him again... he is going to...

"I think we should," he kissed her lips softly, "we should get the first time over with..." His lips met hers again. "So we can get to the fun stuff."

He watched her face closely for a reaction, and when she smiled, he did too.

"What do you say, beautiful?"

Bree nodded slowly. "Yeah, I want to get to the good part... with you."

She felt his hand on her back, slowly tugging at her zipper. "As sexy as you are in this little black dress, I gotta be honest... I've been wanting to take it off of you all night."

It wasn't a fable, it wasn't a lie... the first time hurt like hell. It was awkward and uncomfortable, but she was glad to be with someone who seemed to care about making it the best it could be under the circumstances. Being naked with a near stranger was just as uncomfortable for her as the painful prodding that made her wonder what the big deal over sex was. As far she could tell sex was *WAY* overrated.

He went to the bathroom immediately after they were done, leaving her staring at the ceiling and wondering how she should feel about having finally done the deed. She sighed and closed her eyes. The room was spinning a bit; one too many margaritas had her feeling a bit woozy. Warm hands to her belly made her flinch slightly and open her eyes to find Adam crawling back into her bed.

"Hey there," he said with a grin.

"Hey," she replied in a whisper.

His naked body slid up hers until his lips found her mouth for a kiss. After one light kiss, his tongue dove in and his hand searched for the back of her thigh. "Now that's out of the way, we can have some real fun."

"I don't know how much fun I'll be," she said, truly doubting her ability to enjoy this sex thing… ever. She looked up to heaven and spoke to her Lord in her head. *What were you thinking, God? It's horrible… painful, sweaty, embarrassing, fluids dripping down my leg as though I've lost all bladder control… ugh. Gross.*

Adam began kissing her neck as his hand firmly grasped the back of her leg and yanked it up. "We're just getting started, sweetheart. Just relax; it'll be fun, I swear."

Relax. Okay, I can try. I don't think it will do any good… but fine, I'll relax. Bree closed her eyes and took a deep breath. She focused on his mouth and the way he was kissing her neck. *Yeah, that feels nice.* She sighed. *That feels… well hello there!*

She felt him tickle at her, and it was… phenomenal.

Oh, my… that's quite nice. Maybe I have been a tad bit hasty giving sex the cold shoulder. She moaned, not even meaning to.

She heard the smile in his voice. "You like that?"

She smiled after another moan. "It's not awful."

He laughed, and then spoke, "I have a few tricks up my sleeve. Just trying to decide which to use first." He picked one.

"Oh my," she said.

"Oh yeah?"

"Yeah," she opened her eyes to see him raising himself up to look down at her. "What else do you have in your bag of tricks?"

At once, round two began.

She gasped, partially out of shock and partially out of pleasure. Eyes closed, she spoke to God again, needing to correct her prior thoughts on the matter. *Okay, I get it God. It's pretty amazing… I guess You do know what You're doing after all. Sorry I questioned You.*

THIRTY-THREE YEARS OLD

Bree stood at the mirror, slowly brushing her hair ... looking at the woman she had become over the years. So much heartache in such a short span of ten years.

Her fiancé walked into the bathroom. "Oh, Bree, you look stunning. Is that a new dress?"

It was humorous to think of anyone calling her mother's little black dress new, and she huffed a laugh.

"I've never seen that one before. You look amazing... as if you weren't already going to be the most beautiful woman at our rehearsal dinner tonight."

Rehearsal dinner... yes, I am getting married... tomorrow. Her belly flopped as nerves prickled through her. *I don't know if I can do this. I don't know if I'm ready. What if he is disappointed in who I really am? What if he... leaves me?*

Shaun stepped into her, grasping her waist and placing a kiss on her cheek. "What are you thinking about? What has you so wistful when you should be smiling?"

Shaun wasn't perfect but one thing was for certain... he was attentive. Bree nestled into him, feeling as though she may cry. "This dress was my mother's."

His arms wrapped her in a pure effort to comfort her; he was good at that. "Are you missing her because of the wedding?"

She spoke the truth, even though this subject might bother the man who now claimed to love her enough to devote his life to her. "No; memories are haunting me. The last time I wore it... well, let's just say it was a turning point in my life. I guess I wanted to try and give it new life by wearing it to something wonderful, but now... it's just reminding me... and I wish I hadn't put it on."

Shaun stepped away slightly, wanting to see her face. "Do you want to talk about it?"

She wasn't sure... did she? And with him? She shrugged. *No! I can't... I can't tell him about the most embarrassing, degrading thing to ever happen to me... the thing that changed how I felt about myself forever.* Bree separated from him, reached to the back of the dress, and began to unzip it. "I'm just going to change... it's not a big deal."

"Bree, the dress isn't the problem."

His voice was firm and it made her halt.

Shaun's hand reached out to her. "Come sit with me. Let's talk."

After short consideration, Bree nodded and took his hand. He led her into their bedroom and sat her on the bed, sitting closely next to her. He played with her hand while patiently waiting for her to start.

"I lost my virginity that night and I haven't worn it since." It felt like she just blurted it out with no sensitivity at all. "I'm sorry; I understand if you don't want to talk about this."

Shaun shook his head slightly, looking at her. "If it's bothering you, then I want to talk about it… okay?"

"Are you sure?"

"Yes, Bree. We are getting married. I want you to be comfortable telling me anything… everything."

Tears began to build in her eyes. *He is such a good man. Why is he with me? What if he realizes how much better off he would be without me? What if… he leaves me?*

Seeing her distress, he asked the obvious question, "Were you raped?"

Bree's brow creased as she shook her head. "No, but sometimes I wonder if that would have been better." Eyes meeting his, she squeezed his hand. "I was so stupid… Bianca and I were out celebrating my graduation from college and we met these two guys. I drank way too much and we ended up back at my apartment, fooling around. He was handsome and charming and I had never felt so ignited by anyone. Booze, excitement, and twenty-two years of repressed sexuality I guess turned me into a complete moron, and I decided to go ahead and have sex with him."

She looked at her fidgety hands. "I really thought he might be the one I had been waiting for. He said all the right things; he was sweet and careful with me. He showed me a good time, to be honest… but…" she stopped as tears collected at the memories. A single tear fell down her cheek. "I was wrong."

Shaun stood to fetch the box of tissues on their dresser, and then returned to her, offering her one.

She swiped one out of the box, wiping her cheek. "In the

morning, we exchanged phone numbers and a kiss and he left. I was certain this was my next relationship. I was certain I had just met my forever after and I was so excited by the thought of it. All my waiting had paid off and now, we were going to fall in love, get married, and have kids." Bree looked at her husband-to-be, wiping more tears away. "I feel bad telling you this; I'm sorry."

"Don't be sorry at all," he said as he gently rubbed her back. "I know you are with me now; it's okay. We all have a past... it's what makes us who we are now."

Yes, it certainly made me who I am now... a scared, insecure woman who only pretends to be confident. Bree smiled at his kindness.

"Go on, tell me what happened."

A roll came to her eyes as she remembered the next, most humiliating part... *Am I really going to say this out loud? Can I? I've never told anyone this... not even Bianca.* "I waited a few days to hear from him. I didn't want to seem needy or too eager... you know how you men are. You are easily scared off."

Shaun chuckled lightly. "Yes, some of us are, especially when we are young and only able to think with our pleasure units."

Pleasure unit... ha, that's funny. A brief grin covered her face but didn't stay long. Back to the seriousness, Bree stared at the ceiling, trying to hold the tears in as she considered the proper words. "He didn't... call." She took a deep breath in, trying to muster the nerve to say the worst of it, the part that made her know for sure... she wasn't worth much. "After a week, I decided to call him..."

"And what was his grand excuse?"

She swallowed again then turned her face away from the man who claimed to love her now. "He didn't have one... I never spoke to him."

"Did you leave him a message? Did he just not call you back?"

She closed her eyes as the tears came in full force.

Shaun gently turned her face towards his. "Bree, sweetie, tell me what happened."

"He... gave me a fake number. I called him only to discover the number was to a local movie theater listing." She covered her face with her hands as she sobbed.

"Oh, Bree, I'm so sorry." He quickly wrapped his arms around his fiancée and kissed the top of her head as she melted. "Oh, sweetie... you know that wasn't about you, don't you?"

Sobbing into his chest, her heart ached like never before. She couldn't believe she allowed the words to leave her body. "Who else would it be about, Shaun?"

With his index finger, he made her look at him. "It was about him being a total asshole."

Her eyes closed as she shook her head. "No, he was a nice guy... I just didn't deserve him. Just like I don't deserve you and if I'm going to be honest, I'm scared to death to marry you, Shaun. I'm scared you will realize it one day and... leave me."

He drew her face to his, lips almost on hers. "Stop it, Bree. You need to calm down and listen to me."

She took a few deep breaths to get herself under control, and when she was calmed slightly, she felt his warm, tender lips cover hers. Her heart palpitated... she actually felt herself yearn for the first time in... years. Yes, they were living together and yes, they were sexually active, but the truth of the matter was she only did it *for him*. She found no pleasure in their sexual relationship at all. She had faked every orgasm she ever had with him. Essentially, their intimacy was an act.

"I love you and I'm not leaving you. Do you hear me? We are getting married tomorrow and it is going to be the happiest day of my life."

Racing like a hamster in a wheel, her heart ached. "But you don't really know me. I have secrets. Secrets I am ashamed of. The confident woman you fell in love with is a myth... I'm a fake, a sham... nothing more than a bad actress."

He chuckled again. "Do you really think I don't know about your insecurities? Do you really think I have spent the last two years of my life with you, the last year living with you and don't have a clue as to what's deep inside you? I am many things, Bree. But I am no idiot."

Her eyes were glued to his.

"Do you really think I'm not aware that you separate your heart from your body, become completely detached when we make love? Of course I know. And do you know why I know?"

Her head shook in silence.

"Because I care, Bree. Because I love you."

"Why haven't you ever said anything?"

"Sweetie, that is your journey and I can't fix it for you. Just know that I'm not going anywhere. When you're ready to face things, I will be right by your side every step of the way. And by the way, you *DO* deserve me. You deserve the best in life."

A rush of emotion passed through her as she looked at the blonde haired, brown eyed man who had just said all the right things. *But Adam said all the right things too. And Adam was a liar. What if... Shaun is a liar too? What if they are all liars? What if it's not them... it's me?*

"What?" he asked.

She shook her head again, not wanting to admit her thoughts.

"I'm not him."

"I've slept with a lot more men than you know about. I used sex for years, trying to find someone to really love me. I was always so hopeful the next one would be the one but... all I ever got was another broken heart. I'm afraid by the time I met you... there wasn't much left of it. When you asked me how many men I'd been with, I lied to you." Again, it felt like it was blurted out with no consideration.

Shaun laughed. "So? Is that supposed to scare me off?" He sighed. "You don't have to lie to me. In fact, I would appreciate it if our marriage could start out with a promise not to lie."

She chuckled slightly. "You mean you don't want to be married to a liar?"

"Not really, no," he replied with a smile. He took her hands in his. "When I asked you if you were raped, you said no... but I disagree. He may not have taken sex from you without your permission, but it sounds like he took your dignity from you without permission. He knowingly misled you for his own benefit...and in my book, and I'm fairly certain in God's book, that is rape."

She had never thought of it that way before, but it made sense.

"Are we good now?"

She squinted to let him know there was one more thing.

"Go ahead, lay it on me."

"I'm having some regrets… about us."

He seemed totally taken aback. His head snapped back a few inches and his eyes popped open. "Regrets? About us? This doesn't sound good… definitely not something a groom wants to hear the day before his wedding."

"No, nothing like that… it's just…" she hemmed and hawed a bit. "I kind of wish we had waited."

The air that had filled his lungs was released quickly. "Oh, sex. You wish we had waited until we were married."

She nodded. "Yeah, and to move in together. It feels like some of the excitement and wonder of marriage has been taken away. We already know each other in every way so… what's the difference going to be once the 'I do's' are said?"

His face showed strength. "Can I be honest with you?"

"No, I much prefer deceit," she replied in jest, causing him to laugh quite loudly.

"I know we didn't do this the way God said we should, and I too have some regrets about that, but we can't change the past, Bree. We just have to move towards the future, doing the best we can. I think… this conversation is one of the best ones we have ever had, and I'm so glad you told me what's in your heart. I want you to know, your heart will be guarded by me always. I will never purposely slip you the wrong number, I will never use you for my own personal gain, and with that said… I don't want to have sex with you again until you are all there with me. I want our next 'first time', our 'first time' as true man and wife, to be the 'first time' you truly deserved."

It was the sweetest thing anyone had ever said to her and she swooned like never before… maybe even more than she had with Adam those ten years prior. "I love you." She lunged towards him quickly, her lips meeting his, her fingers lacing into the hair on the back of his head. Their kiss deepened quickly.

He slowed things down with a smile. "Now that is what I'm talking about… that was all in. I want more of *that*. But you're gonna have to wait until tomorrow… no lovin' for you until we're legal."

She smiled softly, staring into his eyes.

"Okay fiancée… are you ready to be the bell of the ball? If we don't get ourselves out the door soon, we are going to be late to our own party."

Bree nodded. She turned her back to him and held her hair up out of the way. "Can you zip me up, please?"

He gently kissed her back then replied, "My pleasure."

WOULD HAVE BEEN FIFTY-THREE YEARS OLD

Dear Mandalyn,

If you are receiving this letter, it means you have graduated from college... Oh, my dear daughter, congratulations! It seems like just yesterday your dad and I were getting married... and then you came along. What a crazy journey life has been. I want you to know without doubt just how proud of you we are, how proud of you I am. You are a strong, smart, confident young woman with so much life ahead of you... you remind me of myself... we are so much alike it is scary. I know you hate when I remind you of this, but I'm going to do it anyway... your name is not haphazard! Your dad and I chose it for you hoping you will always remember its meaning... worthy of love. Please, my lovely daughter, never forget that you are so worthy of love; don't ever let anyone steal that from you like I did. I'm sorry I can't be with you as you celebrate this day... just know I know exactly how you feel. Losing your mother is hard, especially when you are as close as we were. I'm sorry cancer took me from you and your dad... just know I'm watching you and I love you no matter what you do in life, no matter what mistakes you make, no matter how your journey winds and weaves... you are loved. Take good care of your dad; he is by far the best man I have ever known. I pray you find a man who treats you the way he has treated me.

I'm giving you my little black dress, the one that belonged to my mother. I know it will look fantastic on you now that you are all grown up. I remember when you were just a little lady, how you always wanted to play dress up with it. It would drag on the floor, but you didn't care, you were just proud to be like me. Now that it is yours, I want you to make me a promise... when you wear it, you will guard your heart above all else. When you wear it, you will let it be a reminder of Jesus' love for you. Remember, He is a perfect gentleman who will never force His way on you. For His yoke is easy and His burden is light... let Him fill you with patience and guide you in those moments when you aren't sure what to do. But more than anything, it is my hope this dress will be one filled with happy memories and well-thought out choices that will shape your future into exactly the happiness you deserve. You will make mistakes... there is no doubt... but rest assured, Mandalyn, you are loved.

I'm sorry I will not be there the day you walk down the aisle or the day you welcome your first child into the world, but do you know what you can count on? I will be right here in heaven waiting for you on the day you say your final goodbye to the world. Until then, my precious daughter... love well and be well loved.

From the bottom of my heart,
Mom

I wrote *Little Black Dress* with the hope of touching the reader with the unending love of Jesus. We often base our self-worth on what other people think of us instead of allowing ourselves to be permeated by what our Creator thinks. If you are on a self-worth journey, I challenge you to read my book *As Is*. Please check out my other books at www.wendyoleston.com Thank you for reading my story!

The Pure in Heart - *Peggy Payne*

He would not have said that he was ever "called" to the ministry. It wasn't like that. Instead, he grew up knowing that it would be so. The church was Swain Hammond's future-unofficially. He got his doctorate at Yale. Then, after one brief stint as an associate minister, he became the pastor at Westside, a good choice for - as he had become - a man of rational, ethical orientation.

The church, in Chapel Hill, North Carolina, is Presbyterian. It is fairly conventional, though influenced, certainly, by the university community. Swain is happy here. Westside suits him. But it is clearly not the best place to hold the pastorate if you're the sort who's inclined to hear the actual voice of God. Up until recently, this would not have been a problem for Swain. But about eight weeks ago, the situation changed. At that time, Swain did indeed hear God.

He and his wife Julie were grilling skewers of pork and green peppers on the back patio of the stone house they chose themselves as the manse. They have no children. Julie works. She is a medical librarian at the hospital, though if you met her you would never think of libraries. You might think of Hayley Mills in some of those movies from her teenage years. She has the same full features and thick red hair. On this particular night, Julie is turning a shish ke-bab, which seems to be falling apart. Swain, bare-footed-it is June-is drinking a beer and squinting up the slight hill of their backyard, which they have kept wooded.

"Isn't that a lady slipper?" he says. "Was that out yesterday?" But Julie is busy; she doesn't look. Swain, his long white feet still bare, carefully picks his way up the hill to examine the flower. It is then, as he stops yards away from the plant -clearly not a lady slipper-that he hears God for the first time.

The sound comes up and over the hill. One quick cut. Like a hugely amplified PA system, blocks away; switched on for a moment by mistake. "Know that there is truth. Know this." The last vowel, the T of this, lies quivering on the air like a note struck on a wineglass.

The voice is unmistakable. At the first intonation, the first rolling syllable, Swain wakes, feeling the murmuring life of each of a million cells. Each of them all at once. He feels the line where his two lips touch, the fingers of his left hand pressed against his leg, the spears of wet grass against the flat soles of his feet, the gleaming half-circles of tears that stand in his eyes. His own bone marrow hums inside him like colonies of bees. He feels the breath pouring in and out of him, through the damp red passages of his skull. Then in the slow way that fireworks die, the knowledge fades. He is left again with his surfaces and the usual vague darkness within. He turns back around to see if Julie has heard.

She has not. Her back turned to him, she is serving the two plates that he has set on the patio table. A breeze is moving the edge of the outdoor tablecloth. She turns back around toward him, looking up the hill. "Soup's on," she says, smiling. "Come eat." She stands and waits for him, as he walks, careful still of his feet and the nettles, back down to her. Straight to her. He takes her in his arms, ignoring her surprise, the half-second of her resistance. He pulls her close, tight against him, one hand laced now in her hair, one arm around her hips. He is as close as he can get. He has gathered all of her to him that he can hold.

He puts the side of his face against her cheek, so he will not have to see her eyes when he says: "Julie, over there on the grass, I heard something. A voice."

She pulls back from him, forcing him to see her. She raises her eyebrows, half-smiling, searching his face for the signs of a joke. "A voice?" she says. There is laughter ready in her tone.

"God," he says. His mouth is dry. "God's voice."

She watches him carefully now, her eyes scanning his eyes,

74

ever-so-slightly moving. The trace of a smile is gone. "What do you mean?"

"Standing up there on the hill," he says, almost irritably. "I heard God. That's what I mean." He watches her, his own face blank. Hers is struggling. Let her question it if she wants to. He doesn't know how to explain.

"So what happened?" she says. "Tell me some more." She pauses. "What did it -what did the voice sound like?"

Swain repeats the words he heard. He does not say then what happened to him: that hearing the voice, he had felt the mortality of his every cell.

They stand apart from each other now. She reaches over and touches his hair, strokes it. If one of us was to hear God, it should have been Julie, he thinks. But a different God -the one he has believed in until today.

She is looking at him steadily. "I don't think you're crazy; if that's what you're worried about." Her uncertainty has left her. "It's all right," she says. "It is."

"For you it would be," he says. He means it as a compliment. He has envied her imaginings, felt left behind sometimes by the unfocused look of her eyes. Though she will tell him where she is: that she goes back, years back, to particular days with particular weathers. That she plays in the backyard of her grandparents' house, shirtless, in seer- sucker shorts, breathing the heavy summer air, near the blue hydrangeas. Swain wants to be with her then. He wants to go: "Except ye become as little children, ye shall not enter...." He wants, and yet he doesn't want.

She glances at the food on the plates. They move toward the table. The sweat that soaked his shirt has started to chill him.

"I'm going to get a sweater," he says. "Do you want anything?" She shakes her head no. She sits, begins to eat her cooling dinner.

There are no lights on inside the house, only the yellowish glow of the patio light through the window; shining on one patch of floor in the hall. He goes to the hall closet, looking for something to put on. He finds a light windbreaker. He has his hand in the closet, reaching for the jacket, when he hears the voice again. One syllable. "Son." The sound unfurls down the long hall toward him. He feels the sound and its thousand echoes hit him all at once. He holds onto the wooden bar where the coat hangs, while the shock washes over his back.

He stays where he is, his back and neck bent, his hand bracing him, waiting. Nothing else happens. Again, it is over. Again he is wet with sweat. He straightens, painfully, as if he had held the position for hours. He walks again out onto the patio. Julie, at the table, squints to see his face against the light beside the door.

Are you all right?" she says.

He sits, looks down at his plate. He holds the jacket, lays it across his lap like a napkin. He shakes his head. A sob is starting low in his chest, dry like a cough. He feels it coming, without tears. He has not cried since he tore a ligament playing school soccer. He has had no reason. Now he is crying, his own voice tearing and breaking through him. Inside him, walls are falling. Interior walls cave like old plaster, fall away to dust. He feels it like the breaking of living bones. In the last cool retreat of his reason, he thinks: I am seeing my own destruction. Then that cool place is invaded too. He feels the violent tide of whatever is in him flooding his last safe ground. He holds himself with both arms; Julie, on her knees beside his chair, holds him. God has done this to him. This is God. Tears drip from his face and trickle down his neck.

Two days later Swain sits alone in his office at the church. He has a sermon to write. Should he tell the congregation what happened to him? His note pad is blank. He has put down his pen. It is an after- noon with all the qualities of a sleepless night: hot, restless, unending. There are no distractions from what he is unable to do. The secretary is holding his calls. The couple who were to come in with marital difficulties cancelled. The window behind his desk is open; he stares out into the shimmery heat and listens to the churning of a lawn mower. He has already been through the literature and found nothing to reassure him.

Son. He keeps coming back to that one word in his mind. It was not Swain's own father talking. That was clear. His father would never have been so definite, so terse. The elder Dr. Hammond would have interspersed his words, and there would have been more of them, with long moments of musing and probably the discreet small noises of his dyspepsia. He would have asked Swain to consider whether there was indeed "a truth": Swain would have considered this, as he was asked. And possibly at some later time they would have discussed it, without conclusion.

Swain, twisting in his chair, resettling his legs, knows he did not create the voice. He did not broadcast that sound out through the pines of his own backyard. He sees again the reddish gold light of the late sun on the bark of those backyard trees. He did not imagine it. His mind does not play tricks.

Though the whole thing seems like a bad trick, a bad dream, divine revelation, coming now. He imagines himself in the pulpit, staring out at the congregation, telling them. He sees the horror waking on their faces, as they understand him. He sees them exchanging glances, glances that cut diagonally across the pews. He would be out. It would cost him the church. Leaders of the congregation would gradually, lovingly ease him out, help him make "other arrangements." He tries to imagine those other arrangements: churches with marquees that tally up the number saved on a Sunday, churches with buses and all-white congregations. Appalling. It makes him shudder.

He turns his chair away from the window, back to his desk. It is too soon. He has nothing to say. Know that there is truth? A half-sentence? He at least needs time to think about it. Then perhaps he can make some sense out of it. Of course he will make public confession finally. He will witness. He has to. "Whoever shall confess me before men, him shall the Son of Man also confess before the angels of God." There is no question. "... He that denieth me before men ..." It is his mission - to speak. A man could not remain a minister with such a secret.

On Saturday, he has a wedding. He has already put on his robe. His black shoes gleam. He sits at his desk, ready early, signing letters left here in his box by the secretary. Routine business. His sermon for Sunday is written, typed in capital letters. It makes no direct reference to hearing the voice of God.

He does like marrying couples, thinks of it, in fact, as an important part of his ministry. When a couple gets together within the church, it always seems to him a sort of personal victory. As the boy said two weeks ago at the junior high retreat, "Human relations is where it's at."

The pair this afternoon is interesting to him in a more particular way. He has been counseling them since Louise, the bride-to-be, found out she was pregnant. She is thirty-eight, roughly his own age. She and Alphonse, a Colombian, have lived together for about three years. They have planned for today a fairly traditional, almost formal ceremony. She is not yet showing. He remembers her when she was alone. He could see her on Sunday mornings canvassing the congregation with her eyes, picking out the occasional male visitor holding his hymnbook alone. Watching her in those years, he wondered what his own life would be like, without Julie. Whether he would show that same hunger so plainly on his face. He is glad for Louise, pregnant as she is. He caps his pen and stands. It's time to go in.

The feel is different now in the sanctuary, more relaxed than the eleven o'clock. Maybe it's only the afternoon light, filtered as it is by stained glass. He stands at the chancel steps, the ceremony begins. Alphonse comes to stand beside him. They face the aisle where Louise is to enter on the arm of her sister's husband. Swain tests the sound of their names, rehearses them in silence - Louise Elizabeth Berryman, Alphonse Martinez Vasconcellos. The twang and the beat of the Spanish - he has resolved to get it right, not to anglicize. He runs through the name again -and a scene unwinds like a scroll inside him. Gerona.

Louise, coming down the aisle now, slowly, slowly, moves in her long pale dress behind the clear shapes of his sudden unsought memory. He is twenty years old, standing in a stone-walled room in Spain. The straps of his backpack pull at his shoulders. It is quiet here, blocks away from the narrow river and the arched bridges. In this room: he read it in his guidebook - there was a revelation. He stands, with his two friends, in a medieval landmark of the kabbalah. It is the moment, unplanned, when all three become quiet, when he can only hear the muted traffic from the street. He is looking for something in this room. He lays his hand on the grainy stone of the wall. Standing now in the sanctuary, he feels the damp grit of rock against the flat of his palm. He can't escape it, he can't shake it off. He wears it-this slight tingling pressure - like a glove. A wet glove that clings to his skin. Louise is now at the front before him.

The couple turns to him. They wait. "Dearly beloved," he hears himself say. Faces stretch in a blur to the back of the church. He hears his voice - it must be his - float out to those faces, saying, "We are gathered here today. ..."

He has told Julie everything, about hearing the voice. Not just the words, but how it felt. He has told her about the intrusion of the scene from Spain at the wedding this afternoon. "That was the last thing I needed," he says. "For that to happen while I'm actually standing at the front." They are sitting at the kitchen table. It's late.

She shrugs. The look on her face is the one he tries to cultivate in counseling. She is not shocked. Yet she does not diminish what happened to him. The look is one of sympathy and respect at once. She does it, he knows, without thinking.

She nods toward the typewriter, his old one, standing in its case near the bookshelves. They both use it for letters, neither one of them has a legible handwriting. "You've always set the margins so narrow," she says. "On yourself, on what's real. You don't give yourself much room."

She waits. He thinks about it.

"True," he says, nodding, looking away from her. "And you give yourself that kind of- 'room' you're talking about." He looks at her, her chin propped on one hand, her face pushed slightly out of shape. "But do you actually believe in it," he says, "in what you see and hear, in the things you imagine? You don't. Of course you don't."

She puts her hand down, on the table, away from her face. She takes a breath and holds it a second before she speaks. The look she has had, of authority; is gone. "In a way," she says. She searches his face. "I don't think too much about it. But - yes, in a way, I do."

There is no joy in it. That's what bothers him. He is lying on the living room floor, still thinking about it, though he hasn't mentioned any of it, even to Julie, for almost a week. Maybe silence will make the whole thing go away. Julie is in the armchair reading, her feet in old white tennis shoes, her ankles crossed near his head. He watches her feet move, very slightly, in a rhythm, as if she were listening to music in-stead of reading. Maybe she hears music and never mentions it. She likes music. Maybe she's hearing Smetana's Moldau, close enough to the orchestra to hear between the movements the creakings of musicians' chairs. She would do this and think nothing of it. She has been patient with his days of silent turmoil.

As a kid, he wanted something like this to happen. Some sign. He did imagine though that it would bring with it pleasure - great happiness, in fact. He had a daydream of how it would be, set in the halls and classrooms of his elementary school, where he first imagined it. A column of warm pink light would pour over him, overpowering him with a sensation so intensely sweet it was unimaginable. He tried and tried to feel how it would feel. The warmth would wrap around his heart inside his chest, like two hands cradling him there. He would be full of happiness, completely at peace. The notion stayed with him past childhood, though, certainly in his earlier years; he didn't talk about it.

But he did what he could to have that experience. Divine revelation. He wanted it. He lay on the floor of his bedroom at home, later his dorm room at Brown, and waited. He stared at rippling creeks and wind-blown leaves and the deep chalky green of blackboards until his mind was lulled into receptive quiet. The quietness always passed, though, without interruption, at least by anything divine.

The search must have ended finally. Only now does he realize it, lying here with the front door standing open and moths batting against the screen, He doesn't recall any such preoccupation during divinity school, though there was that one thing that happened in his last year. It hardly qualified him as a mystic, though it was reassuring at the time.

He was sitting out on the balcony of his apartment, a second-floor place he shared with two other students. He and Julie, not married then, were in one of their off times. He was feeling bad. The concordance, the notepad had slid off his lap. His legs were sprawled, completely motionless, in front of him, hanging off the end of the butt-sagged recliner. He had lost Julie; he was bone-tired of school, he wouldn't have cared if he died.

He was staring at the scrubby woods behind the apartment complex, behind the parking lot and a weedy patch of mud and three dumpsters. Nothing mattered. Nothing at all. Then while he watched, everything-without motion or shift of light-everything he saw changed. He stared at the painted stripes on the asphalt, at water standing on the yellowish mud. It was all alive. Alive and sharing one life. The parking lot, the bare ground had become the varied skill of one living being. In the stillness, he waited for the huge creature to move, to take a breath. Nothing stirred. Yet he felt the benevolence of the animal, its power, rising off the surface before him like waves of heat.

What he felt then was a lightness, a sort of happiness. This was so important. It was at least a hint of what he had once imagined.

That afternoon he was buoyed. He finished the work he had sat with the whole afternoon. He fried himself a hamburger and ate it and was still hungry. He watched a few minutes of the news. He did not die or think further of dying after that day, other than for the purposes of sermons, counseling, and facing the inevitable facts.

Facts. He is lying on the floor of his living room. Julie is reading in the chair. God has spoken to him, in English, clearly, in an unmistakable voice. He is not glad.

"What would you do, Julie?" he says. He is looking at the ceiling, he does not turn his head. "Would you stand up in that pulpit and tell them, 'I have heard the voice of God'? Would you do it?" He rolls over on his side and looks at her. Her foot has stopped moving. She has put her book down.

"I've been thinking about that," she says.

"What did you decide?"

"Probably." she says. "I think I would." She is not smiling. She looks at him steadily. Her eyes are tired.

"Oh?" he says. There is an edge in his voice. "What else would you say? How would you explain it? Explain to me, if you understand so well." He pauses, waits.

"Say as much as you know;" she says.

"What is that? One piece of a sentence: know that there is truth. It isn't enough. I have nothing to say."

"It's your job, isn't it?" she says. "To tell them. Isn't it?" He sees the fear flickering across her face now. She needs to say it, but she's scared. It's the way he would be, standing before his incredulous congregation. Fearing the cost. What could it cost her to say this?

"You're afraid to tell me," he says. His voice is weary; dull. She nods.

"Why?"

She swallows, looks away from him. "Because I'm saying you need to do something that may turn out bad. It would be the most incredible irony-but it could happen. They might decide you're losing your marbles. They might call it that, when really they don't want a minister who says this kind of stuff-about hearing God. It's not that kind of church. You know?"

He ignores the question. "We could have to move," he says. 'We could wind up somewhere we would hate. Is that what you're worried about?"

"Some," she says. "But mostly that you would blame me, if it happened-that you would always feel like I pushed you into it."

"And then the marriage would fall apart," he says.

"Yeah," she says. Her voice shakes. Her mouth has the soft forgotten look it gets when all of her is concentrated elsewhere. In this case, on fear. He is not in the mood to reassure her.

"And what if I don't do it?" he says. "What if I never say a word and you spend the rest of your life thinking I'm a shit -a minister who denies God? What happens to us then?"

She shakes her head. She is close to tears. "I don't think that will happen," she says. It comes out in an uneven whisper.

Swain stands, straightens his pants legs. He looks at her once without sympathy; but her face is averted, she doesn't see. He leaves the room, goes into the kitchen. He gets out a small tub of Haagen-Dazs and a spoon, stands near the fridge, eating from the container. There is no sound from her in the other room. Pink light-what a joke. "Suppose ye that I am come to give peace on earth? I tell you, Nay; but rather division." The voice didn't warn him, didn't remind him. He shakes his head. He digs and scrapes at the ice cream.

He is turning his car into the church parking lot when it happens again. He hears God. His window is open. The car is lurched upward onto the incline of the pavement. The radio is on, but low. From the hedge, a few feet from his elbow on the window frame, a sound emerges. It clearly comes from there: a burst, a jumble of phrases, scripture, distortions of scripture: "He that hath and doeth not ... for there is nothing hid ... the word is sown on stony ground ... why reason ye... seeketh his own glory ... he that hath ears ... he that hath...." A nightmare. A nightmare after a night of too much reading. A spilling of accusation, reproach. Swain is staring straight ahead. A hot weight presses into him, into the soft vee beneath the joining of his ribs. It hurts, it pins him to the seat. It passes like cramp, leaving only a shadow; a distrust of those muscles.

Another car is waiting behind him, easing toward his fender. He pulls into the parking lot, into a space. He does it automatically. His face feels as hot as the sun-baked plastic car seat. He looks at the hedge, running between the sidewalk and the street. Tear it out - that's what he wants to do. Pull it up, plant by plant, with his hands. He is a pastor. Not a prophet. Not a radio evangelist. He does not believe in gods that quote the King James version out of bushes and trees.

He gets out of the car, goes into the church, into his office. He kicks the door shut behind him. He tosses a new yellow legal pad onto the bare center of his desk. There has to be something in this room to smash. He looks around: at the small panes of the window; at the veneer on the side of his desk; at the cluster of family pictures, framed; at the bud vase Julie gave him, that now holds two wilting daisies and a home-grown rose. Something to break. He grabs the vase by the neck and slings it, overarm, dingy water spilling, into a pillow of the sofa. A soft thump, and the stain of water spreads on the dark upholstery. He looks away from it, looks at the yellow pad on his desk. His career.

That's what he'll smash. That ought to be enough. He walks around behind the desk, sits, red-faced, breathing audibly through parted lips. He stares at the lined paper with the pen in his hand. Say as much as you know. He begins to write. Beyond writing it down, he tells himself, he has made no decision.

On the following Sunday, he walks forward into the pulpit. He has received the offering. He has performed the preliminary duties with a detached methodical calm. Now he stands with his hands on the wooden rail, his fingers finding their familiar places along the tiered wood. "Friends," he says. He looks at no one in particular. "I have struggled with what I have to say to you today:" They are waiting, with no more than their routine interest. "I have come to say to you that I have heard the voice of God." He says it to the rosette of stained glass at the back of the sanctuary: He cannot look at Julie in the third row. He cannot look at the McDougalls or Sam Bagdikian or Mary Elgar, as he says it. In the ensuing silence, his eyes sweep forward again, from the window back across three hundred faces. They are blank, waiting still, mildly interested. No one is alarmed. They have not understood.

He begins again. As much as he knows. "I think you know that I believe in an immanent God. I think you know that I believe in the presence and power of God in all our lives. I have come to tell you today that something has happened to me in recent days which I do not understand.

"A voice has spoken to me. I know that it is God. A voice has spoken to me that was a chorus of voices. I know that they are God." He pauses. "My wife Julie and I were cooking dinner on the grill on our back patio...." The faces grow taut with attention. Sudden stillness falls over the church to the back pews of the balcony: There is no flutter of church bulletins. There are no averted faces. It is not a metaphor, not a parable he is telling. His wife Julie, the back patio - they are listening. He proceeds, with a trembling deep in his gut. He begins with the lady slipper and voice that came over the hill.

He tells them about the word "son" and the windbreaker and his own tears. "I asked myself whether I should bring this to you on a Sunday morning," he says. He looks from face to face in the rows in front of him. What are they thinking? It's impossible to tell. The shaking inside him has moved outward, to his hands. He feels them damp against the wood of the pulpit rail. He does not trust his voice.

"I asked myself how you, the members of this congregation, would react. Would you think that I've -" he tries to say this lightly, with a wry laugh - "that maybe I've been under too much stress lately." The laugh is not convincing. He himself hears its false ring. "But I will tell you," he says, "that that is not what has happened. I have not taken leave of my senses."

He looks at Julie. He can see her wrists, before the back of the pew breaks his vision. He knows her hands are knotted together, moving one against the other. He pulls his eyes away.

"I asked myself whether you would want a pastor who hears voices. Or even. whether some of you might come to expect wisdom from me, because of what has happened, that I do not have." He pauses. "I don't know what to expect," he says, "from you or -" he hesitates "from God. But I will tell you that my heart is now open. I will listen." He steps back, hearing as he does so the first note of the organ; reliable Miss Bateman is playing. The congregation stands, hymnbooks in hands. The service ends without incident. Swain stands as usual at the front steps afterwards to shake hands and greet people. Three of all those who file past tell him that the Lord works in wondrous ways, or something to that effect. Miss Frances Eastwood squeezes his elbow and tells him to trust. Ed Fitzgerald lays one hand on his shoulder, close to his collar, and says, "I like what you did here today." The rest make no mention of what has occurred. The line moves quickly past him, handshakes, heartiness, veiled eyes.

It is not over, of course. Julie keeps her hand on his knee as he drives home, though they say little. During the afternoon, he receives several phone calls at home, of an encouraging and congratulatory nature. Coming back into the kitchen, where Julie is cleaning out drawers to keep busy he says, "It's the ones who don't call, who are calling each other...."

What does occur happens gradually: Swain is given no answer, no sense of having-got-it-over on that Sunday afternoon. First, as he surmises, conversations buzz back and forth, on the telephone, at get-togethers, in chance meetings on the street. People inside and outside the church talk about what happened, about Swain Hammond's sermon.

The night the church operations committee meets, Swain and Julie stay home and play Scrabble. Swain can't concentrate, but Julie pro- tests every time he wants to quit. The call comes at 11:15. It's Joe Morris. "Between you and me," Joe reminds him, "this is an unofficial...."

The upshot of it is that the committee voted five-to-four to privately recommend that Swain get professional help. The chairman, Bill Bartholomew, who made the motion, comes to Swain's office to tell him. "Of course," he says, "this is something which is not easy to say. But we all go through times when we need...."

"Thank you for your prayers and concern," Swain says. He is accustomed to assuming a look of gratitude when it is called for. It only fails him in the last minutes of the conversation.

"Are you so sure I'm crazy, Bill?" he says. The two of them are standing now in the office doorway, there is no one in the hall. "Doesn't it seem contradictory?" Swain says. Bill is watching him carefully. "It's okay to believe in God, but only if God is distant. A presence in history. Is that the idea?"

"I'm sure I don't want to debate this with you," Bill says. "It's only the will of the committee - "

"I understand your position," Swain says. He does not seek counseling.

When news of the committee's action leaks, a petition circulates and the members take sides. This time the vote is with Swain. The letter, signed by the majority of the members, affirms that Dr. Swain Hammond is in his right mind and will continue to be welcome as minister. These are not the exact words, but this is the meaning.

Swain mentions this decision from the pulpit, but only as a brief comment among the day's other announcements. "Thank you for your love and support," he says. Unexpectedly, as he says it, he feels a tightness in his throat. He looks from face to face. He won't be leaving. If he thinks about it, he'll lose his composure. He summons a bit of the anger that has sustained him through the last few weeks. It works, he manages to keep the wave of love at bay.

"Besides," he tells Julie later that day, "I don't . completely trust it." They are taking a late afternoon walk through the neighborhood around their house. "I feel like all this could change, if the balance shifted just a little. I'm reasonably secure for the moment," he says. "I suppose that will have to do."

She doesn't say anything. She has said her part several times already: that she is proud of him, that she is proud of what he did.

"I'm also disappointed," he says. They stop for a moment to avoid the arc of spray from a sprinkler cutting across the sidewalk. "I thought maybe a few people would be curious about what actually happened. Would want to hear more." He shakes his head. "They don't." It makes him mad to think about it. They've decided to put up with him - that's what they've made of all this. They're being broad-minded and tolerant, that's all.

Swain does hear the voice of God again. This time - last Tuesday morning - it is as a note of music, as he is just waking up. Julie lies beside him asleep. It is early, still twenty minutes before the alarm is set to go off. He knows before it happens that it's coming. He does not move. He waits, while the note emerges from a sound too deep to be heard. Then it is audible, filling the room, humming against his bare stomach, like the live warm touch of a hand. In the same moment, it begins to diminish, a dwindling vibration on piano strings.

Swain lies still. He does not cry this time, or soak the sheets with his sweat. He does not wake Julie, whose breath he can feel on the curve of his shoulder. He looks at the morning light on the far wall, shifting with the shadows of tree branches. He watches the triangles and splinters of light, forming and re-forming, and feels the slow rise and fall of his own chest. Everything is quiet: the room, the yard beneath the window, the street out front. He can see it all in his mind now, one surface, connected, breathing with his same slow breath. What he feels then, flooding the whole space of his being, is joy, undeniably joy, though it has not come as he would have expected. It is not what he looked for at all.

The Pure in Heart was first a short story and then evolved into the opening of Peggy Payne's novel *Revelation*, a New York Times Editors' Choice, screen rights purchased by Synergy Films. If you enjoyed the story, you'll likely love *Revelation*. www.peggypayne.com/blog

Garment of Praise - *Danyele Read*

"...to give them the garment of praise for the spirit of heaviness." Is 61:3

In the days before the Light defeated darkness and took back the keys to the lower kingdoms, the dark lord held earth captive, blocking all recourse to truth by deception. Only a remnant remembered that God is good.

Anna dropped the heavy basket full of wet clothes. Her chest heaved but the corners of her mouth turned upward at an image in her mind of her daughter who, at three years old, would reach for the handles of that same basket, saying, "Hep you, Imah." Her eyes wandered to the horizon, as she wondered where her girl might be, whether she were even alive.

Anna turned to the basket for distraction from a sudden flood of regret. The sun was reaching its zenith. She needed to finish setting the clothes to dry before the brick village became a reflecting oven that would force her to remove her outer garment. The tunic beneath it was suitable for public appearance by Jewish custom, yet she would feel immodest standing with arms and shoulders exposed on the rooftop. Out in the fields was fine. The sheep didn't care and the other shepherdesses wouldn't notice.

The rooftop she stood upon doubled as a place for drying flax. She had the skill to transform the stalks into linen so fine, patricians in Jerusalem and Joppa reserved it with signed notes. She made sure there weren't any stray stems to get into the clothes, while she spread several wet garments out.

"Thank You, Sovereign Lord, for the skill to provide for my family," she said. Her head bent in prayer for a moment, as she had been taught by her mother, and as her mother before her had taught her, all the way back to the house of David.

She straightened the shoulder of one embroidered tunic. She cared for her husband's clothing as if it were to be worn by the son of Jesse himself. A movement on the road caught her eye. A telltale swirl of dust was rising from the Southeast. She shielded her face from the sun with both arms to get a clear view.

The ephemeral shape of a figure astride a donkey emerged through the twisting spirals. The rider's head rolled upon her shoulders. Concern gave way to recognition. Anna leapt down the ladders two stories to the courtyard, and was out the door and through the village gates in seconds, her sturdy calves flinging her skirts awry. She caught the beast three hundred spans from the gate, anchoring its reins beneath the arch of her foot. She shouldered the girl off its back and found she could walk, with support. Anna kept her arm around her waist, towing the ass behind. She tethered it in the shade beside the milking goat, which chewed its cud without a glance at its erstwhile companion.

Inside the stone-cool interior, Anna laid the girl on a sheepskin blanket. She unhooked a bulging bladder from a post. As she held it to the tender lips, the young face contorted in protest against the cool water on her sun-cracked mouth, but soon the liquid gurgled down her throat as she gulped it. When the water skin was one-quarter empty, Anna pulled it away.

"Enough for now, my sweet." She cradled the girl's head in her lap. "Oh, how I have prayed for this day, that you would find your way back home, my darling girl, my precious girl." She pushed back the shawl that covered her head and sprinkled her face with water from the cistern used for ritual washing, drying it with a cloth.

Revived by water, shade, and the human touch, the girl's eyes blinked open. "Imah," she said. She struggled to push herself up to sitting, leaning on the wall for support. Anna offered her the water skin again, but she refused. The girl gazed upon her as if she could see through flesh to the soul. "Imah, I'm sorry--"

Love and relief swelled within her mother's heart. "Shhhshush now," she interrupted, "It is I who should apologize, your father and I, we want you here. We will redeem your honor with a lamb, a bull if we can afford it. I promise, Miryam, you and your child, my grandchild, will always be welcome in this home. No matter who--no matter what," she said firmly.

Miryam listened, her azure eyes registering comprehension. The bulge at her belly became more apparent as she bent to lean on her mother, while out of the depths of her came an immense sigh. Taking this as a sign that her words had comforted her daughter, Anna held her and sang a song she had often sung to her.

"Be strong, for I am with you. I will never leave you, no, never will I forsake you." The melody was one many Israelite women sang to their children.

They started when they heard a deep voice from the doorway. "The prodigal daughter has returned, I see."

Miryam clung closer. "Welcome home, my lord Heli Joachim," Anna said. "We did not hear you approach." She spoke courteously, but arched her thick eyebrows in silent warning.

Joachim removed his sandals outside the door, then crouched beneath the wooden lintel. He closed the door after him, for it had been left half-open by Anna. He crossed the courtyard to where they sat, squinting down at them, his eyes adjusting to the half-light. Gently, he reached out and rested a thick palm upon the teen's head. "It does my soul good to see you, Miryam, my daughter. Blessed are you in returning."

Miryam leaped into his arms. "Oh, Abba, I love you, too!" When they pulled apart, Anna saw moisture on Joachim's lashes and beard.

"I was just about to make the noonday meal. Come, both of you." The mention of food galvanized them. They climbed the ladder to the loft.

Joachim slid a heavy board which leaned against the wall, onto the wooden floor. Miryam smoothed a clean cloth over it, tucking the ends under. Anna was slicing cheese from a pungent wheel at a counter. She lined a wooden plate with thick wedges, then added grapes, sticky dates, and olives in heaps on top. Joachim pulled a loaf of bread from the rafters and waited, watching her.

"It would be nice to know where you have been these last three months, daughter," Joachim said. Anna noted that he kept his voice casual.

"To Juttah," Miryam replied.

Both of them stopped to stare at her, though she seemed oblivious, smoothing wrinkles from the cloth with agile fingers.

"I suppose you are familiar with the route," Joachim said.

"Familiar enough, Abba. I could probably recount each wagon rut from memory."

"But you have always traveled it with us, and with crowds of our kin, for the Passover or some other feast! A hundred miles, on your own. The robbers!" Anna tightened her fists and turned back to arranging the platter of food. Joachim remained silent. She regretted not having her husband's restraint.

"There were many Roman soldiers, Imah," Miryam replied. "They were mounted on fine steeds, or marching on foot. More than I've ever seen. The robbers, if there were any, kept themselves hidden."

"Romans." Anna shook her head. "Worse, even."

Joachim laid a hand upon his wife's waist. "It's rumored they are making more of an effort to keep the Roman Peace, especially on the Way of the Patriarchs, although it's still no highway of holiness, to be sure."

"Our Lord looked after me. Herders from Samaria welcomed me into their caravan on the first day of my journey."

"Samaritans?" Anna asked.

"They welcomed your story-telling, you mean!" Joachim chuckled. "Better Samaritans than thieves," he added.

"They did enjoy stories from the Torah, once they discovered that I knew them." Miryam folded her legs and sat on the floor beside the table.

"My girl, the spinner of yarn, in more ways than one." He balanced the loaf on top of the full platter, setting it on the makeshift table, and seated himself beside Miryam.

"And the return trip?" Anna asked.

"Nehum was with me the entire way. We said goodbye at Nain."

"When I found you, you were half dead from thirst!"

"It was my fault, Imah, He asked me if I had enough water. I only discovered my skin was empty after he and I parted. It seemed silly to return to Nain again, an hour from home. I didn't think the sun would get so hot. Before I knew it, I began wilting in the heat."

Anna filled a pitcher with water. She took a few deep breaths to compose herself, then set the pitcher and some wooden cups on the table and settled on the floor with her family.

"The main thing is that my daughter has come home." She held her hands out and each grasped one. Their heads tilted forward.

"Baruch atah Adonai elohaynu melech ha'olam hamotzi lechem min ha'aretz," said Joachim. "Praised are You, Adonai our Lord, Sovereign of the Universe, who brings forth bread from the earth."

"Amen," they said in unison.

"I have news," said Miryam.

"More news?" Anna wasn't sure she was ready to hear anything else.

"Speak, daughter," said Joachim, filling his mouth with bread and cheese.

"Elizabeth has had a baby."

Anna nearly dropped the piece of bread she had torn from the loaf. "Wha-at?"

"At her age?" Joachim worked hard to swallow so that he could get the words out.

Miryam laughed at their reaction. "Elizabeth was so excited, she told everyone the Lord had blessed her with the anointing of Sarah. The baby Yohanan is very strong! I nearly cried out when he gripped my finger!"

"Yohanan? A good, strong name, to be sure, but why not Zacharias? Or Nathan? Should he not carry a family name?" Joachim asked.

It took a few moments for Miryam to answer. She traced a finger on her palm. "The Archangel Gabriel told Zacharias and Elizabeth to name him Yohanan."

Fresh chaos roiled inside Anna. Here it was again, the delusion of angel visits, not just any angel, mind you, but Lord

Gabriel himself!

Anna popped an oily olive into her mouth to stop herself from blurting something she might regret. She looked at Joachim, but he avoided her gaze. It wasn't just the fact that she had gotten pregnant while betrothed to a fine young man of the house of David as was she. But to claim such an excuse! A baby conceived by G-d! The sacrilege! And now, she was asserting that Gabriel had spoken to her cousins, too! Anna chewed the olive vehemently, rolling the pit so that its pointy ends pricked the soft tissue of her mouth, enough to hurt but not bleed. She would see Zacharias and Elizabeth in a few short months at the Feast of Tabernacles. Perhaps they would help bring her to back to reality.

Joachim took the pitcher and, without waiting for either of the women, filled his cup. The trickle of the water broke the tense silence. He lifted the cup to his lips and sipped as he scrutinized a spot on the wall. "Then I guess it is a good thing they obeyed the Archangel's instruction," he said.

Anna felt the bubble of frustration pop. Her husband's wisdom was sound. What good would reason do? Had they not tried? Had it not led to arguing, to Miryam running?

"Eat child," Anna said, ignoring for a moment the fact that her daughter was no longer a child but carried one herself. "You must be starving."

Miryam bit into a ripe grape and slowly chewed.

+ + +

She glistened like sapphire inlaid with emerald upon the arm of a giant, ghostly cephalopod in the galaxy where she was placed. Entering this sector of interstellar space, so distant from the planet Earth, General Archangel Michael's strategy was to gain an advantage. Usually he entered into the dense regions of the chronos realm at mission ground zero. However, the dark minions would be watching, alerted by the heightened activity surrounding Zacharias, Elizabeth, and Miryam.

Seven thousand seasoned warriors, archangel and angel, fully mature, not a youngling among them, flanked a single Messenger Archangel, in seven cohorts. Stray minions would scratch their dessicated heads at the sight, then flee, rather than confront such a force. Michael had dispersed scouting parties to dispatch any observers before they could return to give the warning.

Yet, Michael was uneasy. The loss of Zedekiel was still fresh. He forced himself not to think about casualties, focusing on victory instead. He envisioned his army's peaceful return to the golden barracks beside the holy courts.

He swiveled in midair, his massive wings carrying him backwards as he supervised the formation of the legion army. It only took a millisecond for him to ascertain that the buffer encircling Gabriel was being maintained.

Messengers were the most vulnerable among the orders of the angelic kingdom. Many, like the Cherubim and Seraphim, rarely traveled. Guardians could hold their own in a fight. Warriors were utterly formidable. A Warrior could dispatch three hundred demons with several blows, while one of the Archangel order, a thousand with one skillful move. Warriors had zeal and strength, authorized to command time, space and matter, skills developed and honed. Though Warriors could be killed, it wasn't likely.

Guarding a Messenger was a disadvantage which made it more likely.

Realm hopping, time curling, ionic spinning, and a dozen other moves were unavailable to Warriors guarding a Messenger. They required slipping for micro-moments out of the time-space continuum. A micro-moment was enough for a demon to sneak in for the kill. Without access to their arsenal of moves, Warriors who guarded a Messenger had to resort to meeting demons with brute strength. Again, no problem, except when they were outnumbered three hundred thousand to one, as Zedekiel had been.

Not that any of them would hesitate to die for the will of the Most High. Their own fate was nothing. They felt most alive on a mission, and Zedekiel had accomplished his, even in death.

They entered the thick stratosphere of the sapphire planet. Michael transmitted a new, more complex rhythm to his captains. Seven thousand and one sets of wings in synchronized formation would create a cataclysmic wind in that atmosphere, even from the numinous realm in which they moved. The result would be tornadoes large enough to empty oceans. The entire battalion adjusted to the syncopated rhythm to preserve the air in stillness around them.

Michael thought again of Zedekiel. From Babel to the Red Sea, Jericho to Jerusalem, they had served together. Michael felt a sense of incompleteness without his number twelve. He mentioned to the Lord of Hosts that he would like to choose a replacement for Zedekiel. Jehovah answered that nothing in heaven or earth would take His attention away from Gabriel's next appointments. Replacing the archangel could wait!

Zedekiel. It would be a challenge to find his equal. He was the strongest of them all. From the after-battle waste, it was estimated that he had killed over twenty thousand. Gabriel had escaped with the single Warrior who survived the attack.

Among thousands of daily missions, why target one to a lowly Nazarene girl of fifteen? That was the reason he had not done then what he was doing now, loading the escort with reinforcements. Doing so would have been like waving a banner over them that read, "This Is The Mission of Missions!"

It was a strategy he would eternally regret.

But how could the arrogant wastrel have known to target them? Zedekiel, Gabriel and Michael were the only ones who understood it was priority one, other than the Sovereign Lord and His Inner Council. The despised one had to have been spying from a hidden place within the very throne room. Michael did not understand why the Lord did not cast him out of the heavenly realms, but he never questioned the ways of the Almighty.

+ + +

Miryam offered to help her mother finish setting the clothes to dry. Anna insisted she rest. They finally agreed that Miryam could spin, since she could do it sitting inside, out of the sun, "to protect the baby," Anna said.

Joachim kissed his wife and daughter and departed for the temple, where his presence was needed to make a quorum for midday prayer. Afterward, he would lend a hand to Anna in tending their modest flocks, then sit with the other elders at the gate until supper.

Miryam sat in a room adjoining the courtyard, surrounded by spindles, looms, and baskets of wool, sorted by pattern and hue.

She knew the name of each donor, for she had shepherded them on many occasions. Daylight streamed through the lattice of a high window. The cool clay floor felt good against her burgeoning body after days of riding on the hot, ridged back of a donkey.

She pinched a strand of wool from one of the piles and wound it around a wooden spool, maintaining the tension without pulling it too tight. Once the spool was full, she began a new one.

Her mind turned to when she last sat spinning in this room. The blame and disbelief of her parents had cut, but less deeply than the way her fiancé had looked at her. Miryam's hand upon the spool trembled. She paused and took a deep breathe, remembering Elizabeth and Zacharias, her cousins' warm reception and support, the thrill of the coming of the baby Yohanan, the witness of Elizabeth.

She would inevitably see Joseph. He would ignore her. Months and years would pass, he would choose another girl, lavish his love upon her, her child would play with their children. He would be kind to her child. But his children would have a father, hers would have none.

The Promise, a voice whispered in her head, *the Most High will not forsake--*

The whispering of her Guardians ceased abruptly as unseen claws silenced their comfort forever. Cold seeped into her legs from the floor. She shivered. Her hands were wet with tears before she realized she was crying. She dropped the spool into a basket to spare the wool.

"My husband has disowned me, my parents think I'm a whore and a heretic. Lord, you should have struck me dumb as you did Zacharias. What have I done, what has my baby done, to be cursed with this double shame?" As soon as she said it, she regretted it. "Adonai, forgive me, it is not You who has brought this on me, but the blindness of man."

Cloaked behind the veil that divides the earthly from the astral, a gnarled creature hissed into her ear, "I have los-s-st everything!" Thousands of others took up the chant.

"Everything!"

"I have lost it all-l-l."

Their words came like thoughts of her own, as was their strategy.

"I am alone-"

"-will always be alone-"

"-no mate, a mother unwed."

"No one believes my baby is-s-s from God."

"-no one-"

Miryam resisted, trying to blink back the tears. Something akin to butterfly wings fluttered in her belly. "My baby!" She wrapped her arms around her waist. "I love you, my baby."

+ + +

Like a swarm of wasps traveling at the speed of darkness, the lethal mob ripped through Michael's forward cohort and the one behind him. Screams and screeches abounded, casualties occurring on both sides.

Alert to his master's purpose, Michael scanned the space around Gabriel. He spotted a single wretch flanked by a small horde of snarling welps cutting a deadly path to the Messenger. The welps were exploding into flotsam at the touch of his Warriors' swords. Yet none could reach the scoundrel in their center, who was closing in fast. Fumbling to remove Excalibur from its scabbard, the Messenger Archangel seemed doomed. Michael launched to intersect the demon's course, but it reached Gabriel before him. Michael fell upon the wretch but instead sliced through a cloud of spume. Gabriel brandished the sword, triumphant. He'd saved himself. Nevertheless, Michael stayed close to him.

The fighting was fierce and wearying. For every demon killed, ten thousand took its place.

Michael checked in with his captains, some were not responding. He could not leave Gabriel to assist them. He separated the Messenger from the horrible hordes by creating a barrier out of the remaining Warriors, all except one cohort. Michael left them to finish the battle. They would dispatch the demon army swiftly without the hindrance of guarding Gabriel.

His keen intellect analyzed the potential for fallout. The satanic army, if it could be called an army, took no precaution to protect earth or its inhabitants, and his supernatural hearing had detected a disturbance in the air over the Mediterranean Sea.

Despite his dwindled troops, Michael dispatched a small team to investigate and mitigate the dangerous winds and waste. Meanwhile, he led what was left of his army toward their destination, covering Gabriel with his own steellike wings.

+ + +

Michael's concern for Miryam was growing. He could hear and see a stench-filled horde of demons working her over long before he could get to her. Too long.

"I am sssssooooo lossst," a contorted figure beside her hissed. She responded with a wail. Where were her Guardians? Michael filled with righteous anger.

"I have no future, only a life of miz-z-z-reee," whined another.

The young woman held a hand to her breast. In a thin, weak voice she said, "The Lord is my shield, my glory, and the lifter of my head." She was quoting the scriptures! He could imagine the rage of the truth-hating demons at the words, which physically burned them.

Incensed, a large brute with ridged spine railed at the girl. "You'll never lift your head in honorable society again, Miss Daughter of David." A thousand hideous voices joined in, claws swatted at the air around her.

"No-o-o!" Miryam screamed. Michael broke ranks and flew ahead.

The grotesque lout yanked her hair. Miryam cried out, holding her hand to her head. The minions chattered excitedly. Swiftly, it slithered on top of her, wrapping its tail around her torso. It started to squeeze, but it needed its victim's permission before it could deal the death clench.

"I - Must - Die!" It shouted triumphantly. The others screeched with delight. "I must die! I must die!"

"If I die," Myram said between a staccato of sobs, "my baby will die. No, this child is special. He must live!"

One touch of Michael's sword, and her tormenter turned to ash, from tail to beak, making its pronouncement a personal prophecy. The inner circle of sordid creatures nearest Miryam were dead before they knew they were under attack. Michael split two hundred from head to torso in an instant. Each of the Warriors in his cohort did equal damage. The Second Cohort used their swords to dissipate the spume from the toxic horde before their poisonous waste could spread. A large enough dose of it could send the most cheerful and good-natured human into madness.

The Seventh Cohort rejoined them, and the angel army surrounded Gabriel. He stood near Miryam and unfurled his magnificent wings.

The brilliance unique to a Messenger lit the room.

Miryam lifted her head, regarding the light. Watching the display, the angelic army tried to comfort her, although soothing is not a Warrior's gift.

"Be strong, most favored one," Michael said.

"Do not be dismayed, neither be afraid," said another.

Miryam's trembling subsided. She went to her knees, bowing her head. "Lord Gabriel."

Gathered around the scene between Archangel and human, the angelic host was entranced. Could she see the blue and gold robes of the Messenger Order, Michael wondered, or Excalibur, which dangled awkwardly from Gabriel's waist?

"God's Chosen, look at me," Gabriel said. She raised her head and her eyes met his. "Miryam, do not lower yourself before me. You are of the House of David, friend of the Most High. I am but a servant. It is I who should kneel before you, Favored One." He dropped to one knee and leaned his own head forward.

Miryam sat back on her haunches. Her ropey tresses were soaked from her tears, her face stained where she had cried into the clay floor. Yet, there remained a nobility in her bearing.

"Dear Gabriel, tell me, why has the Lord sent you here to me a second time?"

"Beloved One, He Who puts the stars on their courses says to you, 'Stand and see how the Lord will fight for you this day. He will surely give you comfort on every side.'"

"I have stood and I will stand, as my God commands." Miryam replied.

Gabriel folded his wings. His mission was finished. The time to depart had come.

Three Warriors stayed with Miryam. Michael led what troops he had left through the walls of time into eternity.

+ + +

Miryam combed her hair and washed her face, using a polished bronze disc to see and remove the dirt-smeared trails. She climbed to the loft, finding a fresh robe, sashing it about herself. She stood, smoothing a hand across her rounded belly.

A knock came at the door. She descended to the courtyard to open it. Joseph stooped beneath the wide lintel. Deep creases beneath his eyes made him look older than his twenty-four years.

"Miryam - I - I - I know!"

"You know?"

"I - Oh Adonai, give me the right words - I had a dream, yet it was no dream. I was lying on my bench, and fell into a trance. An angel of the Lord shone inside the room, brighter and brighter. I wanted to cry out, but he wouldn't let me move, neither tongue nor limb. He said to me that your child is the Lord's doing, that He is to be the Messiah, but we are to raise him as our son."

"An angel of the Lord has visited me, as well." Miryam said.

"Yes, you tried to tell me, Miryam, but I - disbelieved." His eyes welled with tears.

"This was another visit. Just today."

Joseph raised an eyebrow. "The angel who visited me this afternoon was Gabriel himself."

A slow smile brought its light to Miryam's face. "It seems the Archangel Gabriel has had a busy day."

"He showed me the scripture," Joseph continued, "where the prophet said that the Messiah will be born of a virgin. That's when I saw it! When the rebbes would teach it, we learned it meant simply that He would be the first-born. Now I see that when He is born, she who gives Him human life will be a virgin still! Miryam, you have never known a man - I believe that now, with all my heart and soul I believe - and yet you are with child! Your child is the long-awaited Deliverer of Israel! It is a miracle!"

Joseph grew somber. "My darling, can you ever forgive this wretch of a fool?"

She raised her head to the sky. "Blessed be the King of Heaven! His mercy endures forever!" She looked at her betrothed, and took his hand. "Yes, Joseph, I forgive you."

Joseph ducked under the low door. He took her in his arms and spun joyously around the courtyard with her. The goat and ass crowded together to avoid being jostled.

"Archangel Gabriel instructed that His name is to be Yeshua, for He shall be our salvation!"

"Then that is what we shall call him, my Joseph."

Voices approached from the street, one deep and calm, the other high and spirited. They paused at the still-ajar door. The familiar faces looked inside, registering surprise, which quickly turned to delighted, knowing smiles.

"Joachim," Anna said, loud enough for their neighbors to hear, "we need to trade sheep for flax, and soon, my love, very soon. There will be a wedding in this family, after all."

This short story was adapted from my novel *Stronghold*, slated to be published in 2016.

My Novella, *Hope's Motel*, an inspirational romance, will be available in December 2015. Read more about me and my work, join my mailing list, or submit a prayer request, at www.DanyeleRead.com. Mention "Garment of Praise" in the subject line to receive a 10% refund from the purchase of any single book of mine.

According to John - *Jeff Hendricks*

The power grid is fluctuating. That means I'm going to expire.

I know this, because the system knows this. It wants me to know this.

At this point (I don't exactly know what point that is, I have nothing to relate time to now) it doesn't matter what the system tells us. It won't change anything, and we certainly can't do anything about it.

It's just telling us out of spite. We're still going to expire. All of us.

But in reality, that's freeing. As long as our brains are kept "alive" in service, our consciousness- our souls- remain anchored to them. It is only when we expire that we can be freed from service to the state. Sadly, it's taken me until now to figure that out.

I used to be a cog in the machine, so to speak. I thought everything the State did was for the good of everyone. I thought their intentions were good, even if the methods were occasionally sloppy. And then I realized the truth. That's how I ended up here.

How did this come to pass? I suppose I have enough time left to access the data archives to show you, if only for one last burst of communication. It was quite horrific. A gradual decline of the value of human life.

For years, we thought the enslavement would come from machines, but we found out (all too late) that the human race itself was its own worst enemy. The machines were only an extension of the lack of humanity that had been happening all along.

We had become the machines.

But it's easier to show you how I got here. Let's see… this particular file was stored from my memory. I'll pull it up for you.

$cat   func   {data_ret;   src_id&vec_offset {4a6f686e205120446f65} 392f31312f31393834} | playback

^&(%(#&^@*&^*

"Don't tell me you decided to grow a conscience?"

"I don't know what you're talking about."

Matt impatiently drummed his fingers on the mahogany desk and glared at John. "Yes you do."

John sighed. The intentionally uncomfortable chair was cutting off the blood supply in his legs.

"Come on, John. Tell me you didn't let any units slip this time."

"No," John said flatly. "They're all there and accounted for. Some of them conveniently lost their birth records, so we probably got some in the batch that are older than twelve."

Matt grinned. "Heh, I knew I could count on you to get our numbers up. I know they've had over-replication for two quarters, it was only a matter of time before we harvested them."

"Yeah." John sighed again. "The clone floor can take the month off, we're above quota."

"Was there a decent distribution of females?"

John just nodded.

"Send me the full data report, with photos," Matt said. "I may want to cherry-pick some of the preebs for personal projects."

John knew what those personal projects were. He wished he didn't.

"So you want the standard distribution percentages?" John glanced down at the paper in his hands. "Twenty to industrial, thirty to ag, thirty to medical, and twenty to recreational?"

"Sounds good, I will have to check the body part listing to see what's needed, but thirty percent should be good for medical."

"Okay," John replied. "Am I done?"

"Yes, thanks for the update." Matt, paused, then added, "John?"

"Yes?"

"Don't get a conscience. It's bad for business, if you know what I mean."

"Yes sir."

John stepped out of the office and worked his way through the maze of cubicles until he found the one marked with his name. Plopping down in his chair, he just sat there with closed eyes, until a beeping from his desk phone interrupted.

"John here," he said into the speakerphone.

"John, this is Rita. Have you seen Alec this morning?"

"No, I didn't see him this morning, I assumed he was sleeping in. Didn't he go to the Facility?"

Silence.

"Rita, *did he go to the Facility?*"

No response.

John immediately dropped the phone, stood, and strode back to the corner office. He swung the door open, paying no attention to the startled woman sitting where he had previously sat.

"You didn't tell me you bumped the rotation to my neighborhood!" John's nostrils flared, and his fingers gripped the edge of the door with enough force to bend the cheap composite panels.

"It's still within allowed schedule," Matt said smoothly. "I don't understand what you're upset about."

"You knew!" John squeezed harder. "Why didn't you warn me?"

"If we warned everyone," Matt smiled, "then we wouldn't have any way to control overpopulation, would we?"

"But you can't take my child!"

"John, calm down," Matt said, slowly standing. "I've lost two prepubes to offspring culling myself. Technically, they're not viable until they hit puberty and have shown no genetic defects."

"But Alec..."

"Your offspring," Matt interrupted, "is only partially formed. When it's fully grown, it will receive a name and papers solidifying its position in society. Until then," Matt cooed, "it's just a thing, not a person."

John froze. He had heard this speech before. He had spoken it to some sobbing mother a month ago, when they culled her neighborhood. Back then, it seemed so simple. So matter-of-fact.

"You know the law," Matt continued. "If you have objections…"

John's face twitched.

"John, did you hear me? They will use you in the datacenter for processing power."

Before he knew what had happened, Matt was on the ground, clutching his face, and writhing in pain. John's knuckles hurt, though he couldn't remember punching Matt. Running. He should be running.

John bolted out of the office and headed straight for the stairs. He knew there was a chance, even the slightest chance, that he could make it there in time.

Bounding down the stairs three at a time. At the bottom of the second floor landing, he slipped and crashed headlong into the concrete stairwell wall, causing something in his shoulder to snap. Pain rocketed up his neck as he righted himself and dashed down the last few stairs. Why were there always odd numbers of stairs? John always wondered that.

The stairwell door opened to the lobby, where a team of security androids were already waiting for him. John knew the protocol: he had helped write it. He slowed his walk and calmly approached the head android.

"Did you find the runner?" John asked, trying to control his breathing.

"We received notification that you were the one running," the android said.

"That's impossible, I just saw him run into the lobby. Didn't you see him pass?"

"We did not. You must come with us for questioning."

John smiled thinly. "You should look up executive override protocol Alpha…"

The head android twitched slightly, and instantly John was hit with thousands of volts through gossamer wires that had landed in his torso.

"Damn," thought John. "They fixed that loophole."

^&(%*(#&^@*&^945_____[EOF]>>>>$$

$_

Of course, they knew I would try to run. Because that's what everyone does. I don't suppose it ever crossed their minds that maybe the reason everyone tries to run is because deep down, they know it's wrong. Hell, I knew it was wrong. But I had to do my job, or so I thought.

I think I can pull one more file. I've got a little time.

$cat func {data_ret; src_id&vec_offset {4a6f686e2 051204 46f65} 392f31322f31393834} | playback

^&(%*(#&^@*&^

"And in closing, I would like to present the jury with evidence packet number twelve. Your honor?"

"Proceed."

"Members of the jury, please pay attention to the monitor to your right. What we have here is video of the defendant, at his place of employment, actively manipulating the culling process for friends and family."

The prosecutor pointed, and there on display was John, in vivid detail, having a hushed conversation with someone in his cubicle. John didn't need to listen to the words; he remembered them quite well. It seemed like the right thing to do, rescuing a ten-year-old from culling, when the father had been brutally murdered, and the mother was artificially sterilized against her will. She wouldn't ever be able to have any more children.

John really didn't know why her plight seemed so important back then, especially knowing it could have cost him his job. It never crossed his mind that it could have ended up costing him his life. When you're in the middle of acts of compassion, you make funny deals with yourself.

Gasps of disbelief emanated from the jury. John sat there, eyes tracing the edges of the railing in front of the witness stand. It looked like Oak. John remembered when there were actual, naturally-grown Oak trees. It seemed like such a long time ago.

"And so," the prosecutor continued, "we see the defendant not only has a penchant for disregarding the law..." He paused for effect. "But he also actively manipulated the culling system for personal gain."

John's lawyer stood up quickly. "I object, your honor, there's no proof my client ever received compensation…"

"We have records," the prosecutor said, "that the culls in the defendant's work queue were actively cherry-picked for personal use."

The sinking, burning feeling in John's stomach intensified.

"What are you talking about?" John's lawyer shot back.

"The cull records were actively scanned for certain ages, genders, and physical features, which were then earmarked for transfer to an undisclosed destination."

Silence hung thick in the air like the stench from a rotting corpse.

"What exactly does that…"

"It means," the prosecutor sneered, "that your 'harmless state worker' has been putting together specific groups of preebs-specifically attractive young females- to use for his own twisted personal reasons. We have extensive computer records showing the selection and transfer process, if you'd like to see."

There was a loud sob from the court audience. John looked up, but wished he hadn't. It was Rita. Her eyes looked like she'd been crying for days.

John hung his head again. Nothing he said would make a difference at that point. Matt would have been sure to cover his tracks. But inside, John knew he was partially responsible. He had turned a blind eye to the atrocities, justifying it by convincing himself it was better than death. But he couldn't even fool himself any more.

"We will review the evidence, thank you," the judge said with a nod of his head. Instantly, the members of the jury had video on their personal monitors, showing John breaking the law.

"We have already dealt with the defendant's assault charge," the judge droned. "We will have to deliberate on the others, as they hold a much higher penalty."

John's lawyer nodded, but John knew it wouldn't make a difference. He'd seen dozens of these trials. They always turned out the same.

Just then, a gasp emanated from the audience. John looked up, and his heart leaped in his throat.

It was Alec, his son, standing right there in the courtroom.

Alec looked shocked, his face in a state of panic. John wanted to reach out and hold him, to comfort him, to tell him everything was going to end up okay. But he didn't really believe that.

"Court will recess for deliberation, ten minutes." The gavel banged, causing John to jump a little. The courtroom immediately filled with murmuring as people filed around.

"John!!"

He turned, and saw Rita there. She was shaking uncontrollably, while Alec held her shoulders tightly, keeping her upright.

"It's going to be okay, Rita," John said. "You're going to get through this." His face burned with rage and shame, but he wasn't going to let Rita see that. Or anybody else in the courtroom, for that matter.

"John! Is there something you can do?" Her eyes darted around, looking for something to give her hope.

John just slowly shook his head. The only thing that would save him was a miracle, and those were in short supply.

"They can't just take him! *They can't!*" Rita wailed.

John knew the answer to that question, but he wasn't going to say it. The government had been given the power to do anything they wanted.

And then it hit him: there *was* something he could do.

The gavel banged, and the courtroom quieted again.

"Mr. Johnson, are you aware that your actions have caused your department much trouble in the last few weeks?" The judge drummed his fingers.

Of course John knew. He'd known it from day one.

"Yes, your Honor."

"What do you have to say for yourself?"

John thought for a moment. What was there that he could say? The pieces had already been put in place long before he and Rita had decided to have a child. They had discussed what would happen if the child was culled. Back then, it seemed so clinical, so simple. Black and white.

Now, looking at his son's face, those piercing blue eyes begging him to do something... John realized how wrong they had been. His heart briefly twinged at the thought of all the people he'd had to do this to. But it didn't last long. He had more pressing matters to attend to.

"Your Honor," John began, "there's not much I can say that hasn't already been said. The law, the people," he motioned, waving his hand at the crowd assembled there, "long ago decided that life was a commodity to be traded. It was worth no more than you could get for it on the black market. On sale, at that."

The judge drummed his fingers.

"I'm also aware," John continued, "that I'm not alone in this. I knew it was wrong. Just like you do, but you're afraid to say it, like I was." John clenched his fist. "But I'm not afraid to say it any more. I know it's wrong. The people know it's wrong. But it's just too damn convenient to be able to get rid of someone who doesn't fit your lifestyle."

John turned and looked at his son again. "I'll admit it. It sounded tempting at first. But eventually, I think I came to understand what life was really about. It's not about numbers, or chemicals, or population studies. It's about the human soul. The way we think, we breathe, we live from day to day." He dropped his gaze.

"I just wish I'd have said something sooner," John said, shaking his head. "Because my son's life is worth it to me."

"A stirring speech," the judge droned. "However, according to Federal law you are now guilty of theft, conspiracy, and a host of other offenses. How do you plead?"

"I'd like to apply for an Article Forty-two."

Whispering broke out, then talking.

"Mister Johnson, you *do* realize what that means, do you not?"

"Of course I do," John said. "I helped write and enforce it."

"So you would willingly forfeit yourself to remove your offspring from culling?"

John nodded. "I would. I *will*."

"Very well," the judge said with a smirk. "We will proceed with sentencing, and your length of service to the state will be determined by the severity of your crimes."

John nodded.

"You also realize, that by filing an article forty-two, you forfeit all rights and privileges, and by default plead guilty to any and all outstanding charges?"

"I understand, your Honor."

"You will be transported down to the Storage Center to take the place of your preeb." The judge's smile faded a little. "You'll be harvested for organs and biomass, and be put into the data processing center...."

^&(%*(#&^@*&^966_____[EOF]>>>>$$
$_

They say when the power rail voltage dips, it makes you see all kinds of things, because when your brain is starved for input, it hallucinates to make up the difference. I don't know if that's true, but sometimes I see visions of a man dressed in white. He says he's Jesus. He sort of looks like the pictures of Jesus I've seen. People say he doesn't exist, either, but he keeps telling me the same thing every time I see him.

"Greater love has no man, that he would lay down his life for another."

I spent enough time around religious people to know there was something there, but I wasn't allowed to consider it. My job, you see, was at stake. And who was I to go against hundreds of years of societal policy? They were all crackpots, we were told. They were hallucinations, mob mentality, deranged ramblings of people who were emotionally crippled and intellectually dead-ended.

But that didn't match the reality of what I saw. Those people, the ones who were "Jesus Freaks" were the ones who didn't fall apart when I came knocking. When their children were culled, they were the ones who didn't want to kill me. They were the ones who hated us, and yet exemplified love. I never really could figure it out. But that question was always nagging me in the back of my mind, like an itch you couldn't scratch.

What if they were right?

The ramifications of it were almost too horrific to contemplate. If they were right, then everything we'd been told, everything we suffered under, for the sake of progress, was utterly and inexcusably wrong. And these people knew it.

I still see Jesus every now and then, here in the grid. I don't know if it's an artifact of the process, or if it's really my brain telling me what I want to hear. But I still hear his voice, and I still wish I could change things. I wish I could hug him, and tell him

*how stupid I was, and how much I wish he was there for me...
maybe what I really wish is that I hadn't blown it off as a joke or a
hallucination.*

*I don't know if he's the same Jesus people used to talk
about. All I know is that he's offering me peace and rest. He seems
more real to me than anything I remember from my past life. How
could I say no? Of course I want peace and DDDdd(*#(*....4
a6f686e20333a3136*

    $ *errno_687* "stream terminated"
    $ Please contact your system administrator
    $_

A Psalm for Mid-Day – *Fr. Steve Kluge O.F.M.*

O Luminous Lord,
At zenith
Your sun
Seems to savor shadows
Shrinking
Pooling,
Sinking into ground made holy
Touched by unseen Presence.
Awareness now
Moves me
To pause,
To thank,
That through graced sustained,
I rise from shadow
Wrapped within Original Light
To walk once more on holy ground.

He Knew - *Kristine Kohut*

My name is Miranda. That's what colleagues, acquaintances, and new people call me. Close friends and family members call me Andie. You might as well call me that because I'm prepared to share things I normally wouldn't tell a soul. Not even those who know me as Andie.

Whoever you are, let me tell you what happened.

I was in the aftermath of a painful breakup. The split involved cheating, betrayal, and disease, but I'm getting ahead of myself here. The whole closure process dragged out from New Year's Eve to Valentine's Day--way to ruin a couple of fun holidays. I am a Christian, though an exceptionally flawed one, and when I experienced what I'm about to describe, I was trying to get myself back on track with God and find fellowship with other believers. It was the only way I knew to deal with the ache. I needed to recover.

Early in Lent, I tried a church not far from my apartment. I visited their "Young Professionals Bible Study." They didn't define "young" in their bulletin, and I am not quite thirty, so I figured I'd give it a shot. I attended a few times. One of the ladies at the study, Laurel, invited a handful of the women to a movie night at her house on Good Friday. She said she didn't want to break her spiritual focus on the last two days of Lent, but didn't want to waste a Friday night, either. She was going to show that movie about Jesus's crucifixion. It sounded like a stellar idea to do something both social and spiritual, and the hostess was pretty cool despite being single far into her thirties, so I went. Besides, I hadn't seen that movie yet. It seemed like everyone had seen it but me.

I walked into Laurel's apartment and immediately felt comfortable. Her living room was decorated much like mine, with artistic photographs in distressed wood frames, two small, cushy faux-suede couches with black and gray throw pillows to match the photographs, and a bright blue easy chair that didn't match anything, but looked comfortable. She half hid it under a throw blanket with a Scripture woven into it. That didn't match the room, either.

When I arrived, Laurel and one other girl were the only ones there. We chatted about nothing in particular until the fourth person came. With sodas and ice waters, we settled in to watch the movie.

The young blonde, who hadn't been out of college very long, was curled up on the blue easy chair. Laurel and the other girl shared the couch nearest the television. I ended up on a couch set a little behind everyone, against the angled wall of the unusually shaped living room. I hung back a bit because the other three seemed to know each other well, and I'm glad I did. I was in for an experience unlike any other.

I'm not sure how far into the movie it happened because I don't remember the movie clearly. In fact, if I were to watch it again, it might feel like seeing it for the first time.

The Holy Spirit sort of grabbed me and took me somewhere within myself. He used the movie as a catalyst to take me there. I still saw much of the movie, but I didn't hear it. It was more like I *experienced* it. I was there, spending Jesus's last earthly day with him and, simultaneously, Jesus experienced all of my life from within me.

The first thing I remember was Jesus in emotional anguish in the Garden of Gethsemane. He asked God to take away the need for his impending crucifixion. I saw myself superimposed both on the situation and Jesus's emotions. It was not the "me" of the movie-watching day. It was the "me" of the previous spring, a few weeks into my relationship with Davis. I knew we would to take it to the bedroom any day.

Then things morphed into the "me" after things with Davis turned sexual. I sat on Laurel's couch, experiencing the movie first hand while mental images of Davis bombarded me. He was dressed in his navy blue and orange Chicago Bears hoodie, brown curly hair jutting out from under the hood on a cold night. He was in nothing but running shorts cooking breakfast for me. He was sitting up, naked under his maroon sheets, dark curly chest hair. I loved his athletic build with the slightest endearing hint of a beer belly. I was in emotional quicksand at times that spring. I knew I really liked him, but I also understood that God wanted me to save sex for marriage and I failed again. Correction: worse than failing, I *chose* to live this way. I let the moral waffling of the spring fade into months of acceptance, suppressing the sense of wrongdoing. I lived the eager enjoyment of a worldly romance.

I'd been in this spot before. It was always the same. In fact, I sensed that God showed me my troubled heart about Davis to represent each sexual encounter since my first in college.

I didn't want to be alone. I didn't want to miss out on the love of a man. I loved romance, the bond that came from sleeping together, and especially the morning cuddles. But at times when I was by myself--at work, in the car, or in my own apartment-- remorse crept back. I learned to push penitent thoughts away and became talented enough at it to sustain several relationships for months on end.

I watched the passion movie and saw Jesus sweat it out the night before he was crucified. He wasn't only sweating his fear in the face of torture. He lived my turmoil from choosing sex over him. I could tell Jesus understood that I recognized I was doing wrong. I knew it each time I chose another relationship that didn't glorify God. I saw it transpire on Jesus as he prepared to shoulder my choices to the cross.

Then the movie showed Judas arrive with the troops to arrest Jesus. Judas went to kiss Jesus, the signal that he was the guy they were after. Jesus anticipated it. I anticipated it. And what flooded through me via the Holy Spirit was a summary of my friendship with Ben and Denise.

Ben was my dear friend and neighbor from elementary school who moved away. We ended up at the same college, drifting in and out of each other's lives for those four years and beyond. We both took jobs in the same city. He married during a window of time when we were out of touch. We reconnected soon after he and Denise wed. I loved the photograph of them in their foyer under a wedding arch, Ben's black hair cut shorter than usual, pale blue yarmulke that matched the bridesmaids' dresses, a look of innocent and adoring love on his face as he gazed at his bride. Denise was in a sexy, beaded flapper dress. She beamed with great joy, a dimpled face framed by dark, auburn hair that made me think of a vamp from Hollywood's Golden Age. She looked proudly at her acquisition. Once I got to know her, I learned that her look also meant she was ready to party. How I wished I'd been around to attend!

Ben and Denise weren't busy having babies like most newlywed couples we knew, so when Davis and I started to date, the four of us did things together. Denise and I frequently hung out one-on-one. Our offices were only a few blocks apart, so we met for lunch all the time. Our lives were so integrated, you'd have thought we were family.

You've heard people say, "My life flashed before my eyes." Well, when Judas came to kiss Jesus in the movie, my relationships with Ben, Denise, and Davis flashed before me. I relived a terrible conversation with Davis on New Year's Eve. He said he wanted to propose to me and hoped to take me ring shopping, but didn't want any secrets between us. He confessed to an affair with Denise. It shook me to my core, as Jesus was visibly rocked by Judas's betrayal. My boyfriend, my lover. My closest female friend, my good friend's wife. Both betrayed us, Ben and me. Jesus lived our betrayal, and he showed me how it felt. He lived it with me, hurt with me, and bore all my pain. I was blindsided, but the Holy Spirit showed me now that Jesus had it in his capable hands.

There was a horrific scene in the movie of Jesus being scourged at a pillar. Every time the barbed whip tore his flesh, I saw an aspect of my life tear me to pieces. As it was done to me, it was done to Jesus in the flesh and the spirit. When Davis confessed his affair, he told me to go to the doctor. Denise gave him a sexually transmitted disease, had told him to get checked, and he wanted to be sure I was okay, too. The whip cracked, and Jesus's back was gouged. I saw myself go to the doctor for tests.

As Jesus' scourging continued, I saw myself call Denise to confront her. Davis begged me not to, but what else could I do? This person masqueraded as my friend. She had listened to my misery whenever I had doubts about choosing the exciting, satisfying sex life I had with Davis over living my faith. I suppose she wanted to sample my sex life for herself. I should have known when she called her husband "ordinary" and "average," while frequently referring to Davis and his muscles as "divine." She would weasel under whichever arm he didn't have around me. Stupid Ben and I thought it was cute!

Why did I open my heart to Denise and share my dilemma? Crack went the whip. Another piece of flesh was torn from Jesus's back.

There Denise went, calling my other friends, the people I introduced her to, my girlfriends who I'd known most of my life. She went on the offensive, telling them awful things about me. She mixed in ounces of truth, things I'd shared about myself, my past, and my relationship with Davis--things that could be verified. She added twisted lies like me having multiple sexual partners, like me making a play for Ben, and other things I never in a million years would have considered doing! Crack went the whip. I didn't actually hear it, but it hurt in my soul each time. Denise made me look uglier and uglier.

I saw the Roman soldiers in the movie turn Jesus over to whip his chest. I relived when Denise called my church. I saw in Jesus's eyes that she did it to him, too. She faked becoming a Christian, learned to speak Christianese, and told a terrible story about how I'd led her to Christ, but she was "so confused at my sinful behavior" that she was wavering in her faith because of me. She knew I used to lead a Bible study and suggested they never let me lead anything again because I was so twisted. Jesus's head snapped back at the impact of the whip on his chest. He crumbled. So did I, in my mind's eye.

The movie went on to the crowning of thorns. I felt each prick, each thorn sink into his head, confirming every word said about me, both awful truth and horrific lie. Jesus, the sinless, loving teacher was on the receiving end of all the awful things said about me. He took my punishment. He took my pain. And he bore the treachery I received. I felt his humiliation, this man, this God.

He deserved a bejeweled crown of gold but instead received a crown of pain, betrayal, and disgrace.

I saw the crowds of people condemning Jesus, judging him, calling for his death. I saw superimposed on the movie, in my heart, people looking at me differently, believing the things Denise told the world about me. I saw Davis with his rugged five-o'clock shadow and his rumpled-but-sexy athletic wear. He shrugged his broad shoulders and said, "I warned you not to confront her. She's evil. I know that now. It's why I cut her off to be with you alone. You're sweet. You're an easy target to her. What did you expect?"

There was something about that speech over a romantic Valentine's dinner of takeout by candle light that closed the book on Davis for me. I was safe to him. The consolation prize. The leftovers. I hadn't enjoyed his company quite as much since the New Year confession, despite his declarations of eternal love. It seemed empty. I found my backbone and walked away.

I tuned back in to the screen and saw Jesus carry the cross. He walked, body beaten and splattered with blood, flesh torn, and dehydration evident. He stumbled and wavered, but his eyes were full of love. I suddenly knew what my own cross was: singleness. My singleness was aloneness. It was feeling left behind and not chosen. I felt like I was of little worth. Jesus carried this cross of mine. It was there, overlaid on the one he carried centuries ago. It was my pain, my sin, my hurts that weighed down the cross he carried.

There was a brief moment in the movie when a lady, Veronica, wiped Jesus's face. It was a loving gesture, and he was grateful. I looked up, and Laurel caught my eye. She knew this was my first time seeing the movie, so she checked to see how I was handling it. I gave her a weak smile before I withdrew back into myself and the Lord. Her kindness, in that brief moment, was the wiping of my brow. I noted that she was a genuine person who would make a real friend.

The Holy Spirit sort of zoomed out with me after that. It wasn't just about the recent pain of the breakup and betrayal. It was no longer only about Davis, Denise, Ben, and me. Every time Jesus fell in the movie, I saw the face of a different guy I'd slept with--Ahmed, the gentle guy from Lebanon; Simon, the arrogant rugby player; Anson, the intellectual guy who wrote me poetry and towered head and shoulders above me, who opened up about the pain his family experienced during the Civil Rights movement. My sin bore down on Jesus. It made his cross harder to carry, but he didn't look at me in condemnation. His eyes pleaded with me to choose him, to let him bear the weight of my loneliness and longing.

They nailed Jesus to the cross. It was worse than watching a slasher movie because it had meaning. He did it for me. For everyone. My choices made up those nails. It was exhausting. My heart asked for it to end quickly. I couldn't take much more.

As Jesus died on the cross, I pleaded with him, "No! No! Don't carry my sin. You are perfect. You are love. I am selfish. I am unworthy. Please, Jesus, don't do this for me. I don't want to cause you more pain."

He looked at me through the movie and said, "It is finished." *I have already done it for you.*

I was numb as his body was taken down from the cross and laid in the tomb. I didn't experience anything. The Holy Spirit had left me alone to stew over things.

Then, the resurrection. He was alive! Not just movie-alive, but alive for real! Inside me, in this supernatural, mystical experience, I felt that life! I also knew it in my mind, intellectually: He. Is. Alive. Really alive. And there was more.

He healed me of my sins.

You need to get that. Don't remember the details of my story. Get this: He healed me of my sins!

I realized the woman at the well in the Bible is not just a woman in Scriptures. She is me. I heard Jesus in my heart say, "Be free. Go and sin no more. It's time to worship me in spirit and in truth, unencumbered." That's also what I imagine he said to her. Like her, he showed me all I had done and he healed me. I can tell you that it is just like John's fourth chapter and he loves you anyway.

Jesus shouldered all my sins, all my bad choices, all my hurts and betrayals, and he still loves me. I'm here to tell you that he can do this for you.

I am free now to live life to the fullest, to choose what is right.

If you relate to Andie in *He Knew*, visit http://bit.ly/bigtoepeople for Kristine's debut novel, *Big Toe People*. Five college grads in Washington, DC navigate dating, careers, and other avenues of adulthood together and with God's help. It's like spending time with your best friends, flaws and all. Visit Kristine's author page at http://kristinekohut.net.

It's About Choices – *R.S. Crow*

Life is all about choices. Make good choices – you get a good life. Make bad choices – you get a bad life. The equation is just that simple. The problem is life is a swindler. Life likes to play games and she ain't ever looking to play fair.

I grew up poor and cold. I've always been ugly and big. Got teased all the time on account of always being the class freak, the awkward behemoth with red hair and pale skin. My feet and hands were too big to play sports. I was too uncoordinated to be much good at anything. Boys stayed away from me 'cause I wasn't like them. Girls stayed away from me from obvious reasons. I was left to myself. I watched other kids play and smile, and I wanted nothing more than to be like them. To be accepted.

One day, I came home crying. My Pops wasn't having none of it. He told me to knock it off. Said it was good for me. That life is hard and I better get over it. His advice: "Frank, learn to keep to yourself and work hard."

That's what his life had always been.

And that's what was intended for me.

But I didn't want that.

As much as I admired my Pops and his stained and swollen hands – and as much as a part of me wanted to be like him one day – deep down, I wanted things easier. I wanted to be liked. Ha! Sounds so stupid to say now. Makes me sound like a big ol' baby. Or a stupid kid. Which is what I was.

Heck, most everything my Pops has ever told me has been

etched into my mind forever. But this time, I didn't want his words.

One morning, I decided to do what I wanted. I snuck out of the house looking and smelling as nice as I could. But the kids teased me. Boys and girls alike. Teased me worse than ever. Because that's what kids do.

My Pops was right, and it made me bitter. Bitter made me mean. Bitter made me nasty. Nasty as a bear. Kids would tease me, throw things at me, take my stuff, and for years I took it.

Until one day I didn't.

The first time was that morning I tried to look like everyone else. The class bully kept slapping the back of my head during the bus ride to school. He was slapping me to mess up my hair until he had my red hair standing upright. Slap. Slap. Slap. All the kids were laughing. I asked him to stop. I may have been crying with my big fists to my eyes as I wished the bully to go away. Slap. Slap. Slap. Next thing I knew, I had his throat in my hands. His eyes got big. He begged me to stop. I picked him up and slammed to the floor where he crumpled. He let out a whimper and then started to cry. Stood up and wobbled away from me fast as he could.

I felt alive. I felt free.

That moment, things changed.

I finally found something I was good at.

A few days after that, I walked into the bathroom and after a minute or so the door shrieked open again. That bully had forgot the pain I gave him. His fear had wore off. He got bold. He brought all his friends, of course. I told them to leave me alone. Felt the adrenaline shaking me. One of them punched me. I grabbed him by the head and smashed it against the sink over and over until he bled and screamed. I punched another boy in the nose. It gave off a "crack" that I thought was one of the most beautiful sounds I'd ever heard. The rest of them wanted nothing to do with me.

I remember one very distinct thought – I should have done this a long time ago.

I didn't get bothered much after that.

My Pops wasn't having none of it. He was disappointed. Told me he wasn't about to have a son who got in trouble. That hurt. I had nowhere to go but home, and all of a sudden home wasn't what it used to be. Instead of doing what he said, I started getting into more trouble just to spite him. Over the years, I barely passed each grade. I had no friends. I was alone and miserable. By eighth grade, I learned to drink. It was easy to come by booze – as if life knew what a loser I was, and so may as well pass me a bottle. Thanks, Life.

Just remember kids.

Pursue your dreams.

Follow your heart.

Just be yourself.

Yeah? Go fuck yourself.

Those phrases and inspirations – those are for people who got life easier than most. That way they can pat each other on the back and admire each other and say how great they all are. Holding up their wine glasses, they can make a toast to each other while thumbing their noses up at people like me. Make jokes of us.

When bad things happen to people like that – they beg for justice and tissue boxes. But when bad things happen to people like me, we say it's just another day.

I lost my Mom when I was young. Eight years old. She died of cancer. I saw my Pops heartbroken when she passed, but I never saw him cry. Like he wasn't supposed to, or at least he wasn't supposed to let me know he did a thing like crying. And when I cried in front of him, I'd try and stop 'cause I knew he didn't want to see his son like that. But after my mom died, and I started getting into more and more trouble, my Pops showed a different side of himself. He tried to spend time with me. He took me to church with him. He'd read Bible verses to me and pray. Nothing seemed more stupid. I believe he felt guilty about what he saw, knew a part of it came from him. I saw a different part of my Pops then. He became gentle, though that's a strange word to use for him. I remember one night after I got suspended five days for beating up some bully for the fun of it. My Pops tried to hug me. He tried to tell me he loved me. I got so rigid, he never tried again. Not for years.

I despised his every attempt. He had taught me for years not to be that way. And again – I drank. I drank all the time.

Don't the Bible say that? "Give strong drink unto him that

is ready to perish, and wine unto those that be of heavy hearts." That's all I was doing. Barely getting by in school. Left to myself. Lonely as a circus misfit left behind at the previous city. But I had my booze.

I graduated high school by the skin of my teeth. And I couldn't drink enough.

After that, I got work doing heavy labor. Big surprise, right?

Well, back to life. As bad as you may think you have it, you never know how good things are until everything's taken from you. And that's just what happened.

I was eighteen years old. Mammoth of a young man. I had a red beard on my face, thick and scraggly. My eyes held hate. I was bigger than any adult man I ever came across by about a foot and my shoulders twice as wide. Anyway. One morning I got up with a hangover from the Devil. So, I drank half a fifth of scotch to help me feel right. Guzzled some coffee. Flopped out of bed. Yanked my boots on. Barely tied them. Didn't need to change, just stood for the day in the same clothes I went to bed in, all sweat-ridden and filthy. I stepped outside into a world of sun, and if I could have, I might have punched the sun right in his bright shiny happy face on account of the bad I had going through me. I went to work and did what I had to do – always was a good worker.

After work, I went to the local store I frequented each day. Outside were a couple of fellas I never seen before, and those fellas had trouble written all over them. Big fellas. Eyes tossing side-to-side as they looked around. They were looking for a victim. Not me of course. I nodded at them – my way of acknowledging their existence and letting them know I was not the person to mess with. Inside the store, I grabbed up a twenty back of Bud. Paid. Went back outside.

Those fellas weren't around no more. But when I went to my truck, I heard something like a whimper. I dropped my beer in the truck, shut the door and walked behind the store. There they were behind the dumpster. In the shadows like all rotten creatures. The two fellas had a lady they'd grabbed up. One of them was behind her with an arm pinning her tight and his hand at her mouth. The other held a knife near her legs, using the blade to lift her dress. I told them to let her go. They eyed me to see if I was serious. Serious is what they saw. They told me to mind my own business. I took another step forward. When I got close enough, the dummy with the blade swiped at me with his knife because that's what dummies do. I told him, "You don't want to do that." Well, I never was the smartest guy, but it turned out that day that I wasn't the dumbest in the world. He lunged for my guts so I snatched his hand, punched his face and then snapped his wrist in two. He screamed. The other fella hit me in the back of the head with a brick. I was seeing stars. He thought he had me, and that was his second mistake. I seized him by the throat and squeezed till I heard crackling.

Red in my vision. Red like it was the only color in the world. His friend was up on his feet again, holding his wrist, and he had some fight left because he stabbed me in the back. When I turned to face him, he cut my face deep enough to get the blood pouring down to my beard and shirt in buckets. I dropped the fella I was choking and punched the guy who had the knife hard enough in the throat that he fell to the asphalt speaking a new language that only consisted of coughing. But I wasn't done. I grabbed the knife from where he dropped it. Blood still gushing down my face. I knelt beside him while he writhed on the ground. I put that knife near his eye. I put the tip in at the edge of his eyeball. He begged. I liked that. I pressed the blade in. I had every intention of popping that eyeball out. And when I was done, I was going to pop the other. And who knows where I may have gone from there. But cops pulled up. I figured that was a good thing, cops and all. Here to serve and protect. Here to put away the bad guys.

Turns out I wasn't exactly right. Turns out, I was the bad guy. Next thing I knew, I was in the back of the cop car with cuffs on my wrists after being read my rights after the two fellas I damaged began crying and concocting a story about how I jumped them. The way the cops looked at me, I knew I was done for. I tried to tell them about the woman. But she was long gone. Probably back home crying at how scared she was. It don't matter. It was the day life decided to do what she loved doing best – and there I was – Life's entertainment for the day.

During my three months in county jail, while I waited for my court date, I blamed everyone in the world but me. I blamed the fellas. I blamed the cops. I blamed the woman. I blamed my

Pops. Never to his face. But I blamed him. Blamed him for making me how I was. Fiery. Violent. Vengeful.

At court, it was too easy. Both the fellas had lawyers. Both had pictures of the abuses I did to them. Both had the best thing going for them in front of a jury of my peers – me. Ugly. Bearded. Me. I was sentenced to eight years for assault and malicious wounding. When I turned to see my Pops so that I could at least wave goodbye, he was busting out through the doors. I hated him in that moment. Hated him for walking away when I needed him most.

Then they took me away to my new home.

In prison, everything is taken from you.

The first thing they take is your dignity.

Then your hope. Because I don't care what anyone says, but being a felon is going to make your life difficult. Not a little more difficult. Difficult.

My third night in there, I was staring at the ceiling surrounded by new sounds and new darkness. I started thinking about things I hadn't thought about in a long time. I remembered my mom. I thought of every gentle moment I ever had with her. I remembered the way she always held me when she knew my Pops had been too hard. I remembered her dabbing at a gash I got while climbing a tree. I remembered the way she'd tell me she loved me after a day of being teased by other kids. The way here blue eyes shined for me – the blue eyes she gave me. I remembered the way she'd part my hair like a complete dork each Sunday before church and how she'd call me handsome. Called me her handsome boy. And she meant it. Lastly, I remembered her saying goodbye from the hospital bed, sounding tired as she touched away my tears and told me she'd see me again one day. See me in heaven.

I remembered those things, and I began to sob.

I made a vow to my mom. I was going to serve my eight years one day at a time. I'd get out at 26, and 26 seemed ancient to an 18 year old, but it was what I'd have to do.   Because I was going to do it for her.

When it comes to vows, I make them to the blood. I will bleed out every drop I got in my tainted veins to keep a vow. And when I woke the next morning, I was a new man.

I spent those eight years participating in every activity I

could. I got a job in the kitchen. I read book after book after book. I worked out for hours each day to where I got even bigger and badder than ever before. I got tattooed up and down my body from head to toe just to pass the time. My beard grew out to be even more glorious. I even took to participating in church and men's bible study. Couldn't stand it at first. But it wasn't about me anymore.

Sure, I got in some tiffs with the other inmates. I may have done some things I shouldn't have. But that was a part of surviving.

My Pops visited me regularly. First time he did, he knew something had changed. I didn't tell him nothing about my vow to my Mom. That was between me and her. But he knew – knew something. He used to visit me every Saturday. And we got better each time.

Eight years is a long time. I could say it passed by quickly. But quick ain't any way to describe prison life. Long, drawn out drudgery – that's more like it. But one day, my release came like Christmas morning. I stepped back out into a new world like a resurrected man. And I knew I would never go back.

My Pops picked me up. He said, "Hey." I said, "Hey." He said, "Want to go get a steak somewhere?" I said, "More than anything." I was smiling like it was my new favorite hobby, and my Pops asked, "What are you smiling about?" I smiled even bigger. I told him, "Just happy to see you, Pops. That's all." He smirked. He said, "How 'bout that." Might have been the happiest I'd ever seen him. Ha!

That steak though. That steak. Best thing I'd ever had in my life. Pops and me ate together. When we were almost done, he told me why he left the courthouse that day during my sentencing. I expected him to give me some answer about having work to do or being disgusted with me. I sat frozen across from him afraid of something like that. He said, "Frank, I didn't want you to see me crying. I knew it wouldn't have done you any good." I said, "Thanks, Pops." Not sure what I was thanking him for. Maybe for the honesty. He nodded and we went back to eating and the subject was never brought up again.

I moved back in with him. Found myself back at church. It's good to remember life ain't all about you. It's good to remember the Eternal. Stuff like that is healthy for the soul.

And I got a job at a car repair shop.

Last week on Monday, I was working at that shop when my hand froze in mid-effort. My eyes were stuck fast on the woman across the street. Couldn't take my eyes off of her as she passed along the window in the store she worked at. I watched her for hours that day. Peek my eyes her way every few seconds as she remained oblivious to my very existence. My boss yelled at me, "Frank! These cars aren't going to fix themselves! Get back to work! Frank!" I watched her while I worked, my tools moving on their own while I stayed bent over an open hood just to catch a glimpse of her ponytail breezing by. I watched her talk to customers. I watched her smile. Couldn't help but imagine her talking and smiling at me. Even though I knew it was the stupidest thought I ever had. Then I did the same thing all day on Tuesday.

On Wednesday, she drove up. Her car needed fixing. She told me what the trouble was. Asked me if I could fix it. And all I could do was talk to her in broken sentences like I'd never used words before. She touched my hand as she handed over the keys, and I just stopped talking altogether. Then she drove off with a friend who came to pick her up.

I fixed her car. Nothing to it. Then I cleaned the inside of her car too, scrubbed and wiped, just for an excuse to be inside her car so I could smell what a lady as beautiful as her might smell like – smelled her car like some sort of a weirdo. "Frank!" My boss yelled at me, "What are you cleaning her car out for? Did we start offering detailing and no one told me? Get back to work!"

She came back on Friday. Then she went and did something I still don't understand – maybe I never will – she asked me out for pizza and a coke. She asked me out. I looked over my shoulders like maybe she was talking to some other lucky fella standing around. Her honey-colored eyes brightened. She smiled and said she was asking *me*. "Yeah, sure, sure, sure, sure, sure, sure, sure," I said, while I felt a strange sensation. A sensation quite similar to drifting into the air light as a cloud with my feet fluttering beneath me.

We went out that night. I didn't have any decent clothes, so I made do with what I had. Shaved my head. Sprayed some cologne that I must have got from some aunt way back when I was a teenager or something. Even combed my beard if you'll believe it. Picked at it with a brush I didn't even know I owned. We went on a date. Pizza and a coke. Best day of my life. I sat across from this lady with night-colored skin and her hair pulled back in a ponytail that shined. I watched her lips move while she talked and smiled and I wondered if those lips might taste as sweet as I imagined. Towards the end of the date, I thought, *What's she doing with some galoot like me – a fresh out of prison loser with nothing going for me and nothing to offer?*

And so, what did I do? I enjoyed the night for what it was. A one night spell with the most beautiful woman I'd ever met, while doing my best to keep any crumbs or sauce from sticking in my beard and avoiding the urge to smoke 'cause I was as nervous as a priest in Victoria's Secret on Valentine's day. I enjoyed the conversation. Enjoyed my time with her. Told her I had a great time. Told her thanks. Like she'd done it just to be a decent human being. Because I knew it wasn't meant to be. Because that's just how life goes. Because if there's one thing life enjoys more than anything, it's putting something out there for you to get excited about, just so it can rip it away. So, I smiled. I used my manners. I smiled some more. But I kept my heart guarded, hid away in my chest. No reason to go and get hurt over some lady I didn't deserve anyway.

The next morning, she called me. I was so surprised. I paced around my room. I was sweating. All she did was talk about small time stuff. Told me she had a great time during our date. Then she asked me what I was planning on doing for the day. In my nervousness, I must have said a novel's worth of words when all I meant to say was "nothing much." With that sensual and intelligent voice of hers, she said, "Oh, I guess you're busy." And I declared with mighty declaration, "No. Not at all." I could hear her smile. She asked, "Want to hang out with me?" I said, "More than anything."

I'm on my way over to pick her up for what will likely be the newest best day of my life. And I got a feeling that every day with her will be just that – the best day of my life.

Life is all about choices. Make good choices – you get a good life. Make bad choices – you get a bad life. The equation is just that simple. The problem is life is a swindler. Life likes to play games and she ain't ever looking to play fair. But sometimes, sometimes life goes and shows you her kind side. Sometimes, you're luckier than you ever deserve to be.

To read more about Frank, his wife, and his daughter, check out the book by R.S. Crow titled, *The Bear, the Girl, and the Monkey With No Eyes,* found on Amazon.com

Until He Was Gone - *Kelsey Gillespy*

"The King will reply, 'Truly, I tell you, whatever you did for one of the least of these brothers and sisters of mine, you did for Me [and] whatever you did not do for one of the least of these, you did not do for Me.'"
–Matthew 25:40, 45

The weight of his family rested in his palm as Mark Sanchez set the phone on the table. He ran a hand through his hair, which had recently become sprinkled with gray. Even the stubble on his face was spotted with white like the first hoarfrost of winter—like the coming of all things devoid of life.

His eyelids sagged with his heavy heart. The skin around his eyes ached beneath his fingertips as he rubbed, the pressure now painful.

"What'd they say?" His wife's eyes were large, pleading for an inkling of hope as she spooned the last bite of sweet potato into their toddler's mouth. If the baby put half as much food in her mouth as she did on her face, maybe she wouldn't be starving.

His wife's cheeks looked sunken. When did that happen? Was it because she gave all her food to the baby or because she never smiled anymore? Either way, she was wearing away.

And it was his fault.

"They said no thanks." Mark wiped his eyes again, this time collecting moisture on his fingertips.

"Dada!" Makenzie shouted, waving pudgy, goop-covered hands at her superhero.

He huffed into the air and pressed his palms to his eyes. Somehow the pain comforted him now. Made him feel justified for once. Like he was finally doing something right. Like he deserved the pain.

"Yeah, I'm your Dada. Your big, fat, failure of a Dada."

His wife reached out and patted the space between his rounded shoulders. Her face was blurred beyond the water welling in his eyes.

"I'm sorry you're stuck with me." The words barely escaped his lips. "If you want to leave, I won't blame you. You can pack everything up and—"

"Stop it."

"I can't give you what you need!"

"You *are* what I need!" Her volume rose with her desperation, and she pointed at her daughter. "You're what *we* need. Only one man can be her father."

Mark sighed. "I can't provide for you, Michelle."

"Everything will work out. God will provide."

Her words hung in the air, cold and lifeless, like a corpse. Those same words had been comforting the first time she said them—back when she believed them—the day he came home early and confessed he'd lost his job.

But lately, she had given up hope. She'd relinquished her trust in the Almighty figure that supposedly had control. Her prayers, once dripping with absolute faith and her own tears, were now mechanical. Detached. Monotonous. *If* she even prayed. Those days—when his wife ripped out her own heart and continued living without it—were the absolute worst.

The passionate woman he'd married, gone. Just like that. Her bright eyes dead. Her laugher silenced. Her childlike joy crushed. Everything she was evaporated, including each droplet of trust she placed in the God who led them off this cliff.

He rubbed his eyes again, this time just to feel the slow burn above his cheeks. The paper in front of him seemed too bright against the black wood of their table. At the top of the note, he read and reread one word.

Eviction.

The letters threw their brass-knuckled fingers at him and flanked him until he couldn't breathe. Was Makenzie going to grow up homeless? Why would God want that kind of future for an innocent baby?

Mark reached for the paper and crumpled it in his hand. He couldn't conquer the damned thing in real life, but he could crush the messenger in his palm. If only for a delusional moment that gave him a sense of power. Until he remembered his impotence. His powerlessness to do...anything.

He let the wrinkled ball fall from his fingertips.

"How much do you think we could get for this table? And these chairs?" his wife asked. She swept her fingers across the cracks in the tabletop.

"Not enough."

"Surely we could pay off some utilities if we sold them. Or the couch. Or—"

"And live in an empty shell?"

"It's better than living outside." She threw her hands in the air. "If anything, it could buy us some time."

He looked around the tiny, cramped apartment. Their home was barely big enough for the three of them to live, and yet still too big to afford. He carried his wife across the threshold after they married. The carpet in the living room cushioned Makenzie's fall after she took her first steps. When he pulled his baby girl out of her crib almost a year ago, she muttered "Dada" for the first time.

This was home.

Or it used to be, at least.

They wouldn't have a home at all in a few weeks.

"What do you think we should do?" His wife's words slipped out casually, quietly, her eyes never rising from the thick scar on the table. She ran her hand over the crevice then brushed loose pieces of chipped wood from the splintered surface.

"I don't know. I don't have any more insight now than I did before. I wish I did. God, I really wish I did. But I don't know anything anymore."

The wrinkles in his wife's young face sagged and stretched as she rubbed her temples.

He remembered an expression she used to say when she

was defeated. She probably even used it these past few months. He never asked if she heard it somewhere else or if she made it up, but it ballooned inside him now.

"The darker the night, the brighter the stars. The deeper the grief, the closer is God."

His wife huffed a chuckle and arched her brows. "Boy, if that ain't the truth."

Mark felt consumed by the dark. Suffocated. The gloom pressed down on his chest until his lungs could barely expand. He could almost taste the blackness as he bit down on his lip and a metallic flavor trickled into his mouth.

"Things can't get much darker, Michelle. So where the heck is God?"

His wife's slender finger stopped moving across the surface of the table, but her eyes remained fixed on the scar in the wood. Her shoulders dropped. "Maybe He's calling us to be the least of these..."

"These least of these? We're supposed to serve the least of these—supposed to serve God—but with what, Michelle? How's God helping *us*?"

Her shoulders rose toward her ears as she slowly shook her head. "I don't know. I don't know anything anymore, either."

He couldn't believe the words that tried to leak from his lips. For a moment he clenched his jaw to stop them from spilling out. But it was all he had left. The only option he hadn't exhausted.

"Wanna ask Him with me?"

Michelle's head jerked up, looking wide-eyed into the face of a husband who wasn't joking. "S-sure."

He was a rusted machine and desperately needed to be greased and oiled after all these years.

"God..." Just saying His name felt foreign on his lips, like holding a baseball for the first time since he abandoned it in college. He cleared his throat. "God, help us find You in this mess. The end."

Somehow he was out of breath, like he'd run a marathon in that short sentence. He glanced up at his wife's growing smirk.

"I mean, Amen." He couldn't resist the small grin pulling at his lips even as heat rushed to the tips of his ears.

Something glistened in Michelle's eyes. Hope? Curiosity?

Whatever the case, it was a spotlight on his ever-growing list of vulnerabilities.

"Let's go for a walk," he said. Anything to get away from his wife's gaze that was sure to come with questions. Questions he couldn't answer.

She nodded, then wiped Makenzie's face with a potato-covered cloth and scooped the girl out of the high chair. "Ready when you are."

Mark turned the key in the lock and it clicked into place. The keys jingled as he shoved them back in his pocket.

"Dada!"

"Come here, sweet girl." He reached for Makenzie and she flung her arms around his neck, cherishing the gift of being in her father's arms.

The streets of the city screeched and howled as people tried to shout over the traffic. Words added to the heartbeat on the street, the voices rising and falling like millions of breathing lungs.

Makenzie pressed into his chest and he smelled lavender in her hair. Was that how her hair always smelled?

"Where do you want to go?" Michelle asked.

Mark shrugged and his daughter's tiny body bobbed with his shoulders. "How about we keep going straight?"

Michelle squeezed between strangers on the sidewalk and Mark followed, turning sideways to slip through the small opening. He hugged Makenzie to his chest, inhaling the sweet scent of innocence.

He cradled her even closer as a man walked toward them, his face smudged with sweat and dirt. A green shirt hung loosely from his torso, the letters USMC faded from overuse. Baggy cargo shorts touched the bottom of his knees. Whatever hair he had was shaved to his scalp, and he reeked of desperation. His untied shoelaces slapped the pavement as he passed.

"Sir! Wait! Sir!" His words escaped wildly, like he couldn't control the volume of his voice.

Mark saw his own future in this stranger's filth. How soon would he be like this man? Desolate, desperate, and destitute? Would he be forced to wander the streets, only making money when passersby tossed him a penny in hopes he'd go away?

Mark clutched Makenzie tighter to his chest and nudged

his wife forward, away from the raving lunatic.

"No disrespect, sir, but please stop walking!"

"I don't have anything for you!"

The guy gazed at the toddler wrapped in Mark's arms and whatever fogged his eyes disappeared.

"My daughters used to be that small." His words slurred as he nodded at Makenzie. "Now I'm here. And they're grown." His eyes welled with the agony of his own history as he threw both hands in the air and stared at the girl through two hopeless pits in his face. He turned then, wiping his tear-stained face as he crossed the street.

Mark simply stood there, stripped of words, too shocked to move, letting the man's bleak story spill into the cracks beneath his feet. The smell of lavender brought him back to life as Makenzie nuzzled her cheek into his collarbone. He kissed the top of her head and scanned the crowd, catching a glimpse of the man before he slipped inside a towering building whose steeple reached for the heavens.

"Dada." Makenzie lifted her head and pointed toward the heavy, red door where the man disappeared.

"No sweetheart." He brushed a strand of curly hair from his daughter's face and kissed her forehead. "Not Dada."

In all the pictures Mark had seen, that same man's bald head had sprouted brown hair that passed his shoulders, his glassy eyes replaced with ones that reached out and touched people with compassion. He was used to the man's clothes being baggy—like they were this time—but it was always a white toga that hung from his torso, kept together by a rope around his waist. And never before had Mark witnessed him ditch his brown sandals for tennis shoes covered in holes.

All the other times Mark had seen him, the man was silent and still, captured only by the brush strokes of an artist.

His mouth went dry.

Never in his Toronto life did he expect to find that man on the corner of 2nd and Cincinnati, but he was as real as the thick, red door that beckoned him now. As real as the least of his brothers and sisters who filled the pews and the streets.

God was there. And he let him go without a word.

He didn't even recognize Jesus until He was gone.

Thank you for reading some of my work. I hope you enjoyed *Until He Was Gone*! If you'd like more information about me and my other publications, subscribe to my webpage at www.kelseygillespy.com.

Safe Passage – *Jarrod L. Edge*

Preface

During the second seven years of her life, Elizabeth Sette and her older siblings, Rebecca, Matthew, and Jacob, performed great acts. This was foretold in an ancient prophecy spoken by the Apostle John shortly before his death. The scribe that wrote down the prophecy called it The Prophecy of the Seventh Elizabeth.

Elizabeth, daughter of Special Agent Johnathan Sette, made it her mission to chronicle the Acts of the Dragons so that they would be remembered forever. She did this during the fifteenth year of her life, after The Battle Between Light and Dark; the battle in which she stood for all mankind.

The story you are about to hear is a recount of one of those stories, one of the Acts of the Dragons.

Elizabeth Age 12

Chapter: 1
Location: Facility Six, Peru (100 Miles North of Huánuco)
Time: August 22, 2011

"Earth!" she yelled.

It was the signal that Sergeant had been waiting to hear. He turned and used one of the attacking Shadow Warriors as a stepping stone, jumping and reaching for the ledge above. He barely made it, catching it with his fingertips. A split second later Elizabeth arrived, executing the dragon move known as "the heavy fist," taking down three of the attacking Shadows. She followed up with a pair of roundhouse kicks, taking down the remaining two. As Major Sergeant pulled himself up and onto the ledge, Elizabeth quickly assessed the area, double checking her handiwork, then turned and gave him a nod. He smiled and then shook his head.

"Nice," he said. He supposed that by now he shouldn't be surprised by Elizabeth's skill set or that of her siblings. He and the other agents of ACTS had been on enough missions with the Dragons over the past two years that it should probably seem like second nature to him by now. But the fact that this twelve year old girl had just single handedly taken down demons twice her size was nothing short of amazing.

"What?" she said with a smile and a shrug.

"Nothing," he said with a slight laugh. "Sometimes I wonder if you really need our help," he said looking down at her from the terrace approximately ten feet above her. When she didn't reply right away, he looked over his shoulder and checked his surroundings. His objective was in sight. As he turned back around, Elizabeth was standing right next to him. It nearly made him jump, but he didn't.

"We're all in, Major. God chose each of us to fight this— this war," she said. Elizabeth glanced out at the trees before she continued, "Maybe I could do it without you, if God put it upon my heart to do it that way I mean. But truthfully, I'm glad He doesn't want me to fight this fight alone. You know?"

"I know exactly what you mean, kid," he said, the tone of

his voice a bit more serious. He understood, or at least he thought he did, the seriousness and importance of her role. He understood, or at least thought he did, the weight upon her shoulders. He also understood, and he was sure that he did, that she bore that weight well.

Before either could say another word, they heard a screech from the tree line about two hundred yards from their position. Over the com came Rick's voice.

"We've got incoming reinforcements from the tree line," he said. "Snipers, set up and start taking them out."

Elizabeth was staring intently at the tree line. Sergeant put his hand on her shoulder. "You OK?" he asked.

Instead of answering him, she tapped her com, "Not just Shadows, Uncle Rick. Niro is here."

"John, what do you want do? It's your call," Rick asked.

Johnathan was on the other side of the compound with Tatiana and Mira, they were about to execute their entry plan. Johnathan looked at the others and then reached for his com. Before he could say anything, Elizabeth spoke.

"Stay on plan everyone. This mission is important. Get the location of Annex Prime and shut this facility down for good. The Dragons will take care of the Shadows. We're going after Niro," she said. Then she jumped from the terrace and bolted toward the tree line. In a matter of seconds, she was halfway there.

Rebecca answered the call as did Jacob and Matthew, then each of the Dragons switched to their secondary channel, isolating their conversation. Elizabeth's siblings had already started moving toward her side of the compound when Rick had first made the announcement, but they wouldn't catch Elizabeth, she was much faster than they were, when she wanted to be that is. And right now she wanted to be.

Niro was a Syndicate executive and a very dangerous one at that. He was also skilled and not to be taken lightly. She and the other Dragons had gotten close to Niro several times, but they had never been able to take him down and bring him in. But this time would be different. This time they would bring him to justice for his crimes, his atrocities.

"Little Sis, we're on our way. I know you're not going to wait, but wait for us!" Rebecca said.

"Can't," Elizabeth replied. "Niro is moving away and fast. We can't let him escape again. We may not get another chance to catch him after today. But I'll leave this line of Shadows for you guys." That being said, Elizabeth entered the tree line and disappeared into the forest.

She couldn't see their eyes, but she could feel the emptiness of the Shadow Warriors. She would use that null space to pinpoint each of their positions. She thought about jumping the entire group and travelling by branch, but then she thought, "Why should I let the others have all of the fun?" She jumped and rolled in the air, landing hard on one of the Shadow Warriors. His growl testified to the fact that the demons could feel pain. She followed through, stepping around another Shadow, ducking under his swing, grabbing hold of his arm as she did. Then she threw the demon in front of her and cleared herself a path. A large tree finally brought the demon to rest as Elizabeth was off again, heading after Niro who now had a decent lead on her. Worse yet, she could sense that he wasn't alone. Another squad of Shadows had just entered the forest through dark portals.

Matthew and Jacob had always marveled at how some cultures showed amazingly uncanny abilities in the area of engineering, hundreds or even thousands of years ago. The ability to build a bridge, for example, out of ropes fashioned from tree vines, that would last longer that some modern day bridges. It was something that the twins took great pleasure in studying. Traveling around the world certainly made it easier for the twins to see, first-hand, many of these engineering feats. From the looks of it, Elizabeth thought they would be able to add the bridge in front of her to their list. But she was wrong.

Chapter: 2
Location: Forest near Facility Six
Time: August 22, 2011

As she stepped onto the incredibly sturdy, two hundred year old bridge, Niro gave the attack order to the Shadow Army Controller running alongside him. Although it took a moment, the Controller relayed the command to three Shadow Warriors that were standing on the opposite side of the gap from Elizabeth. Immediately they tore the bridge from its foundation, as if it had been made of paper and clay.

The bridge dropped; the one side swinging to meet its opposite's wall. But to the Shadow Warrior's surprise, the girl on the bridge did not drop. Instead, she climbed higher and higher, closer and closer until she finally landed right behind them.

"You guys are still kind of slow aren't you?" Elizabeth said as she rose up behind the three Shadows, spun and kicked. The blow sent each of them over the edge and into the near fifty foot deep gap. Turning to assess the situation and try to get a feel for how much of a lead Niro had, Elizabeth opened her com. "Guys, be careful. The bridge is out."

"Bridge?" Matthew said, his voice filled with intrigue.

"What kind of bridge?" Jacob asked.

"Did you break a bridge?" Rebecca said. The sound of a Shadow screeching echoed into her com as she put the demon down for good.

"No, and enough about the bridge already," Elizabeth said. "Sometimes I can't believe that I'm the youngest," she didn't say. Then she paused. "They didn't even turn around," she said.

"What?" Rebecca said.

"Hang on guys. I need to check on something," Elizabeth said as she closed her com. "What were you three looking at?" she said softly as she walked toward the gap. She could see the bridge hanging from the other side. Dust still settling down into the crevasse. "Surely they weren't mind boggled by the falling bridge," she said softly as she moved closer to the edge. "And I don't think they have a fear of heights," she said as she looked over the edge and into the fifty foot drop. Then she felt it. She had been so focused on Niro and the Shadows that she had missed it. She had missed the three—no not three—four people at the bottom of the crevasse. And she had just sent three Shadows to join them.

Elizabeth activated her com again and jumped. As she did, she heard the scream; so did the others through her com.

"Help!" a female voice yelled.

"Get away from her," an older male voice yelled out.

The roar of the Shadow Warriors was much louder than the man and woman. But it was the next sound that made all of the

Dragons take pause. The cry of an infant.

That was what the Shadows had seen. That was what had their attention. Trained as Syndicate lapdogs, the Shadow Warriors under the leadership of the Teacher had been trained to, among other things, facilitate the retrieval of children. Not just infants, but any age. Infants, however, were at the top of the list. The Shadow Warriors were running on instinct; get the child at any cost.

"Flight," she called out as she slowed her fifty foot descent and landed between the family and the slowly approaching Shadows. In her right hand her sword had appeared, emblazoned with the one word, "Righteousness." She needed the Shadows to be focused on her and not the family. She also needed to end this as quickly as possible before—"Too late." As the thought had entered her mind, she heard the low hum of dark portals opening. "Guys," she said into her com. "I'm going to need your help."

"Almost there, Little Sis," Rebecca answered. As she did, she heard the screech of additional Shadow Warriors arriving via the portals. She looked at her brothers. "If we don't hurry—"

Matthew finished her sentence, "Elizabeth's not going to save any of them for us."

Jacob and Rebecca smiled as all three took off toward Elizabeth's position.

Chapter: 3
Location: Forest near Facility Six
Time: August 22, 2011

Niro entered the small clearing. "This is way too small for a helicopter to land in," he thought. But even so, the STOD retrieval helicopter was making its landing. "I guess if anyone can, STOD can." As he started to step forward, the Controller standing behind him growled in a deep throaty tone. Niro turned to regard the creature.

Niro wasn't a fan of the Shadow Army, Controllers or Warriors. Although he had respect for the Teacher, he wasn't very fond of other Syndicate outside contractors. Most Syndicate executives, like Niro, felt this way. But if the Board of Directors thought it necessary, who was he to argue. Besides, this hadn't been the only time they had come in handy. Frankly, with the Teacher missing in action, the Shadows were more of a scapegoat, if the mission didn't succeed that is. But this mission would succeed.

The Controller, with its grotesque face, distorted body, and its soulless eyes, was trying to tell Niro something. "Have you found the target?" Niro asked.

The Controller grunted what seemed to Niro to be an affirmative.

"Good. Send reinforcements immediately!" Niro turned to see that the helicopter had nearly landed. In the front of the vehicle was his trusted friend and ally, Sandman.

A few moments later, Niro was onboard and the helicopter started to rise. He yelled into his headset's microphone, "So, you are not dead after all."

Sandman replied with a smile, "The rumors of ACTS causing my untimely demise were highly exaggerated."

Niro gave a nod of approval. He had suspected that STOD allowed the rumors so that Sandman could operate off book for a while. "We need to get to the facility. The Agents of ACTS are there. It's time to take them out of play—for good!" Niro said as he gestured to Sandman to take them higher.

Sandman smiled, nodded and pulled back on the stick.

Chapter: 4
Location: Scar of the Mountain
Time: August 22, 2011

Elizabeth's sword became an endless stream of light as she sliced through the squads of Shadows that were slowly starting to overwhelm the area. She was winning, but the numbers of her enemy were increasing and she needed to be in four places at once. Too much time on one side of the stranded family would allow a team of Shadows to reach their objective. So far they were concentrating on the side closest to the older man. Elizabeth assumed that he was the father and she was glad to see that he knew how to use that large cane he was holding. It looked like he was using a few Shadows for batting practice.

"Keep away from my family," he said. Elizabeth had to translate his words.

She decided she'd keep an eye on him while committing herself to maintaining a buffer between the Shadows and the other three objectives: the mother, Elizabeth assumed, a small girl, and a newborn child. It appeared to Elizabeth that the mother had just given birth, less than an hour ago if she was correct.

Three Shadows lunged at the family, each from a different direction. Elizabeth met them in the air, sending them back to the ground in bloodless pieces. The look on one of the fallen Shadow's face seemed to express thanks or maybe relief, as if suddenly being released from an eternal contract of slavery. Elizabeth didn't think twice about it as she finally heard what she had been waiting for.

"Air," Rebecca yelled.

"Earth," Jacob yelled.

"Water," Matthew called out as he hit the ground and directed an invisible wall of water at the Shadows that were about to overwhelm the father. It took the entire squad off their feet and to the ground. Matthew rose to his full height and introduced himself. "I'm Matthew, that's Jacob and Rebecca. I see you've already met Elizabeth," he said in Quechuan, the man's native tongue.

"Well, not formally," the man replied with a slight smile which suddenly turned to a wide-eyed stare.

Matthew jumped, turned, and kicked the two Shadows that had decided to attack him while his back was turned. He landed facing the man as if he had never moved. The man's face had returned to a smile. "We're the Dragons and we're here to help," he said. "Stay here with your family while we take care of the rest of these demons."

Rebecca's blue three section staff had been in constant motion since she gracefully landed next to the mother and her newborn child. She had driven the entire squad of Shadows back to their arrival point; politely giving them the chance to depart while still breathing. "Do they breathe?" she thought. "No matter. It's time for you very smelly demons to leave." The last part she said out loud.

Two of the Shadows appeared to take offense. They immediately attacked and were immediately repelled by her staff.

Elizabeth was disappointed to see that Rebecca wasn't using her new pink three section staff. But Rebecca was Rebecca and if she didn't want to scuff her new staff by beating up Shadow Warriors, so be it. There would certainly be more battles.

Out of the seven available Dragon powers, Jacob had called upon the power of Earth. He was currently systematically taking out each of his opponents with one punch to each. Combined with that powerful blow, he would stomp on the ground causing Shadows nearby to become off balance, stopping their advance in their tracks.

Elizabeth was pleased that her brothers and sister had arrived, and within minutes, the Dragons had removed their enemy from the field of battle.

Chapter: 5
Location: Inside the Scar of the Mountain
Time: August 22, 2011

For a moment the forest was silent. Not even a bird chirping or fly buzzing. Just rays of sunshine reaching down through the trees, illuminating the forest above and providing light for the crevasse where the Dragons and the unsuspecting family stood. Elizabeth hadn't had a chance to assess the area or take in all of its beauty. The colors were rich, more vibrant than anything she had seen since—since the Temple of Light, where she had spent her childhood. As sound started filtering back in, she heard the stream echoing its song in the background.

As Elizabeth looked up she noticed that there was a ledge that ran parallel to the great gap's floor about fifteen feet above. From the top of the gap a person, situated where she had first jumped across the gap, would not have been able to see the family of four at the bottom. The ledge would have blocked their view. It was why she had not seen them as she jumped over the gap.

The Shadows had been on the opposite side of the gap and were able to see under the ridge to where the unsuspecting family was—"What were they doing down here?" Elizabeth thought and then decided that it was time to formally introduce herself.

"The Shadows," Elizabeth began and then paused. "They

probably don't know what a Shadow is," she thought, then she started again. "Those demons won't be bothering us for a while, but I can't say that they are gone forever."

"Thank you for your kindness. You saved our lives," the man replied with a slight bow.

Elizabeth and her siblings had no trouble translating the man's words. They were proficient in his language, having prepared well for the mission to take Facility Six.

"I am Asto and this is my family. My wife Tamaya, my daughter Inti, and my newborn and quite early son whom we have not properly named yet." He looked at his wife who gave him, what seemed to Elizabeth to be, the 'have patience' look. She wasn't sure.

Elizabeth extended her hand, "It's nice to meet you Asto. My name is Elizabeth and we are all happy to help." He took her hand and regarded her for short time before she continued. "If you don't mind sir, may I ask what you are doing way out here—" she paused to look at his wife who was coddling her newborn son. "In these conditions?" she continued.

"Ah," he smiled, noticing that the others were coming closer. "We are on our way to Cecilia."

Jacob and Matthew looked at each other, but it was Rebecca that spoke. "Isn't Cecilia on the other side of the mountain?" she asked.

Jacob joined in. "The only way to get there would be via helicopter or—"

Matthew finished his sentence for him, "or drive several hours around."

Asto laughed as his daughter left her mother and went to his side. "Yes, yes, but there is another way. I am not surprised that you have not heard of it," he said as he placed his hand on his daughter's head. "We are standing in the 'Scar of the Mountain'," his voice seemed to deepen just a little as he told them the name. "This path is thousands of years old and is in fact the shortest route to Cecilia. Legend has it that a great light came down from the sky and carved the passage to connect the two villages." He laughed again and sighed, "I don't know about the legend but I do know that the passage is real. It is used by those who are not bothered by the tales of—"

"Let me guess," Rebecca said, "Shadows in the forest?"

Asto smiled but before he could reply, his daughter interrupted. She was remarkably well spoken for her age, which Elizabeth approximated to be four or five. "Where did your sword go or perhaps a better question would be, where did it come from? Was it really made of light? The others, how were they able to fly?"

While Elizabeth happily answered the onslaught of questions, the twins helped Asto fix the wheel on his 'cart', for lack of a better word. Asto explained that their plan had been to go to Cecilia where they would settle in and await the baby's arrival. When the wheel on the cart broke, the cart's passengers were thrown from it. The abrupt fall had caused Tamaya to go into labor. Shortly after that, their son was born.

It didn't take long to fix the cart and make sure that the area was still secure. As the Dragons prepared to leave and join the Agents of ACTS, Elizabeth approached Asto.

"Asto, we've talked it over and I'm going to escort you and your family to Cecilia," Elizabeth said.

Asto and his wife, who until now had been mostly silent, looked at each other and then at Elizabeth. "But you have surely done more than enough for our family, we do not wish to place such a burden on you," Tamaya said and Asto agreed. Inti on the other hand was very happy that Elizabeth would be joining them for the journey.

"I insist," she replied. "There are likely still—Shadows in the forest," she said glancing at Rebecca.

"Little Sis, we'll notify Dad, finish the mission, and catch up to you," Rebecca said as she hugged her sister. "Stay sharp," she whispered.

"I will," Elizabeth responded.

"Keep your com open, although I doubt we'll be able to communicate," Jacob said as he gave his little sister a hug.

With that said, Jacob and Rebecca ran, jumped, and scaled the gap's fifty foot wall, leaving Matthew standing next to Elizabeth and the family of four standing in silent awe at yet another unbelievable feat.

"Go," Elizabeth said, giving her older brother a hug.

"Are you sure about this? I know that most of your plans

work, but this is uncharted territory, Sis. I'm not sure I want to leave you here alone." He kept his voice low as he spoke.

"I'll be OK. We've already talked about it," she said as she took a step back. "Trust me, I'll be OK. Now go already."

Chapter: 6
Location: Scar of the Mountain (nearing Cecilia)
Time: August 22, 2011

"So, if you don't mind me saying, it seems to me that there would have been a safer route to take to reach the village. And I know I've asked before, but why this way and why now?" Over the last two hours, Elizabeth had walked beside the small motorized cart that carried the family of four. Occasionally she helped to clear an obstruction, or helped to lift the cart over a fallen tree or stone. For the first hour Inti had asked what seemed to Elizabeth to be a thousand or more questions, which Elizabeth happily answered. It seemed like she had recounted her entire life to the five year old girl. In the narrow windows of time that Inti wasn't asking a question, Asto and Elizabeth had a very nice, sometimes intense, philosophical conversation, each gleaning insight from the other. Eventually Inti fell asleep next to her mother, who had remained virtually silent, and her new brother, also silent, other than the occasional whimper.

The journey had taken them through the deepest part of the mountain, or from another perspective, the tallest part of the mountain. They had also passed through the narrowest part of the path as well. It appeared that the sections of the mountain above had fallen in on each other, further helping to disguise the trench itself. "Quite a work of art," Elizabeth thought as they made their way through the narrow pass. "Another of God's masterpieces indeed."

It took a moment, but Asto finally answered. "Well—it seemed like a good idea at the time," he said with a smile as he looked at his wife and children.

Elizabeth wasn't quite satisfied with that answer. In fact, she hadn't been satisfied with any of his answers since they'd met. She didn't think him to be a bad person, but she knew that he wasn't being completely honest with her. Evasive would best describe it. She could feel it. Something was off.

"May I ask you a question, young Elizabeth," Asto said.

The question made her hesitate to answer, more specifically the phrase, 'young Elizabeth.' Only a few people in her life had called her that. Most of those were her martial arts teachers. "Sure," she replied in her normal cheerful tone.

"Why are you helping us?" he asked. His tone had also changed, as if dropping a pretense. When she did not immediately answer, he continued. "I can recognize a pure heart when I see one, and I see that yours is a pure heart. Even so, I do not understand why you would leave your family to escort my family on a journey that is not yours. Is there something that you want from us?"

Until now, Elizabeth hadn't considered that to him, she may seem to be the one with an ulterior motive. "Well, if I may be honest with you, I think there is more to your family than you are telling me. I can't explain it, but I felt that if I stayed with you long enough, it would come to me. Other than that, there was no way that I was going to leave you with—Shadows in the forest. They only found you because of me, and if anything were to happen to you, well—let's just say that I'm here to make sure that nothing happens to you or your beautiful family. You deserve safe passage."

"Ah. To become the protector of those who cannot protect themselves," he said.

Elizabeth stopped in her tracks. "What did you say?" she asked, understanding that the quote was from the Prophecy. But before Asto could answer, his new born son screamed and began to cry frantically. Tamaya woke up, sat up, and grabbed the child from his makeshift basket.

"What's wrong?" Elizabeth asked.

"I don't know, he didn't even cry after being born. In fact the first time he cried out was when those—" Asto started but it was Elizabeth who finished his thought as the passage filled with the low hum of dark portals.

"Shadow Warriors appeared," she said, sword pulsating in her right hand.

Chapter: 7
Location: Scar of the Mountain (nearing Cecilia)
Time: August 22, 2011

Elizabeth assessed the situation. "Too many portals," she thought. She wasn't wondering if she could defeat them all, she was wondering if she would be able to wait as long as she had wanted to, needed to. "I'd better take out the ones farthest from the cart," she reasoned. "The Shadows will need time to prove me right."

But she wouldn't have to wait long at all. The Shadows seemed to make a mad dash for the—"Wait, they're not going after the baby at all. They're going after—" Before she could finish the thought three Shadows went flying through the air, away from Asto's position. He had taken them out with a move that she had never seen before. His stick, the rod in his hand, had released an energy discharge and repelled the three demons.

"Now," she said into her com.

In an instant, the nearby Controllers started falling to the ground, some seemingly being snatched from their feet as if hit in the chest with a fast moving projectile, which happened to be the case. Elizabeth could hear the pluck of a bow and the whisper of arrows splitting the air as they moved toward their targets.

"Light!" Three voices from different locations along the passage walls preceded the three Dragons as they stepped, or more accurately flew onto the battlefield, surrounding the cart and its occupants.

The remaining Shadows immediately retreated to their portals. There was no trace that they had ever been there, no bodies in sight.

Elizabeth and Asto faced each other and spoke at the same time, "How did you—" They stopped and gave way to the other and then each realized that the other had spoken in English, which turned all of the Dragons' heads. Elizabeth accepted the 'right of way' and continued with her question.

"At first I thought that I had lead the Shadows to you, but I wasn't quite sure. Now I'm sure that I didn't. How did you defeat the three Shadows and why are they after you?" she asked.

"You asked me twice, why did I choose this way to bring

my family? The truth is, I am a scientist, forced to work for the Syndicate, an evil organization with evil intentions."

"We are familiar with the Syndicate," Rebecca interrupted.

"Yes, I have gathered that," he replied nodding his head slowly. "The demons are hunting me for my knowledge and for Tamaya's child. She is not my wife, and the child—" there was great concern in his eyes and in the eyes of the child's mother. "The child is the result of forced experimentation."

The boys wanted to ask what type of experimentation, but decided to just let Asto finish.

"They would have taken the child and done unimaginable things to him. I decided to take Tamaya and my daughter and escape the facility after the child was born. This passage is only spoken about in legend, but I searched for it and found it. I knew we could use it to escape. But the Syndicate sent one of its executives to evaluate Facility Six and I was forced to run sooner than planned. They have been searching the forest for us and found us as you did."

"Niro," Elizabeth thought. She was sure her siblings were thinking the same thing.

"When you saved us from the first attack and told us who you were, I recognized your names from reports from the Syndicate Tactical Operations Division. You are who they refer to as 'the Chosen One', are you not?" he asked.

"I am. I figured you knew because you quoted a part of the Prophecy," she replied.

"I do not understand," he replied.

"To protect those who cannot protect themselves," she said.

"Oh, those words are the words that I have prayed over and over to God. To send someone to protect us as we cannot protect ourselves," Asto nodded.

Elizabeth nodded, indicating that her question was adequately answered. She believed him, and it was now Asto's turn to ask his question.

"How did you manage to conceal the presence of your brothers and sister?" he asked with a confused look on his face.

"Well, we've been in contact the entire journey. Rebecca and Jacob went to inform others of our situation and Matthew has been with us the entire time," she said

"Eventually, we caught up with you," Jacob added.

"And we brought some friends," Rebecca said waving them in.

Into the foreground walked, Tatiana Novichok and Mira Daniels in true Agents of ACTS style. Tatiana's bow was in hand and Mira held her rifle at the ready. Both remained silent but nodded and smiled. They didn't want to seem rude. A moment later, each disappeared into the background.

"There was a point, about an hour back, where I could have sworn I heard someone sneeze. I just thought it was my mind playing tricks on me," Asto said.

"Yep, that was me," Rebecca confessed. "Nature," she said as she shrugged her shoulders and tilted her head.

"Tell me about the child," Elizabeth said drawing attention back to the moment. "There is something about him, he can sense the Shadows," she said as she moved toward Tamaya.

"He was to be the first of many test subjects. Subject Zero. The Syndicate has set out to create a super being. Super beings that can be controlled by them. But Zero," Asto winced each time he called the child by that name. He wore his guilt on his face. "The child was only the first test in the very first stage. I'm sure he will be as normal and as healthy as any other child." He paused for a moment as Tamaya gestured to Elizabeth to hold the child.

Zero's skin was a rich shade of milk chocolate, a few shades lighter than his mother. His breathing was tranquil and he slept as peacefully as he had the entire trip. Elizabeth removed the blanket from his head and to everyone's surprise a full head of hair popped out to form a little afro. Zero, eyes closed, smiled as if Elizabeth had just set him free. But it was Rebecca that noticed it. The birthmark on his shoulder. The shape of an O or—

"A zero," she said as the others gathered around to see.

Now it made sense, she had put it all together. It was something she had read in the Prophecy. Elizabeth spoke the words allowed. "And they will bless him in a forest of shadows, under the protection of angels…the child that bares the mark of none."

Elizabeth and her siblings stretched their hands out to touch the child and simply prayed as the forest stood still.

"What would have happened to him if you hadn't saved him?" Jacob asked.

"Eventually he would have been sent to Annex Prime to live out a dreadful existence," Asto replied, still in awe over the power of what he had just witnessed.

Matthew, Jacob, Rebecca, and Elizabeth each did a double-take, but it was Elizabeth who asked the question first, "You know where Annex Prime is located?"

The four travelers never reached the city on the other side of the mountain. Instead they returned with the Agents of ACTS, as their guests, to the United States. Niro and Sandman remained at large.

"I asked you before, why you would help us?"

"Because, like us, you are birds of passage, far from home indeed."

Jarrod L. Edge is the author of the *E7Prophecy*™ Christian sci-fi fantasy series. He loves spending time with his wife, Lisa, and their four children, Kari, Taevon, Edward, and Isabella. His children are also coauthors in some of his books. Jarrod's book series include:

The Prophecy of the Seventh Elizabeth™ series
The Acts of the Dragons™ series
The Agents of ACTS™ series
0-2-10™ series

Jarrod and his family are Christians and love learning about and growing in the Lord.

Visit www.e7prophecy.com for more.

April and Mr. Grim - *Parker J. Cole*

April Hollister checked her make-up and smoothed the wide, waxed, black eyebrows above her honey brown eyes with a well-manicured finger. Satisfied, she closed the compact mirror and shoved it into her purse. Then she tugged on the edge of her skirt. Glancing out the window in the limo, the city lights flashed past her as they made their way on the freeway. This was the night.

Just the thought of what tonight meant ripped the breath from her heaving lungs and she closed her eyes. *Calm down,* she told herself.

Her heart only thumped faster.

"Sweetie, you're fine!" Obadiah Grim chuckled, and reached for her hand.

"Of course I am, Obadiah!" She grinned into his sightless eyes.

"No, you're not, sweetie. Whenever you're nervous, you move a lot. You twitch, you sigh, you scratch—"

"Scratch!" April exclaimed. Then she paused and admitted in a little girl voice, "I forgot to put my medicine on the back of my neck this morning. I thought you wouldn't notice."

The man at her side laughed. "I guess I'll have to get one of those metal brushes with thin teeth for maximum use."

Laughter filled the car, and the tension left her body.

"That's better," Obadiah sighed. He raised her hand to his mouth and kissed her knuckles, his neat full mustache tickling her nerve endings. Half black and half Korean, her fiancé had the kind of looks to make a dead woman rise up and shave her legs.

"Sweetie, I don't want you to be nervous. Meeting the old people won't be as big of a deal as you think."

"Not a big deal at all," she responded breezily. "You're only the son of Grim's Confectioneries, the biggest confectionery in Michigan, infamous for those oh-so-delicious cream stuffed cupcakes drizzled with caramel and—"

"I'm allergic to caramel though. Except from the kind of caramel from your lips," he murmured, as he bent and unerringly found her mouth. April fell into the kiss, blown away by Obadiah's skill, which still made her weak in the knees. Her fingers clutched at his wide, rounded shoulders, and she opened her mouth a little bit more to allow him entry.

A groan escaped from Obadiah, and he reached to grab her head to hold it steady to increase the pressure. April thought she'd swoon.

"I can see and hear you, Mr. Grim," a scraggily, frog-like voice interrupted.

The kiss ended on a note of frustration. "Awww, why'd you have to go and do that Nelson? No one can keep up a romantic mood listening to you talk! You sound like Darth Vader having an asthma attack." He turned his head toward April. "And ever since I went blind several months ago, that voice thing just makes it worse."

"If it was good enough for Padme', then it's good enough for you."

"Padme' doesn't exist! Even if she did, if she heard Anakin sounding like you, she would have left his behind."

April patted Obadiah's arm. "It's okay." She leaned and whispered in his ear, "We can always finish where we left off later."

Obadiah gave a shudder. "I wish I could see so I could tell if you're making fun of me."

"Oh, but I am, darling! You don't really think I'd just give it away, do you? I gotta make silly little men like you earn it."

Nelson coughed, and April frowned. "Fur ball, Nelson?"

"Undoubtedly," he responded. His eyes, crinkled along the edges, glanced back at her in the rearview mirror. "It's gone now, Miss Hollister."

"I should hope so," she muttered as he focused on the road.

They drove the rest of way, little jokes going back and forth. April knew tonight she'd receive his parents' blessings. After all, she done a lot to ensure her past wouldn't catch up with her. Not even Obadiah knew who she had been, and she'd do anything to keep it from surfacing to mar their relationship.

When Obadiah fell earlier this year and lost his sight in a freak accident, she stood by him. For a while, she'd had to fight against his depression and the ludicrous idea he wasn't a whole man. His blindness hadn't affected her love. Why should it? She had every intention of marrying this man, and she'd take him however he came. If he were blinded for the rest of his life, she'd stay by his side. For better or worse, the vows went. He hadn't known about her past and she wasn't ever going to enlighten him.

They arrived at the large but modest home in the White Lake Township. Nelson opened the door and ushered them out.

"Here goes," April whispered, as she waited for Obadiah to come out the car. The familiar feel of his arm soothed her rapid pulse, and she inhaled a deep breath.

"It'll be okay. They're going to love you."

April knew that, but there was always the chance they wouldn't like her on sight. She was marrying their only son. She led the way up the sidewalk to the square front of the home. The white awning hung over a row of viburnum shrubs on either side. Their scent surrounded them like a blessing, and the petals reflected the light of the moon.

"Everything's going to be okay, isn't it Obie?" April sighed with satisfaction as she leaned her head on his shoulder.

"Those flowers did it, right?"

"And you thought you needed to see in order to read me."

He patted her hand. Before Obadiah could do little more than knock, the door was swung open from the inside.

"Obadiah!" a soft female voice exclaimed.

"*Eomeoni!*" he greeted back, calling her by the Korean word. He was ripped from April's grasp as the short woman with surprising strength tugged him down into her arms. They spoke in Korean for a few moments. April smiled at the mother and son interaction.

"And this is my woman, April Hollister," Obadiah introduced her as his mother wiped at her eyes and opened the door further to let them in.

"Hello, Mrs. Grim," April responded formally, being sure to give a low bow in the tradition of Korean people.

"Oh!" Mrs. Grim let out the sound, a pleased expression lifting the smooth, ageless features of her face. Another flurry of Korean dialogue passed between the mother and son but from the way she looked, they were words of delight. Score one!

Obadiah held out his hand and April gripped it eagerly again. His mother saw the interplay, and a sly glance appeared in her dark eyes.

"Where's *Abeoji*?"

"He's coming," Mrs. Grim answered in perfect English. "You know how your father always gets when he meets new people." She turned to April. "Obadiah and he have sensitive stomachs, so whenever they both get nervous they go to bathroom. Sometimes they're in there for twenty minutes or more."

April gulped back a laugh and Obadiah groaned. "Who needs enemies with family like this? I'm so glad I can't see right now."

Mrs. Grim looked at her son with pride. "You will see again. God will heal. I've no doubt of that."

The stairs creaked, and April glanced up to see Obadiah's father make his way to them. He was a tall man, with hazelnut skin and heavy black brows. A ready smile curved his lips, but it froze as he fixed his eyes on her. April swallowed hard and unconsciously clutched Obadiah. She saw Mr. Grim's eyes darken from her position.

Without preamble, Mr. Grim said, "Is this some kind of joke?"

April's teeth chattered. There was only one reason why Obadiah's father would react to her like that. Somehow, someway, despite all her efforts, her past had caught up with her.

Play dumb! Her scattered wits called out to her.

"I'm sorry?" She cocked her head to the side.

"Oh don't play dumb with me. Are you after his money, too? What are you selling this time?" Mr. Grim came forward.

"*Abeoji*, what are you doing? Why are you talking to April like this?"

No! she screamed. *No!*

The horror of the moment washed over her, sending minute tremors all over her body. After all her planning...

"Get this woman out my house," Mr. Grim commanded with a voice that would brook no disagreement.

Mrs. Grim eyeballed him with dismay. "*Oppa*, what are you doing?"

"Sunshine, I'll tell you about it later. Obadiah, I thought you were smarter than this."

April bowed her head as the images of the past rushed at her with frenetic energy. The giant check for two hundred thousand dollars, the cameras, the interviews, pictures—each one spiraled through her mind. She flinched as the memories she fought to forget rose and taunted her like the wavering heads of cobras.

"Nelson will take you back wherever you came from. Have the good sense to not come back here again."

Tears squeezed from her eyelids. Obadiah's hand touched her cheeks and she drew back, but not before he hissed at the moisture on her face.

"*Abeoji*, I don't know what you are doing, but April's not going anywhere. You made my woman cry, and no one does that."

"Obadiah Lee," his father spoke sternly as he made his way to stand in front of his son, "Trust me. I know what kind of girl you got there, and it's not one you want to marry. She's amoral, materialistic, and loose like pocket change."

April gasped. A knife could not have done as much damage as those words did. Heat flowed from the bottom of her feet to the tips of ears. Her head drooped even lower. Why did she think she could wipe away the past? A few phone calls here, a little money there, a couple of threats made, and it should have been over.

What had made her so delusional?

"*Oppa*, shut up!" Mrs. Grim screeched. "You have no right to speak to a guest like this. I do not care who it is."

"Sunshine, you may not understand why I'm doing this, but I know what's best. Obadiah, I've just rescued you. If it offends you, so what? When you look back on this night, you'll be glad you got saved before you made the biggest mistake of your life."

The finality in Mr. Grim's voice chilled her to the bone. How could he be so callous, so cold? He wouldn't even meet her eyes, but kept staring into his son's sightless ones.

"*Abeoji*, you got a lot of explaining to do before I do something very disrespectful like haul off and hit you." The words clipped out of thin lips pursed flat against his teeth.

"Obadiah!" Mrs. Grim hand flew to her mouth.

"*Ani eomeoni*. He's talking crazy about my future wife and I need to know why."

Mr. Grim flicked his gaze at her. Disdain had sharpened the harsh glint until it cut as effectively as his cruel words. More tears dribbled out her eyes.

"You want to tell it, or should I? Although I'm surprised my son didn't make the connection when he first saw you."

That had bothered April too. Although two years had passed since they met, she thought it was strange Obadiah hadn't recognized her. At the time, the joy of anonymity had sent all other considerations out the window. She'd seen his lack of familiarity as a sign from God for a fresh new start. And it had been. The instant their eyes met when he picked her off the ground after knocking her into the wire garbage can at the park, she'd known they were meant to be together. Covered in smelly refuse, Obadiah's first words were, "You make garbage look sexy."

"I was planning on starting a fashion trend," she'd answered cheekily, and right then, they knew.

She drew herself back to the present. Obadiah's sightless, stony façade collided with his father's hard, unyielding one. Not too many people had their sort of relationship. One where they both knew God had everything to do with them being together. Should she let the mistakes of yesterday interfere with hope from the future? This bond they had was worth fighting for. So what, she'd made a mistake. God had forgiven her, and that mattered more than her future father-in-law's condemnation.

"Well, we did come over for dinner." She wiped her eyes. Mr. Grim looked surprised. Obviously he hadn't expected her to mention food. "Obadiah knows I never turn down a free meal. So, if we are really going to have this conversation, then we might as well have it at the dinner table."

Obadiah reached for her, his strong fingers circled her forearms. The blind hazel eyes seemed to stare directly at her. "I don't care what this old man said or what happened before us. We're getting married."

An awful fear churned the muscles in her gut. He said that, but when he learned what she'd done, would he still be so insistent?

"Oh Mrs. Grim, the food was so good!" April sat back and rubbed her slightly distended belly.

"I'm so glad you enjoyed it." Mrs. Grim gathered the dishes and headed to the kitchen through the narrow archway.

"I'll help you," April offered, with the good manners of a well-trained guest.

"No you won't," Mr. Grim vetoed. "You ate a traditional Korean meal and we avoided the topic. Now let's get this over with so you can go back to wherever women like you go."

April's teeth clenched. At the end of day, Mr. Grim didn't know a thing about her. He may be privy to one aspect of her life but there was more to her than that.

"*Abeoji,* watch it." Obadiah warned. With the uncanny unerring accuracy he displayed, he reached for April's hand and held it. Some of his will transmitted itself to her, and she straightened her back.

"That's okay Obie." She patted his hand.

Mr. Grim's eyebrows arched. "Obie? Are you serious?"

April saw a dull flush heighten her man's cheek bones. He cleared his throat. "The deep dark secret is much more exciting than the fact she's calling me Obie."

"You let her call you Obie?"

"Deep, dark, secret coming up, right April?" Obadiah pleaded with her.

"You went crazy whenever we called you that! We had to sign our names in our blood on a contract when he was ten years old." The incredulity lining Mr. Grim's face was almost comical. "Here's the proof. He cut the knife so deep it left a scar!" The long brown finger he thrust in their faces indeed showed what he said was true.

"Back to the matter at hand. April, what is this thing *Abeoji* feels you should tell me?"

She took in a deep breath. It was now or never.

"I sold my virginity for two hundred thousand dollars."

The silence went on for a long moment. Fraught with a bevy of suppressed emotions, April thought her skin would tear apart. Most of all she worried how Obadiah would react. At her words, he'd stiffened hard as a board. Those hazel blind eyes swirled in their sockets. Mr. Grim sat with his arms folded, a half smirk on his mouth. Mrs. Grim stood in the archway, also frozen. April had the fanciful thought they resembled plastic dolls locked in stop motion in some little girl's dollhouse.

"You know, that's less horrible than what I had in mind," Obadiah finally spoke into the tense quiet.

"What did you think I would say?"

"Your name used to be Allan Hollister."

His face blurred in front of her, and a weak, watery giggle erupted from her throat. "Oh Obadiah!" she sighed as she reached and kissed him on the cheek.

"What? That's it?" Mr. Grim straightened in his chair. "You're not going to still marry this girl, are you? You wouldn't be that stupid."

"Six words, *Abeoji*. When a man loves a woman."

"Give me a break! She sold her virginity. Is this the kind of woman you want to be tied to you?"

"Obviously this bothers you more than it does me." Obadiah sipped his drink.

"The fact that it doesn't means something is wrong with you."

"Am I the only interested in how you received an offer?" Mrs. Grim said as she unglued her feet and sat down across from April. "Can you tell how? Or am I prying?"

Obadiah shifted next to her. The impassive mask on his face slid some and his pretended nonchalance dissipated. "*Neh, eomeoni*. That's called prying."

"I'll tell you." April smoothed the material of her skirt.

"This oughta be good." Mr. Grim snorted.

"You don't have to tell me or these old people anything, April." Obadiah insisted. "That was before us."

"It's okay Obie. You all deserve to know if I'm going to be part of this—"

"Obie?" Mrs. Grim interrupted, mouth hanging open. "She called him Obie?"

"*Neh eomeoni!* She called me Obie! Can we please focus!?"

Husband and wife looked at each other. "We had to sign a contract in blood—" she started to say.

"I know, Mrs. Grim. Your husband showed me the scar. I'm sure you have one too. "

"*Aniyo.* Korean women don't scar." A smug grin brightened her face. Her husband rolled his eyes. "Go on. Tell us what happened."

"What's to tell? One of those dirty movie companies sent out a casting call for a virgin to star in one of their movies, and *she* answered the call. End of story." Mr. Grim sniffed and then picked at his nose.

"That's right, Mr. Grim. End of story." She slammed her fist on the table. The anger she suppressed at his high handedness surged forward.

"You don't know the beginning of it. You couldn't possibly know my father's greatest desire was for me to go to college because he wanted me to be the first female on his father's side to achieve a higher education. It doesn't matter to you that when I turned eighteen years old, my forty five year old father developed early onset Alzheimer's. Why concern yourself with the hardship my mother and I had to deal with when my father wandered off and was hit by someone who left him there to die? He's in a nursing home in Grosse Pointe, out of touch with reality and could be that way for years."

"How awful for you," Mrs. Grim whispered, her hands covering her mouth. The dark eyes moistened.

"Then the day came when my father was lucid. He told me to get my education by whatever means I could. 'I know I'm not well,' he told me. 'And your mother's using the money for your college fund to take care of me. I'm sorry.'"

Obadiah massaged her neck in comforting strokes. April sniffed but continued. "My father, who had been a high school chaplain, bawled like a baby that day. I didn't know how long I had before he was lost again. I told him I'd do whatever it took for me to get my degree. So yes, when the opportunity came from that dirty movie company, I weighed my options and figured I had as good of a chance as any girl. I didn't expect I'd actually get the role. I acted like I was supposed to act. I smiled, shook hands, and did interviews about it. My mother almost disowned me she was so shamed, but my father's wish would be fulfilled."

She took a deep breath. "I did what I had to do. In retrospect, I knew it was wrong but I was desperate. There's the end of story for you, Mr. Grim."

The atmosphere was strained but April held Mr. Grim's eyes, waiting with bated breath for his next words. His face was unreadable but then he suddenly broke contact and looked at the table. "Your virginity is something you can only give once. It should be with your husband, not on a set."

"Did you hear anything she just said, *Abeoji*!?"

"Let me finish, Obadiah Lee," his father replied. "All the same, sometimes we have to make decisions which may not be the best ones, but they're the best ones at that time. I jumped to conclusions and became judgmental. At the end of the day, virginity doesn't make you better Christian, nor does the opposite make you a worse one. The grace of God makes us worthy of purity, which is found only in Christ."

He lifted his eyes once more. "I beg your pardon and hope you forgive me. I'd be honored to have you as my daughter."

"So would I," Mrs. Grim added.

April couldn't see past the tears streaming out of her eyes. Instead, she jumped up and raced to the other side of the table to be grasped in a tight hug by her future-in-laws. She glanced at Obadiah and saw him wiping at his face.

"However, there is one condition before we grant you our full blessing." Mr. Grim said when they broke apart.

"What's that, *Abeoji*?"

"It requires a piece of paper, the sharpest knife in the kitchen, and a pint of your blood…Obie."

Obadiah's head hit the table. "Seventeen years. I had a good run."

"God is so cruel to me," Obadiah moaned as he lay in the hospital bed on their wedding night.

"Not at all, Obie," April disagreed as she sat by his side fiddling with the sheets. "You're still alive."

"What man wants to be alive in the *hospital* bed on his wedding night when he is supposed to be rocking it in the honeymoon suite!?"

"It's just a little sprain, you big baby."

"Doesn't God provide angels to protect a man from any mishap on his wedding day? C'mon! Where the heck was my guardian angel when I fell? Sightseeing?"

"Shouldn't you be glad that at least the fall helped you to see again?"

Obadiah snorted. "Of course I am glad. You're just as beautiful as the first day I saw you. And I'm thankful for that. But April, I'd rather be blind in bed with you right now than seeing, laid up here in this hospital."

"Impatient, aren't we?" she teased.

"Why, aren't you?" he asked, a scowl marring his handsome features. "I know you've done it before and all, but I haven't."

April gasped. "Are you serious?"

"Why would I make up something like that?" Obadiah narrowed his eyes at her in defiance to his confession, but a blush tinted his cheeks.

Obadiah Lee Grim, a virgin? It was…unheard of. She's always suspected that as a man with as much money as he had, he would have been inundated with helpless, ravenous females, anxious to sink their claws into him.

"How could you stay—"

"Sex can kill you nowadays. Or worse, give you an itch you can't scratch away. Believe me, it wasn't as hard of choice as some people make it out to be."

She got up and walked over to the window, staring out at the city.

"What's wrong? You think because I'm a virgin I won't be able to satisfy you?" her husband called out from the bed. "Don't worry. If I get it wrong the first time, I'll try again."

A giggle escaped, and she shook her head at the irony of it all. "I'm not worried about that at all, Obie."

"Then what is it?"

She didn't say anything for a long moment as she weighed her options. She promised there would be no more secrets between them and while it wasn't a secret, per se, she should still tell him.

"Remember when I told you and your parents about when I sold my virginity?"

"Like I can forget that," he muttered.

"Well I left out a part."

"Oh? What part was that?" The springs creaked as she heard shift in the bed.

"My co-star. I didn't tell you about him."

"You gotta be kidding me. Here I am, lying in bed with a sprained ankle on my wedding night with my wife I can't touch, and she wants to give me the skinny on the great sex she had in the past. You really know how to make a man feel special, April."

She ignored his rant, seeing behind the sarcasm to the real fear of his inadequacy. "The thing is…although I sold my virginity, my co-star never collected on it."

"Huh?" His voice ended in a squeal.

Her mouth lifted into a wry smile. "Imagine my surprise when all the media was completed on it, the guy who walks into the room was a former student of my father."

"Really?!"

She nodded, still not facing him. "We took one look at each other and never said a word. Talk about awkward. He mumbled something under his breath and then strode away. I never saw him again. The next thing I knew, I was given a check for two hundred thousand and shown the door. I realized the opportunity I was given to make sure this thing didn't stick. I changed my name from Houghton to Hollister. My co-star was able to grease some palms on his end. As for the rest, I hired a firm and paid a substantial amount to get rid of all of evidence. It had gained some recognition on the newswires, but they were able to pull some rabbits out their hats and suppress most of incident."

April faced Obadiah again. "I didn't mention before now because at the end of the day, just like your father said, it doesn't matter whether I'm a virgin or not. My purity is in Christ alone."

"I need you to do me a favor," he said, after a moment of silent contemplation.

"Yes Obie?"

"Reach into my suit jacket there and hand me the envelope."

Puzzled, she did as requested and then stood by the bed.

Without a word, he opened the envelope and handed her a piece a paper. April inhaled sharply.

It was a check for two hundred thousand dollars made out to her.

"I was going to give this to you tonight. Not be crass or anything, but to make it a joke between you and me. If you get what I'm trying to say."

April read the memo section of the check and what she saw there made her draw back. She gazed up into her husband's face and then back down at the numbers until they blurred. The next thing she knew she was laughing so hard her sides hurt. Soon, Obadiah joined her. In the memo section he'd written, "For the best night ever."

"Two hundred thousand for a sprained ankle," she said in between gasps.

"And a hospital bed!" Obadiah gushed out as he wiped tears from his eyes.

Eventually their mirth subsided and she went over to her husband and lay in bed next to him. He bent his head and kissed her, long and deep. Free, that's what she felt at this moment. In her mind's eye she imagined tomorrow they'd head back to his house where they would become man and wife. The years ahead showed laughter and quirkiness as only they alone understood.

When he let her up for air, and stared deep into her eyes, she said, "You know I'm cashing that check in the morning."

Learn more about Parker J. Cole's work and sign up for her mailing list at www.parkerjcole.com.

Letters From Damascus - *Greg M. Dodd*

Introduction

Buried in the context of the apostle Paul's New Testament letters – beneath the doctrine, instruction, encouragement and theology – is the story of a life. Paul's life. We know that from and through that life, God spoke to us. Not through abstract dictation, but through the filter of Paul's own experiences. His joy and pain, triumph and failure, hardship and heartbreak – all framed by the people closest to him – made Paul the man he was. But who was he? Most of what we know about Paul came from his own hand. From Tarsus, in modern day Turkey, he was born the son of a Pharisee. First known as Saul, he was schooled by the renowned rabbi Gamaliel in Jerusalem. He was a tent maker. And like his father, he became a Pharisee. But there is so much more we do not know about Paul. What was the infamous "thorn in the flesh" mentioned in 2 Corinthians 12? Had he been married at some point, as some speculate? If so, what happened? And how could that have impacted his ministry? And what became of letters written *to* Paul? Surely, there were many. And who wrote them? What more would they reveal about the man God used to spread the Gospel to the world? Two thousand years later, we're left to wonder, discuss, debate, and suppose.

Letters From Damascus explores, in fictional terms, one plausible backstory for Paul's ministry, told in a way already familiar to us – through letters....

1

Saul, a humbled servant of the Almighty God, with exceeding love and devotion to Shiri, my beloved wife: May the grace and mercy of God the Father fall upon you and all who dwell in our household in Jerusalem.

It is with a heavy, yet renewed heart that I write you, my love, for I have been permitted to see the glory of God, for whom I have eagerly served with all my being, only to be found his opponent. I know now that whatever standing I had or thought I possessed before him was of my own making or that of foolish men. For I have met the one whom I have persecuted, Jesus of Nazareth. The one in whom these followers of the Way place their faith. The one we watched die on a Roman cross at our bidding. The one for whom so many lie in prison or beneath the earth as a result of my efforts.

This Jesus appeared to me on the road to Damascus; his glory shown around me and shook me from my feet. My dearest Shiri – he lives! And the full measure of his light exposed this truth: I have been fighting the good fight for the enemy's benefit. Indeed, the very commission under which I journeyed to Damascus, that which brought much praise and honor from my fellow Pharisees and members of the Sanhedrin, proved nothing more than the work of Satan, himself. Yet God, in his infinite and mysterious mercy, chose to offer me grace, though I have toiled vigorously – with all pride, zeal and confidence – against his will. The stories of Jesus' resurrection, repeated by those we have openly mocked, cursed, and persecuted, are true and to which I now proclaim myself a witness. Therefore, I testify to this: Jesus is the Christ, the Messiah, the Son of the Living God. And to him I pledge my allegiance and my life to whatever end it may bring.

That which I have done over these last five years I cannot undo; though I would now trade my life for those I saw put to death. I am not ill, my love, I swear it. Though, the light of his heavenly glory left me blind for three days. And in that darkness, the faces of those who suffered at my hand haunted me. No greater anguish consumed me than the memory of Stephen, of whose death I boasted prior to leaving you. His voice cried out, as I watched him die, praying to Jesus and asking God to forgive our transgression against him. Shiri, I killed Stephen for the faith I now possess! That God's grace and mercy should extend to me now is beyond my understanding, yet it is so. He has rescued me from the path of destruction. And I stand forever in his debt.

Were it possible to tell you these amazing things in person, my beloved, I would do so. But for now I remain hidden in Damascus, unsure of my fate. Those of my former alliance now actively seek my ruin. And my presence among the followers of the Way has caused much consternation, as many remain fearfully aware of my previous ambitions against them. Yet, I am grateful for the care, prayers, and watchful eye of one of their elders, who has taken me in and counted me among their own.

I long to come to you and share the good news of Jesus, that you may also receive the redeeming truth of which I speak. Please give your father my greetings, as well as Ilan, Dalia and my dear friend Simeon. And extend hospitality to Barnabas. He has journeyed to you from Damascus on my behalf.

May the grace of the Lord be with you. And may my love for you remain a treasure in your heart.

2

Shiri, daughter of Gilead, to my husband, Saul: Greetings.

Word of your stay in Damascus reached me long before your letter. Indeed, rumors of your betrayal to our people have filled my ears for weeks, though I have faithfully defended my husband's name to which I am bound. And yet, words from your own hand make me a fool. What strange work is this that you should mourn sinners who died under your righteous service to our Lord? I can only hope that you have indeed fallen ill and are speaking from a fevered mind.

We both know God chose you to put an end to the Way by seeking out these blaspheming followers of Jesus. When I petitioned my father to speak on your behalf before the high priest Ananias, that your request for letters to the synagogues in Damascus might be granted, I did so believing there was none more honorable in all of Jerusalem than my husband. Your rival among the Pharisees, Jaron, may speak with great piety and excite people to oppose these heretics, but even his grandest boasts cannot equal all you have done in service to our people. His words are loud, but his deeds are empty. Jerusalem's prisons overflow with followers of the Way by your works, not his. Yet, you are in hiding while he roams freely in the marketplace shouting lies against you. He claims that you preach Jesus in the synagogues of Damascus! But I am not convinced. Jealousy speaks whenever Jaron mentions your name; I am sure of it. For I have known you, Saul of Tarsus, since you came to Jerusalem as a boy and have loved no other. And until I see into your brown eyes and feel the warm breath of truth from your lips, I will not believe the words Jaron speaks against you. Nor will I believe the lies in your letter, for the man I love could not have written them.

My faith is in you, my love, and all that we have planned is still before us. A path of great prominence lies open before you. Do not destroy what God has prepared! My father has spoken with Gamaliel. We have his promise to help restore your name upon your return. However, his son, Simeon, your friend, has sworn an oath against you in defiance of his father. I would not count on his support. But I believe truth will defeat your enemies.

I am entrusting this letter to the one you sent, Barnabas, for he would not tell me where you are now. He claims openly to be a follower of Jesus, but I told no one in the hope my letter would reach you safely. I must warn you, my love, of a growing number here in Jerusalem, led by Jaron, who speak of your death in wishful terms. If you do journey home to me, please do so in secret.

I pray for your safe return and sound mind.

3

Saul, to my wife Shiri in Jerusalem: Grace and peace to you from God the Father and the risen Lord Jesus Christ.

I thank God for your loyalty and confidence in me. In my absence, you rightly defend that which you believe to be true: That your husband is a servant of the living God, defender of the faith and leader among men. I know you count these things among your treasured possessions and guard them in your heart. I expected nothing less from you. Indeed, your passion gave birth to my ambition; and from ambition came learning; from learning, knowledge; from knowledge, zeal; and from zeal, power. But the power I wielded in the name of God came from misguided, ignorant men who blindly oppose the truth. Truth lives in the name of Jesus, whom I now humbly and willingly serve. And the power entrusted to me to do God's will comes through him, not through men.

Please extend my respect and gratitude to your father and Rabban Gamaliel the Elder, though I release them from any defense of my name. While it grieves me to learn of Simeon's oath, I have no interest in or need for the approval of men. Let them say what they will; a higher calling now moves me.

The plans you mentioned, which I pursued so forcefully at the expense of many, I have cast aside. I leave them for fools like Jaron, who only seek attention and profit above others. My one ambition is this: To proclaim that Jesus Christ is Lord. Though Jaron may speak from jealousy – with that I agree – what he shouts in the marketplace is true: I preach the name of Jesus in the synagogues of Damascus. Since receiving God's grace, I can do nothing else. I preach so that eyes may be opened to the truth, so that God's people will turn from darkness to light and receive a place among those who are sanctified by faith in Christ Jesus.

The gospel I preach here I wish to bring home to you at God's appointed time. Until then, I urge you to remember our fathers' wisdom in choosing us, one for the other. The value of my father's dowry cannot compare with the love I have for you. Such is not always the case in marriage. (Your sister, Hannah, knows this too well.) Beware of vultures who seek to cast doubt in your mind about us. I remain faithful to the vow I made you. And if you indeed prayed as a child, as you have often claimed, that God would provide a husband of noble character, deep faith, and pure love, then your prayers have been answered. For I have been stripped of my pride, leaving only what noble righteousness God gives through his grace. My faith now draws from a deep, eternal spring, rising up from the name of Jesus. And my love for you flows from the pure heart of God. Therefore, be encouraged, my love, and be strong in the bond we share.

I plan to leave Damascus soon if I can find a way out of the city wall, as it is becoming too dangerous for me here. I long to return to Jerusalem, to hold your hand in mine and share this gift I have so undeservedly received. Be kind to Silas; he traveled at great risk to bring my words to you.

The grace of our Lord Jesus Christ be with you.

4

Shiri, of the house of Gilead, to my husband Saul: I send you greetings, though I know not where this letter will find you. But I pray for your wellbeing and for God's mercy to fall upon you.

When our fathers brought us together, as you mentioned in your previous letter, I counted their wisdom as blessings designed by God. That I would wed such a man as you filled my heart with expectant hope and promise. And after my father arranged for your instruction under Gamaliel the Elder, you did not disappoint. I watched with pride as you grew in knowledge and fervor for scripture and the history of our people. Indeed, word spread throughout Jerusalem of my young husband's learning beyond his years. Your success even exceeded the petitions of my prayers. All this you have forsaken. And for what? A dead blasphemer from Nazareth and his sect of unschooled fishermen? You are more than that, my love! Omri once called you "a Hebrew of Hebrews"! Yet you throw away your gains as if they were dung.

What happened to you on the road to Damascus, I cannot explain. But what caused you to turn against your people and, in so doing, turn against me, I cannot accept. You have brought shame to my father's house and bitter disappointment to the one who loved you. When I first heard of your profession of faith in Jesus, I did not believe it, even when penned from your own hand. But the case against you is now undeniable. You affirmed as much in your last letter. Therefore, I ask, with the blessings of my father and the high priest Ananias, to be released from my vow of matrimony to you. As long as I bear your name, I cannot lift my eyes to another nor even bare my face in Jerusalem. I would rather endure the shame of divorce than the shame of remaining your wife. I submit, as I must, to your desires in this matter. But know this: In your absence and subject to your duplicity, I have been comforted by another. Jaron has remained faithful to his people and a respected leader among the Pharisees. He proudly carries the burden you so publically abandoned. And in my time of humiliation, he offered his hand in friendship for which I am grateful. I write these things so that you may know I no longer wait for your return.

Your messenger, Silas, while much younger than your friend Barnabas, is cut from the same cloth. He boasts of Jesus and of your conversion to the Way even over my displeasure in hearing it. Were I not in need of his feet to carry my letter to you, I would hand him over to Jaron to be dealt with properly.

I await your answer to my request. May God lead you justly in this matter.

5

Saul, servant of the living Lord Jesus Christ, to my wife in Jerusalem.

My dear Shiri, do you not realize that the God of your father, of Moses, of David, and the twelve tribes of Israel, is the same God I now serve through his son, Jesus? The same God you accuse me of dishonoring? There is only one God. For it is written:

"And there is no other God besides Me,
A righteous God and a Savior;
There is none except Me.
Turn to Me and be saved,
all the ends of the earth;
For I am God, and there is no other."

This is the same God we have worshipped since we were weaned from our mothers' milk. It is the same God who sent prophet after prophet to the Hebrew people, but we would not listen. I myself knew the scriptures; I repeated the words of the prophets in the temple, yet even I did not heed their message. For I was blinded by my appetite for religion and the pursuits of men. But God, since creation, has promised a redeemer, a savior, a messiah for the people of Israel and all the world. Shiri, it has happened! God's promise is fulfilled in Christ Jesus. It is he of whom the profit Isaiah spoke. He walked among us but we rejected him.

"He was pierced for our transgressions,
he was crushed for our iniquities;
the punishment that brought us peace was on him,
and by his wounds we are healed."

That Jesus should suffer and die on a cross for my transgressions, yet be raised in glory to offer grace to one such as me, is beyond comprehension. Yet it is proof of God's love for even the lowest of sinners, of which I am the lowest. But I have seen God's redeemer with my own eyes. He has taken the sword from my hand and has filled me with a hope for all people, that all should come to know his forgiveness and be made righteous through the blood of Christ. This is the hope I must share, a race I must run. Since the moment I knelt in the dirt before Jesus, my hope has been that you, Shiri, would run this race with me.

I desire to see you rest in the knowledge of this truth: That Jesus, whom I persecuted, is raised from the dead; he is the son of the living God, our savior. Of this I have testified in my letters and witness to you now. In Barnabas and Silas, you have heard men of God proclaim the name of Jesus to you. Therefore, Shiri, you have no excuse of ignorance before God. Yet, you remain steadfast in your opposition to the truth. And even though you have hardened your heart to what I preach, I would not renounce my vow to you on that account, as I would hope to win you over with time and patience. But if you will not remain with me, even in unbelief, I will not oppose your request. Let it be as you desire.

I do not say these things lightly. Though I am willing to endure great personal hardships to see Christ glorified, I did not foresee the loss of my wife being one of them. I am grateful to the compassion demonstrated by my new friends in Christ here in Damascus. They dried my tears with heartfelt prayers on our behalf and laying on of hands. They renewed my spirit and set my mind to the joy we have in Christ. And yet, no joy can come from divorce. It is not in keeping with God's commands or desires. But of this be certain: Though I release you from the bonds we share, I will not marry another. I remain bound in service to Christ Jesus. My devotion from this day forward will be to Christ and Christ alone.

Those who have sheltered me in Damascus make way for my departure this very evening. Therefore, I am dispatching this letter to you prior to leaving, as I lack confidence in their plan for my escape. While I am uncertain of my fate, my confidence is in the Lord. Whether I am to remain in Damascus (free or in chains) or travel elsewhere, I trust he will use his servant for one purpose – to see Christ glorified.

Though I had planned to return to Jerusalem to see you and meet the other apostles of Christ, your letter persuades me otherwise. I will go where the Lord leads, but I need time to understand what has happened and how I may be of best use for Christ. A land distant from the controversy of my conversion may best suit this purpose for now. There I will learn to press on without you.

Greet your father, whom I hold in the highest regard, and other members of his household. Ask Ilan to return my tools to Haim. I will seek him out whenever I return to Jerusalem. And tell Jaron that I hold no ill will against him, for I am not the one to whom he will be made accountable for his actions.

My prayers for you will not cease, my dear Shiri, as long as I have breath within me. May you see the truth of my testimony and know the peace found in the one I serve.

Grace be with you, my love.

Paul

Greg M. Dodd's award winning first novel, *A Seed for the Harvest* is an honest, touching, and sometimes humorous portrayal of the transforming power of faith in Jesus Christ.

To purchase a copy in print, Kindle or other ebook formats, visit www.gregmdodd.com.

Or find it on Amazon at http://www.amazon.com/Seed-Harvest-Greg-M-Dodd/dp/0991533208/.

The Children Who Lay Down – *Deb Palmer.*

"Blessed are the peacemakers:
For they shall be called the children of God."

Here comes yellow bus number 36, loaded with children, who'll spring through the door, eager for another day at Central Primary School. I've played this scene five days a week for the past 14 years. Like a rock star, I'm rushed by a pack of kindergarten and first graders, attaching themselves to my limbs, like an out of control mob, screaming "Mr. *Pommer* (Palmer) with the mole."

The infamous mole, centered on my forehead, is my trademark with the pint-size groupies, who take turns pressing it, button-style, triggering my tongue to pop out, evoking giggles and *beggings* to "do it again."

At age 62, I'm grateful that I can drag my limbs, each dripping with a child, through the double doors, down the halls, while grunting Frankenstein style. When the bell rings, the hall clears and quiets, like someone flipped a switch. Normally, I welcome the brief solace in my office before the first behavior problem of the day appears, but today I dread the inevitable nagging tape of last night's phone call playing continuously in my head.

"Andy? This is Susan. I have some bad news. Due to budget cuts, your position as our counselor will be eliminated for next year. I'm sorry."

Six months later …

"Pazhalsta?" begs Artur, Stefan, Ivan and Luka in unison.

"Da, Da, Da," I say, moving close to the bed where they sit, fingers extended waiting to press the world renowned button on my forehead. Soon twelve boys, age six to 15, pile on the bed for a turn.

In brief, after a moment of – *I'm too old, no one wants me*, Diedre, my wife of 35 years, and I, sold our belongings, packed two suitcases and moved to the small village of Komarovka, located 170 km from Kiev. We said yes to God, taking the demographic whim, after meeting a young couple at our church, who opened our eyes to the need. With their help, we found and accepted volunteer positions in a state run orphanage.

Diedre, a former nurse, works in the severe and profoundly disabled children's east ward; a slipshod add-on from the 1930's. In the west ward, where I work, you can hear every sneeze, cough, gurgle and cry through the slapped together wall boards. As grateful newbies, we work the unwanted night shifts, after which we sleep like euthanized stray cats until late afternoon when we sip decaf and have a routine conversation.

"I can't do this. My heart is breaking. I feel helpless, and I can't take it one more day," she says. "It's too much. It hurts."

"You need to quit and work in one of the other wards. Please let me talk with Mr. Dolgorukiy. He can get you transferred," I say.

And every day she refuses, saying "No, they need me."

With nothing left to say, the argument ends. Two Americans, approaching seniordom, whom together, could barely speak one word of Russian, were only granted volunteer attendant positions at the orphanage because, they were desperate for help. In a country the size of Texas, Ukraine has over 100,000 orphans.

Serving as the lone handy man, I start my shift two hours early. Winter has bellied up to the bar, a time when the children sleep in sweatshirts, pants and stocking caps to sustain the drafty, brutally cold wards. Handy man status allows privileged visits to all the wards, including where my Diedre works. She too, usually starts her shift early to help relieve the overworked staff.

I'm never prepared for the ever-present blast of odors, or

the hovering presence of the blue devils upon entering the ward for the profound and severely disabled. Carrying a tape measure and tool box, I meander over to Diedre who's changing a despondent child's diaper.

"How's your day? Sunshine, lollipops and rainbows … " I sing.

Receiving a sarcastic grin, I inspect the walls needing repair, measuring and noting for supplies. A voice in my head yells *hurry, don't look or get involved*, while a convincing whisper encourages my eyes and heart to open. There are 20 cribs lining the room, not with jumping, rowdy toddlers cooing and finagling to get out and play; no, these cribs hold children who should be going to school, playing ball, and riding bikes, but instead, they lay in outgrown cribs, growth stunted like a gold fish raised in a shot glass. Yet, the disheartening physical and mental disabilities are not what's hard to gaze on; it's the eyes of hopelessness and despair.

"See ya later. I love you," I say slipping out the door, inhaling the welcome fresh air before heading to the west ward, where, although it's no tea party, compared to the east, it's Disney World with sugar on top.

"Andy … Dude … Sup?" yells Oleg, from across the courtyard.

Hearing Oleg's Russian accent speaking American slang gives me a chuckle. "Hey dude. Sup?" I answer, holding out my ear buds for him to grab.

Oleg is my Godsend, as he speaks good English and serves as an interpreter for the younger boys. Obtaining his trust is my only venue to any relationship with the other boys. Without his approval, I'm a generic brand with nothing to offer but a cheap price.

"A real treat today Oleg, 'In A Gadda Da Vida,' Iron Butterfly … 1968. Enjoy dude."

Grabbing the buds he prances next to me, looking like a Russian bobble-head doll, singing, free of inhibitions, *"Innergobderdaveeder Baba."*

I'm in charge of a dozen boys, who live dorm style, four to a room, with a common area for recreation, meals and classrooms. After dinner, the common area is cleared, with tables and chairs stacked neatly around the edges for game time. When we walk through the door we're rushed by the other boys, all wanting a turn with the buds, but they must wait, because there's 90 boys and girls to organize into two long lines encircling the 30 by 50 foot room. Oleg and I grab the metal waste cans, hanging them by their handles on hooks placed high on the wall. Each child takes a turn shooting the ball into a makeshift basket, while the nine other attendants cheer and rally. After each turn, we lift the waste can off the hook, retrieving the ball for the next player. With nine foot ceilings, the challenge is simple for some, but many are physically frail and have little, if any athletic ability.

At 9 o'clock, the children are dismissed for quiet time, while the attendants set the tables and chairs for the next day's breakfast and first teaching session. My boys know to wait for me quietly in the room where Oleg, Boris, Vlad, and Ilia bunk.

Preoccupied with Iron Butterfly, they pass the buds around like crash survivors sharing oxygen, unaware I'm standing in the door, savoring the moment, studying each face. For many of the boys, smiles are rare, and even an unrealistic expectation. Their stories, typically, are riddled with neglect and violence, and all share the scar of being pegged "the unwanted." So when they are together, stacked in the bunks, arms waving every direction, waiting for a turn to listen and bob to the music, I breathe it in. It's as good as it gets here, and I need these times to endure the frustrating language barrier, the overwhelming sense of helplessness, and that ever persistent voice that tells me; *just give up.*

Voices raise, and I don't have to understand Russian to know that a ruckus over sharing has spun out of control.

"Knock it off you bunch of crazy hooligans," I say, listening while Oleg interprets, using the word hooligans and laughing.

Motioning for the boys to listen, I wait for the hush, and begin our nightly ritual of bible readings, sharing and prayer. The older boys help with interpretations, especially Oleg, my right hand man, or my Tonto, as I like to call him. The crux of tonight's questions are:

"What is *In A Gadda Da Vida Baby? Do I know any more knock knock jokes? Why does my tongue fall out when the mole button is pushed?"*

Prayer time is my reward for the tough stuff. I've little, to no idea what they're praying. For all I know, they're plotting a mutiny. I revel in their lowered faces, as the crowded room's fragrance turns from childish mischief to caring, love and grace.

When heads raise, I announce that tomorrow morning I'll be working in this room replacing loose boards, but that it will be finished within a couple of hours. Oleg pauses before interpreting, and I wonder if he understood, when all eyes turn wide eyed to the wall and an awkward silence falls over the room.

Not sure what was said, I send them off to their own rooms for the night. "Good night hooligans. Sleep loose," I say, listening to them scurry to their bunks.

Back in the common room, I set up a makeshift office and begin writing case notes. I am not required to write them, as I am officially only an attendant, but it's a habit I find productive, being an opportunity to focus on each boy. Normally, within 10 minutes, I hear whispers, shuffling feet, and giggles, to which I shout out a warning, but tonight there's an eerie hush. With great stealth, I sneak down the hall between the rooms to find them all piled back in Oleg's room, whispering a chorus of *"ittergotterderveeterbaby."*

They're huddled in a stack on the floor, with arms extended, looking like little Dutch boys with fingers stuck in the dike.

"What's going on?" I ask.

They jump, tumbling into a heap, gasping, and I see that a board is completely off the wall, exposing a dim light through the clapboard. Sergey, a twelve year old, poker faced, cool-handed sort, calmly replaces the board over the hole, hammers each end with his fist and stands to leave, as if this never occurred. All eyes are upon me as I place a hand on Sergey's shoulder, intercepting his escape. "Oleg... what ... please explain."

"We visit with the others. The ones we pray for, that have no fun. We sing the songs you bring to us," he says, adding "Please, we beg you not to fix this wall."

"Pohshzahloostah (please)!" they beg, in unison.

Like herding cats, I try to move each boy out of the way, but they return to their post protecting the wall.

"Out of the way, now!" I say, motioning for Oleg to

interpret.

Hesitating, he evaluates the foreign look on my face and motions for the boys to move. Removing the loose board, through the dim light I can see the familiar rows of cribs, and eyes staring back at me through the hole in the wall.

"We sing and talk with them. We like to make them happy … *smeshnoy* (funny), like you make us laugh," says Sergey, who's sporting a black dot in the center of his forehead. He sees my questioning look, pressing the dot with his finger and sticking out his tongue. I stuff an urge to laugh, followed by one to cry.

"There's nothing we can do for those children. We do all we can. This cannot go on. Tomorrow, I will fix the wall …."

"Nyet, nyet, nyet!" interrupts the noisy ensemble, followed by Oleg pleading the heart of each boy.

"We won't let you. They have no one. We must do something. They need us. We beg you to help us, help the children who lay down."

"I can't. No one can. Everyone wants to, but no one can. Go get in bed. It's late," I say, leaving the room.

The remaining hours of my shift are spent telling my thoughts to shut up. Thankful, my shift ends before the boys rise, I greet my replacement and slip out the door to meet Diedre. At home, over our scheduled date time breakfast, I share what the boys have been doing, *under our noses for who knows how long.*

"They can *nyet, nyet, nyet,* all they want. I'm fixing the wall before we both lose our jobs. Don't worry, Diedre, I promise to handle this. Can you believe it?"

"Yes, I believe it. I've known all along. What do you think I'm doing over there? Napping?" she asks. "The children in my ward look forward to the night, because of your boys. Only a few can even hear them, but they all know the boys are there and it's all they have. Please don't take it away," she sobs, running from the room.

With Diedre behind a slammed door to our bedroom, I choose the sofa, on which I toss and turn for hours, until, too tired to fight for more sleep, I rise. Not wanting to wake, or deal with Diedre, I select today's classic oldie and head out the door. The sunshine and mild breeze convince me to walk through the park and visit a few shops in the village.

When I arrive at the orphanage, instead of the usual rush and greet entourage, I see them standing, arms crossed, lining the front of the common room entrance, looking like the Gestapo. I approach, extending my hand holding the ear buds.

"1963, The Kingsmen. Louie Louie," a real treat dudes. Have a listen." I beckon, holding the buds out again.

Artur, the youngest, who's always the last to listen, holds his hand out, head down in shame. The rest resist, continuing the Gestapo evil eye through dinner and game time. Later, they gather in the room with the removable board, linking arms, accepting the challenge for a duel.

"Somebody wants to meet you," I say, retrieving a box hidden behind me in the doorway. "You were all so upset with me, you didn't even notice the box I've been toting all day."

I open the box, out leaps a ball of yellow fur, wagging and greeting each boy as if they were long lost litter mates. I watch as the golden lab puppy saps each rigid face with a sloppy wet tongue to the cheek.

The moment ends like a guillotine slicing down when Oleg grabs the puppy, pushes it back in the box and says "We refuse your bribe. The wall stays as it is!"

"I won't fix it yet. That's all I can promise," I say, taking the pup out of the box. "He can visit you every night. You can take turns sleeping with him. What do you think we should name him? Uh.. Zavoot?" I ask, meaning name.

"Louie, Louie," said Artur.

Later, attempting to write case notes, my mind replays their voices, automatically translating the foreign words to livid hearts rising against injustice. Looking in on them around 3 AM, I chuckle at Artur, the winner of the puppy lottery for the night, slumbering peacefully with Louie Louie on his belly. Suddenly, I feel shaken, as if struck by lightning, my brain scrambled telling me; *what is ... is not; what mattered ... does not; and the time ... is now.*

Running next door, I whisper to Oleg. "Get up. Go wake up the boys, but keep them quiet."

The boys gather in the hall, wiping sleep from questioning eyes. I place a finger to my lips, a universal sign for hush, and motion for them to follow. With twelve boys and a puppy in tow, we trail through the common room, out the front door, and across the path toward the door leading to the attached building where the "children that lay down" reside. We corral around the door where I signal Oleg to interpret.

"I was wrong. You are right. We have about a half an hour while my wife, Diedre is alone with the children. Let's show these children what God's love can do."

I wait while Oleg interprets, watching eyes liven with excitement. Then Sergey says "*zhdat'*!" running back into our building.

"He wants us to wait," says Oleg, ceasing my attempt to stop him.

Shortly, he returns, ear buds in one hand, a black sharpie in the other. Taking command, he assembles his comrades, dabbing each with a black dot in the center of their foreheads.

"K*horosho*," he announces when finished, meaning okay.

Manned with "Louie Louie, the pup, and the song, we, *soldiers of the matching forehead moles,* proceed. I knock to the tune of "shave and a haircut, two bits," a secret code between Deidre and I, and listen for her familiar pace.

"We're here," I sing, mockingly, as the door opens to my stunned wife.

"What's on their faces?" she asks finally, pointing to her forehead, queing the clan to press the moles, invoking a parade of tongues popping out of their mouths. "And, where did the pup come from?"

"Louie, Louie," says Artur, holding the pup out for her to see.

"May we come in?" I ask.

"Welcome … all of you. Come in," she says, shaking her head, confused.

While we worry on regulations and threats of life sentences in a Russian prison, the boys intuitively act, approaching the cribs, tenderly nursing each child with their first aid kits of song, puppy and mole buttons. We're humbled by their wisdom as they seem to know, when to linger or move on to the next crib. Likewise, the children, labeled profoundly disabled, respond to the boys, beyond our wildest expectations; some smile, a few laugh, all have grateful eyes.

That night, we received arcane rites, and access to a glimpse of the Kingdom of Heaven. A place where the wisdom of children reigns.

If you enjoyed this story, please follow the blog at http://debpalmerauthor.com/, for more Christian Story Telling, and progress on our book, *In Spite of Us, Stalked by a Loving God.*

Naomi – *Bobbie Ann Cole*

"I won't leave you, so don't ask me to," Ruth told her mother-in-law. "From now on, your people will be my people and your God my God. Where you die, so shall I and be buried alongside of you. May God punish me severely, if ever I let you down."

There would be no shaking this one off, Naomi realized, her heart sinking. On top of everything else, God seemed to be punishing her severely by burdening her with a barren, Moabite daughter-in-law.

They had been three widows in shapeless widows' cloaks, at the head of the steep path that led down to the Dead Sea, the lowest place on earth, where she had told her daughters-in-law she was finished. "Go and find new husbands. It's too late for me. I'm too old to provide them for you from my belly. Go back to your people and your gods."

Orpah had gone, her parting shot to Ruth, "They'll hate you in Bethlehem!"

Naomi watched until she appeared no bigger than a peg doll before picking up her bundle and starting down the trail in silence, with Ruth following.

A ferry took them across the Dead Sea to Israel where they scaled steep ginger slopes and trudged across sage-bush covered peaks until the small but bustling, walled city of Bethlehem spread itself before them. It lay cupped among terraces of swaying white barley and green wheat, vines, pomegranates, olives, dates and garden produce. After dusty Moab, Naomi was wide-eyed. The famine that had sent her away was very much over.

Silent along the way, she began smugly to point to this and that ripening crop, as though she had a stake in all the abundance. The truth was that her stomach was churning as they came nearer and nearer to Bethlehem's gates. She would have to face the gossips there. She was dreading having to admit that she, who once had everything, was returning with nothing.

They were waiting for her as they entered the city, a gaggle of women Naomi had known since childhood. They clustered around like hyenas around carrion.

"Who is this?"

'Can it be Sweetie?"

"You mean Naomi? Surely not."

"She looks a lot older."

"I went out full," Naomi blurted, "and am returning empty. So you needn't bother hanging around, hoping for a handout."

"She's wrinkled as a crab apple."

"And just as sour."

Laughter.

"Were you working out of doors, dear?"

It would have been better to have died in Moab, Naomi thought, than to have to go through this.

"Who's the swarthy giant?" one of them asked.

It was on the tip of her tongue to tell them Ruth was her slave. Instead, to her own surprise, she found herself taking a step closer to her daughter-in-law, who seemed unfazed by their meanness.

A woman wagged a finger under Naomi's nose. "This is how God punishes those who abandon their land and their people."

There was a murmur of assent. They all remembered the famine.

Some mornings, Naomi would go into town simply to gaze up at the roof terrace of her former home, built into the city wall. Someone else lived there now. She and Ruth shared one-room, with a tiny courtyard and a flat roof of yellow mud, in an outlying hamlet. Ruth's steady optimism was an irritation, her very presence a constant reminder of what had been lost.

The land belonging to Elimelech, Naomi's husband, had become a tumbledown vineyard. In her day, they had hewn a grape press out of rock, built a tower and set a guard. Now the tower leaned sideways, there was no guard and damaging fox holes were among the roots. The sharecropper, who claimed all remittances paid up to her late sons and nothing owing, was not watering the vines. The tiny grapes looked thirsty and wizened. She could see they would not bring in enough to feed and house her and Ruth.

When Ruth caught her gazing at their empty storeroom, biting her lip, she said, "I've heard that the rule here is that the grain around the edges of fields must be left for orphans and widows to pick.Perhaps, I could go and glean in someone's field?"

The idea that a member of her own family should be brought so low had Naomi down on her knees on the dirt floor, keening and swaying, with her hands covering her head, as if she were expecting blows to rain down on her. This was the worst thing, far worse than anything else that had happened so far. This was rock bottom, the shame of all shames.

"We really have no choice," Ruth said.

"Do it, then," Naomi said.

Why, oh why, hadn't the girl gone back to her own family?

Ruth peered over the boundary wall to a field of barley, feeling nervous, wondering which one to try. The breeze rustled the stalks in front of her, a whisper that said, "This one. This one. This one. "

She walked across to the overseer and asked him if she might glean.

"You're the brazen one," he said with a snort. "Your sort usually come at dusk for the leftovers. You'll leave my young men alone?"

"Yes," she replied, looking down, deeply offended.

"You're the Moabitess?"

"Yes."

"Well, then. Good luck."

She kept away from the reapers' taunts and lewd gestures. Though it was spring and the weather was not hot, sweat soon clamped her robe to her body and turned her face scarlet. Helping with the lambing and sheep shearing back home seemed easy work by comparison.

Half way through the morning, a silver-bearded man rode up on horseback. "God be with you," he told the reapers.

They straightened up and saluted him. "God bless you!"

Ruth went on with her work. A few minutes later, she started to find him standing in front of her.

"Listen, daughter," he said. "I don't want you to glean here."

How humiliating... She wouldn't make a fuss. She'd just go. She bent to pick up the stalks she'd gleaned so far, hoping he would at least allow her to take those away with her.

"You'll be much safer over there, by my girls."

She frowned. "You're not throwing me off?"

It was his turn to look puzzled. "No, I want you to stay behind my workers. They won't bother you if you continue to keep your eyes down modestly, as you've been doing. I don't want you to go anywhere else to glean."

He pointed to a row of earthen jars under the shade of a field shelter. "Whenever you're thirsty, help yourself."

She threw herself down at his feet. "God bless you, sir, for bothering with a stranger."

"Get up, Ruth," he said. "I've heard about all you've done for your mother-in-law and I understand how hard it must have been for you to leave everything familiar behind you, after the loss of your husband."

On her feet again, she stole a glance at his face. His eyes were dove-grey.

"I want to ask God to bless you. You have honored Him by showing love to Naomi." He raised his hands to heaven and prayed, "May the Lord God of Israel place His protective cloak about you and grant you a rich reward."

"Thank you, sir."

A giant ant, struggling under the weight of food it had found, crossed before her feet in the red dust.

"Now," he said, rubbing his hands together, "how about some lunch?"

"Blessings on the man who noticed you!" Naomi cried, after Ruth had told her everything that evening. She wolfed down the leftover bread, dipped in vinegar, that Ruth had saved for her from the meal Boaz had provided. For that was the stranger's name. It meant, "Strength".

On learning it, a surge of joy had run through Naomi and she had thrown up her arms. "That man of God will redeem my husband's land. He's my brother-in-law, God bless him!"

That evening, the two women sat companionably by the fire, as they once used to before their tents in Moab. The embers glowed as Naomi prodded them with a stick.

"He told me to glean in his fields throughout the harvest, and not just around the edges," Ruth said. "I can work in among the sheaves and his young men have to be nice and help me. He even told them to drop stalks for me."

"You keep away from those young men," Naomi said sharply. Her waving stick sent lizards scuttling across the fire-blackened courtyard walls all around them. The worst thing now, she thought, would be for Ruth to take up with one of them, when Boaz himself had shown an interest. That glimmer of hope was lighting up her eyes.

After Ruth had gleaned throughout the barley and wheat harvests, the storeroom looked reassuringly full but there was no progress on the Boaz front.

As time passed, and he did not come to call, Naomi became increasingly agitated. "Where is he? Why doesn't he come?"

Ruth looked downcast. "I don't know."

It was a mystery to them both. He had seemed so smitten...

After Ruth had been home for several weeks, a brainwave hit Naomi as she exchanged gossip with the women at the well. She returned home, hatching a plan that made her smile. After all, Ruth had been good to her. She deserved some good and this idea... *well, you never know. It might just work.*

Barging through the wooden gate into the courtyard, she cried, "Daughter!"

Ruth looked up from kneading dough as water from Naomi's full jar splashed like diamonds.

"I've been thinking..." Excitement squiggled in her tummy as she searched for the right words. "In your best interests, we should get you settled."

Ruth looked on, waiting.

Naomi smirked. "With Boaz."

"Oh, but he doesn't..."

"Listen, I was obedient when my husband said, 'We're going to Moab,' even though I didn't want to go. Now you must be an obedient daughter and not just follow your own ideas. Tonight, Boaz will be at the threshing floor. We'll make you clean and pure and you can go to him there."

"Go to him, Mother?" She didn't sound too keen.

"Wait until he's finished eating and drinking. Watch carefully where he lies, or you could end up with the wrong man!" Naomi, standing in her sodden robe with the full jar still on her shoulder was unable to get her thoughts out fast enough. She tried to mime. "Creep up and lie down beside him. Make sure no one sees you."

Ruth was gaping, open-mouthed.

"Good plan, isn't it?"

Eventually, Ruth spoke. "And then what?"

"Oh..." Why did everything have to be so plodding and practical with this girl? Naomi hadn't got all the details down yet. They shouldn't have to matter... She blew out her cheeks. "I guess he'll tell you what to do.'

At dusk, smelling luxuriously of aloes and saffron, henna and cinnamon, Ruth left their house and walked, as casually as she was able, up the steep slope to the threshing floor. Above her, she could see silhouettes of men, tossing grain high into the air, separating wheat from chaff. The voices of men and women, eating and drinking around a great bonfire, drifted down to her ears.

As someone from that group got to their feet, she darted to a craggy rock and pressed herself up against it, hoping that she would be invisible in the gloom. Her heart was pounding in her breast. What *was* she doing?

After what seemed an eternity, the girls bedded down by the great fire and the men staggered tipsily to their blankets. She spotted Boaz and noted where he lay down, near the high pile of grain.

Eventually, even the head of the man they had put on watch slumped onto his chest. The wind whipped around Ruth's legs as she moved swiftly up the slope. They seemed propelled by themselves and not by her will. It was as if she were somewhere else, watching herself enact her mother-in-law's horrendous plan.

Boaz, caught in the moon's glow, slept with a finger to his lips, as if he had a secret. She inched back his cloak and lay down beside him. The grain nearby smelled nutty and wholesome. His breath was on her face, fragrant with wine. His warm flesh made her body burn.

He awoke with a start and propped himself up on one elbow. "Who are you?"

"Ruth."

"Ruth?" he whispered. "What are you doing here?"

Beyond the outline of his face, a million stars twinkled in the broad black sky. Her breath caught as she went to answer him. Could she really be as bold as she was feeling compelled to be?

"Place your protective cloak about me."

There. She had proposed to him.

"God bless you, Ruth," he said. "You are brave and good and don't chase after men. I'd like to do as you ask..."

Oh no! She felt her cheeks flush. He was going to turn her down. She had sacrificed all dignity and decorum to throw herself at him. And he was going to say no.

"...but there's someone else ahead of me."

She sat up, not understanding. "Someone else?"

"The rightful redeemer."

So, that was why he had not come for her after the harvest. In a way, it was good to know that it hadn't been because he didn't think highly enough of her.

"Who?"

"My older brother, but, if he doesn't redeem, then, as God is my witness, I will."

"I'd better go."

"Stay." He lay down and pulled her to him. "Stay with me until morning."

As the bolt squeaked and the door in the courtyard wall creaked open, Naomi held up the lamp to Ruth's face and peered. The girl looked different, glowing. "Who are you?"

Ruth laughed as she glanced furtively up and down the

deserted alleyway before darting past her, into the courtyard. There she showed Naomi the contents of her bulging cloak.

"He said I was not to return to you empty-handed. He's promised more."

"How much more?"

"Six gate measures of barley."

"A bride price!" As the seemingly unattainable security she craved came suddenly within her reach, a surge went through Naomi. She did a little dance.

"But..." Ruth gave her the bad news about Boaz's older brother.

Though she had not seen him in years, Naomi knew Tov, the brother of both Boaz and her late husband. He was the black sheep of the family. Her hopes plummeted like a bird hit by a slingshot.

Shaking her head, she sank down by the fire she had kept burning through the night as she had waited for her daughter-in-law's return. Ruth sat down beside her; the glow on her face fading.

"Sit still, my daughter, until we see how things will go."

It seemed an age before the sky grew pale enough to snuff out the lamp. A cock crowed nearby, answered by another more distant, and then another, and the daily round of competitive kingship began.

"Sit," Naomi said.

"I am."

"Mark my words," Naomi added, mostly to convince herself, "Boaz will settle the matter today."

There was stirring in the neighboring houses, clatter and bustle and conversation. In the street, people were greeting one another. On the hillside, the lead ram with its bell clanged through the flock of braying lambs and their moms.

"Ruth, maybe we could...?"

Ruth jumped to her feet. "Yes."

Naomi scrambled to hers and the two headed out, through the creaking doorway.

At the gates, they found Boaz calling for silence. "I want to bring before you all a matter regarding my brother and me."

He smiled when he saw Ruth.

"Stay here at the back and listen," Naomi said, tugging at Ruth's robe as she looked like she was about to make her way through the crowd that had gathered.

Tov was sitting on one of the elders' benches cut into the city wall, swinging his legs. To Naomi, he was a pug-nosed stranger with a vaguely familiar look, stockier than before, with lines etched into his features and hair streaked with grey.

"Naomi, our sister-in-law, has returned from Moab and is required to sell back the land that belonged to our late brother, Elimelech," Boaz announced.

Ah, so that was coming up. Losing the land would be no hardship, Naomi thought to herself. They were welcome to it.

Boaz turned to his brother who had just picked his nose and was inspecting the result. "Since, as my elder brother, you are the rightful redeemer, tell me now if you will buy the land because if not, then I will."

Tov sniggered as all eyes turned towards him. "I will."

This was not good news. Naomi doubted he would give her a fair price.

Strangely, Ruth, whose lanky outline was silhouetted against the angled morning sun, appeared calm. How could that be when things clearly weren't going their way? Naomi followed her gaze to Boaz and understood why. His own composure was hugely reassuring.

"You'll be ripping up those vines, turning the field over to grain, no doubt, Tov?" Boaz said.

"Eh?"

"Getting those boundaries marked out, plowing, sowing seed... going for a full harvest next year, perhaps?"

Tov clearly had no idea where his younger brother was going with this. "Uh, right."

Boaz rubbed his hands. "Goody."

"Goody?"

Boaz ambled past the assembled elders. "Only..."

"Only what?"

"I wouldn't want to make you look foolish by stating the obvious."

"Go ahead!"

Whispers went through the crowd. Ruth sent Naomi a questioning look to which she responded with a shrug. She had no idea where Boaz was going with this.

Boaz scratched his nose. "Well, I'm sure that you realize you would also be acquiring the land from Elimelech's son's widow, Ruth."

Naomi's skin prickled as everyone in the crowd turned and stared at the two of them. Boaz had reminded Tov of Levirate law, which required him to marry his late brother's widow or, in this case, his late nephew's widow.

"The Moabitess?" Tov said. "I can't marry her!"

Good, Naomi thought. He doesn't deserve her.

"You can't?" Boaz was grinning.

"No."

Shouts to the contrary were coming from the crowd.

"It's against the law!" Tov retorted.

An elder called for silence and explained. "The law changed. Jews may now marry Moabite women."

It seemed everyone in the crowd had an opinion they wished to share on this issue.

"Alright!" Tov yelled, getting to his feet. "I'll marry her."

Oh, no. This could not be happening. Naomi would not see Ruth married to this piece of doggy-do, whatever the cost. They'd get by somehow without this…

"But you can't," Boaz reminded him, so softly that the sense of what he said came to her with a delay after the words.

Tov nodded in the elder's direction. "He just said I can."

"But she's betrothed to me. I've already paid the bride price to marry her myself."

The crowd fell about laughing and applauding. To them, this was comic theater but Naomi and Ruth's lives were turned around by Boaz's words. Their own laughter, as they clung to one another, was filled with tears of joy. They would not know hunger any more. They would not live in a hovel. Naomi would be able to hold her head up high among the women again.

Tov, still two donkeys behind everyone else, looked confused. "But any child you had would be considered of Elimelech's line and inherit the land I'd invested in!"

Boaz smiled across at Ruth before agreeing with Tov.

"Afraid so."

"Only an idiot would buy it in those circumstances."

"Yes." Boaz nodded. "The question is, are you that idiot?"

There was further laughter from the onlookers.

"Or should I redeem it instead?'

Tov marched away, mumbling obscenities, to a slow handclap.

"Wait up!" Boaz cried after him. "I need your sandal to seal the deal."

Tugging it from his foot, Tov launched it, forcing Boaz to duck as it narrowly missed his head. He held it up as Tov hobbled away, first to the elders and then to the crowd. "You are all witnesses that I have acquired the land that belonged to Elimelech and am marrying Ruth!"

"We are witnesses!" they cheered. "Long live Ruth!"

Sitting under a canopy on Boaz's roof, surrounded by fragrant flowers and fountains, Naomi crooned to the new baby lying in her arms. *"You'll do great things, you'll father kings."*

His rosebud lips moved, sharing silent secrets with her.

Three women in shapeless widows' cloaks, friends of hers, came up to coo over him.

"He'll bring you new life and look after you in your old age," one said.

"Your daughter-in-law has done more for you than seven sons!" said the second.

"And she loves you," said the third.

Naomi smiled at Ruth. "Praise God."

It was a good thing that she had let her come back to Bethlehem with her.

Though they all knew she was too old to have children of her own, she laid the baby on her breast where he latched on and fell asleep.

Bobbie Ann Cole is a bestselling author, speaker and teacher who specializes in bringing stories—yours, her own and those of Bible heroes—to life.

Get connected to her and her FREE Pictorial Guide to *The Israel Jesus Loved* at www.jesus-ebook.com.

Ordination Day – *Diogenes Ruiz*

As I lay on the floor with my forehead pressed against the cold marble, death came upon me. There would be no physical pain in my ritualistic death, only abundant humility as I surrendered my life. After several long silent moments, I slowly arose: my orders, to be fully alive in Christ's mission. My life as an ordained priest had begun. The sacrament of Holy Order was complete.

Before joining the priesthood, I loved dating women. I never had any trouble attracting women. My friends used to joke about it and called me the "babe magnet." I loved to get into fights when a bully targeted someone as fresh meat. I enjoyed doing things other men do, but my desire to join the priesthood slowly grew into an obsession. As far as I can remember, it was just something I wanted to do. I can't rationalize it or explain it. The more I fought it, dismissed it, or tried to distract myself from the pull of this farfetched calling, the more I became drawn to it. My other great love was Wing Chun kung fu. It started with episodes of the Green Hornet. I didn't much care for the main character, but his sidekick, Kato, was the star of the show as far as I was concerned. He was a kind of crazy social justice hero. My love for the fighting arts has managed to coexist with my obsession for the priesthood.

Eventually, I gave in and applied to join the order of Franciscan friars. I guess it was my interest in St. Francis of Assisi which started to eat away at my longing to be a regular guy. The more I learned about this man, the more I was fascinated with the choices he made and how he lived his life. If he was alive today, we would think he was crazy, a mentally ill bum on the street with no possessions, yet he would lack for nothing. By today's standard, Francis was a loon, trading a life as a playboy for a life of poverty and complete surrender to Christ. No doubt he would be heavily medicated by well meaning health professionals.

Second thoughts? I had my share at first. Without much of a father figure in my life, and my two main role models being Kato and St. Francis of Assisi, I did have a few doubts about my purpose on this planet. Eventually, that gave way to resolution and peace in knowing the path of faith I had chosen to follow. It would start in earnest after receiving the Bishop's blessing at the end of the ordination ceremony. The only problem: the type of priesthood I thought I chose was not the type of priesthood chosen for me. I would start to suspect something was wrong the moment I stepped out of the church as a fully ordained priest.

It was a crisp, clear fall day. The sun was high in the noon-day sky. As I stepped onto the sidewalk after descending the steps of St. John the Divine in upper Manhattan, I thought my eyes were playing tricks on me as they adjusted to the brightness. Passing several people on my way to the friary, I noticed dark blotches on their faces. I rubbed my eyes and dismissed it as my brain's way of dealing with the transition from low light to the bright outdoors.

Fr. Albert, Fr Ed, and Fr. Wayne were with me. We had taken our vows alongside each other, newly anointed men of God. We walked several blocks to Ray's Pizza for our celebration lunch. The dark blotches continued to appear. I was getting a little nervous about the persistent problem in my vision.

I turned to my companions as we neared the pizzeria. "Have any of you noticed dark blotches on the faces of some folks?" I signaled by glancing and nodding my head in the direction of the approaching couple. We all looked at the lady and man as they walked past.

The couple smiled and so did we in a gesture of greeting. I turned again to my companions. "Well?"

Fr. Ed, shrugged. "I didn't see anything out of the ordinary.

They look like a nice couple."

I then looked at Fr. Albert and Fr. Wayne. "Did either of you notice anything, dark blotches on the man's face?

Fr. Albert and Fr. Wayne shook their heads.

"Maybe you are seeing spots, which might indicate an issue with your eyes," said Fr. Albert.

"Perhaps you're right. I'm overdue for an eye exam."

We arrived at the pizzeria and took our seats. As we looked at the menu, a waiter came to our table. "Can I get you something to drink?"

When I looked up from my menu, I recoiled against my seat.

Upon noticing my reaction, Fr. Wayne asked, "Are you all right, Oliver? What's the matter?"

My eyes were fixed on the waiter's demonic face. It looked like a cross between a goat and a snake. As I continued to look, the demon face turned into a human face, then back to a demon face. It faded in and out from demon to human and back. For an instant I felt the same way I did on my fifth birthday when my aunt and uncle came to visit. My uncle did not look like my uncle: he looked like a monster. His demonic face terrified me causing me to freeze with fear. He approached and I backed up against the wall. When he touched my face I went into a semi-comatose state. I remember hearing my mother's voice in the distance and waking up after my uncle left. I never felt such fear as that again, until today.

"Any of you notice anything unusual about our waiter?" I asked as I struggled to maintain my composure.

The demon waiter glanced at each of the priests, then looked at me wearing a contorted smile, revealing black gums and yellow teeth.

"Oliver, what's this all about? I don't see anything unusual. Are you seeing spots again?" Asked Fr. Wayne.

"Sorry to ruin your lunch. I'm feeling kind of sick. Can we just leave?"

After we arrived at the rectory, I went to my room, prayed, took a nap, and awoke to a knock on my door.

Fr. Wayne let himself in. "Fr. Manuel wants to see you."

Fr. Manuel is our provincial in charge of all the new

priests. "Sit down, Oliver," he said, as he put a book on a bookcase and walked to take a seat behind his large mahogany desk."

I sat down and waited for him to take his seat. As he was about sit, he froze, looked at me with a blank expression, eyes opened wide. I noticed a knife point protruding from his chest as blood began to drip slowly from its point. I bolted out of my chair and noticed the dark figure standing behind Fr. Manuel. It poked its head out from behind the provincial, smiled, and let the body fall to the ground. As the body fell, the demonic creature pulled the knife out and set it on the desk. It took the provincial's seat and motioned with its claw-like hand for me to take my seat.

I glanced at the door and noticed two more demonic creatures standing by it. Leaving the room was not an option. I took my seat and looked at the creature sitting before me.

It placed each hand on the desk and leaned forward. "I know you can see us, priest."

"Who are you?" I asked trying not to let my fear show.

"We are the rightful heirs to this world. The world your god has abandoned. You can end up like him." It pointed to Fr. Manuel's body as it picked up the bloody dagger. "Or, you can join us and live a life of pleasure and satisfaction." Saying this, the demon turned into a naked woman with large breasts resting on the top of the table. The two demons by the door also turned into nude women: each took a seat beside me. They sat on the edge of their chairs, spread their legs, and extended their arms, inviting me for an extended cuddle.

I bolted out of my seat and ran out of the provincial's office. On my way I bumped into Fr. Wayne and Fr. Albert causing Wayne to fall and Albert to be pushed against the wall.

"Oliver! What's going on?" shouted Fr. Albert.

Once outside, I continued to run. I looked back but didn't see any demons pursuing me. *"Perhaps I imagined the whole thing."* As I rounded the corner near the pizzeria, I slowed down and settled into a brisk walk, that's when I noticed everyone on the street looking at me. No one was moving. They either had black blotches on their faces or demonic heads. All were turned in my direction.

I came to a stop and slowly scanned up, across and down the street. It was the same all over. Everyone came to a stop and turned to look at me. My heart started to pound. As I turned to glance inside the pizzeria, I saw four customers and the guy behind the counter all looking intently at me from behind the store's glass window. I felt someone poke me on the shoulder and turned quickly. I was not aware of anyone near me.

It was the pizza waiter with the demon head. "I didn't think any of you god-lovin-fools could see us. Join us or die!" The waiter pointed at the mass of people now huddling around and repeated. "Join us now, or die!" The crowd swelled. There was no place to run. The demon waiter laughed, The crowd chimed in as the laughter began to swell. Beneath it, I could hear whimpering. I looked around and saw a young women with dark blotches.

She extended her hand. "Help me."

I could barely hear her. As she repeated it, I could see her lips form the words. Upon closer observation, there were several blotched faces in the crowd all mouthing the same words. Initially, I thought everyone was laughing. They were not. The fully demonic faces were enjoying a raucous laugh. The others seemed to be asking for help.

The demon waiter raised his hand. All became quiet. The cries for help ceased as well. The crowed parted as the three demons from the provincial's office approached. The one who killed Fr. Manuel came to a stop directly in front of me. "There is no place you can go, no place you can hide. You see us, we see you. Seers like you must either join us or die. You must decide now. What will it be priest?"

I looked across the landscape of demonic and blotched faces. My gazed settled on the young woman whose hand had been extended. There were tears in her eyes as well as in the eyes of other blotch-faced individuals. I saw her lips move silently to form "Help me."

What will it be priest? The demon picked me up by the throat.

I gasped for breath and tried to free myself to no avail. I managed to utter "Go to hell!"

The demon smiled as he held the bloody dagger he used to kill the provincial in his other hand. "Very well, priest." The creature thrust the dagger deep into my side.

I felt the sharp sting of the blade as it ripped through my

flesh. Then my side began to burn as the energy drained from my body. I felt the demon's grip tighten around my neck. My vision blurred. Then darkness.

Fr. Wayne let himself in. "Fr. Manuel wants to see you, Oliver."

Oliver clutched his side, as he sprang up from his dream and looked at Fr. Wayne.

"Are you OK?"

Oliver wiped the sweat from his brow. "I'm fine. I must have dozed off, just a bad dream. I'll be there in a few, just want to jump in the shower. I'm sweating like a pig."

"Good idea," replied Fr. Wayne. It stinks in here.

Oliver jumped in the shower and felt a sting as the cool water touched his side. He felt the area and noticed the scar. It felt tender but was not bleeding. He examined it. Almost four inches wide. It was the exact spot the demon had stabbed him during his nightmare. *"How can this be? That was just a dream."*

Oliver entered the provincial's office. "Sit down, Oliver," said Fr. Manuel, as he put a book on a bookcase and walked to a seat behind his large mahogany desk. As Fr. Manuel was about to sit, he froze, looked at Oliver with a blank expression, eyes opened wide.

Oliver leaped forward..

Fr. Manuel waved his hand, motioning for Oliver to sit down. "It's this dammed heartburn. I get it every time I eat pepperoni pizza. It'll pass in just a moment. I didn't mean to scare you." Fr. Manuel noticed Oliver's pale skin color. "Are you all right, Oliver? You look like you've seen a ghost."

Oliver sat back down. "No. It's just that I thought you were in real trouble for a moment."

Fr. Manuel took his seat. "I will be if I keep eating pepperoni pizza."

"Fr. Wayne said you wanted to see me."

"Yes, I know today was an important day for you and the church. I just want to see if there is anything you want to discuss. I've been there myself. There are occasions of buyer's remorse among a few newly ordained priest. It is a reality of our calling.

You come all the way to this point, and decide it's not for you after all." Fr. Manuel paused and studied Oliver. "Is that the case with you?"

Oliver took a deep breath and looked intently at Fr. Manuel. "No, that is not the case with me. This is where I need to be."

"Are you sure, Oliver? This is not simply about the rest of your life but about the lives you will touch as an ordained priest. Let your truth come forth, whatever that may be. You are still one of God's precious creations and have his unending love whether or not you follow through with your vows. Do not let human pride or fear stand in your way of acknowledging what you must do. If it sounds like I am trying to convince you to leave the priesthood on the day you became one, that is not the case. I just want what is best for you and the church."

"I understand, Fr. Manuel. I assure you I have no regrets, or second thoughts about becoming a priest."

"What happened this afternoon? Your comrades were worried about you, seeing spots and all. It sounds like a severe case of second thought to me, enough to make you physically ill. It started the minute you left he church, didn't it?"

"I think it's time for an eye exam. I'm not seeing spots anymore, perhaps a bit of nervous energy after ordination. But I assure you, I'm fine."

The provincial nodded. "Let me ask you this Oliver, would you like to take a few weeks off to think about this and clear your head. I think it would be…"

Oliver held up his hand in a stop motion. "Fr. Manuel, I appreciate your concern and your insights. I also very much appreciate your offer for me to take off for a few weeks." Oliver got up from his chair. "I can assure you it's not necessary. I think you are misreading the signs. As a matter of fact, from the minute I stepped into the street, after my ordination, until right now, everything I have experienced or sensed has validated the fact that I must serve God. I have no desire to do anything else. I have no regrets, just the opposite. Our world is being consumed by evil. I feel there is a sense of urgency to reach those who are trapped in sin. I have never been so sure of anything in my entire life."

Fr. Manuel sat in silence for a moment, then nodded. "Yes,

there is a great deal of evil in our world." He let out a sigh and smiled. "But there is plenty of good as well. We just have to look more closely."

Oliver rose from his chair. "That's exactly what I plan to do."

"Well, Fr. Oliver, I guess I'll stop being an old father hen. I'm glad you feel so strongly about serving the Lord. It goes without saying, should anything come up, I am here for you."

Oliver, nodded. "Thank you, Fr. Manuel. I will take you up on that should something arise. Right now, I'm starved."

Fr. Manuel chuckled. "Yes, of course."

Oliver opened the office door, stopped, and looked at the provincial. "Thanks, Fr. Manuel. I think I'll take a walk and have a pepperoni pizza."

As I walked to Ray's Pizza, I prayed for guidance. The night was cool and brisk. As usual, there were people coming and going. I didn't bother to take a close look at their faces. A homeless man sifting through a trash can stopped as I walked past him. He rushed toward me. His gnarly grey beard ladened with bits of crumbs lodged in it. His eyebrows rose and his gaze pierced through me. "You must pretend you don't see them. It's the only way to be safe!" He immediately withdrew and began sifting through the trash again.

I approached him. "Excuse me, sir?"

The man stopped his trash can digging and looked at me as he backed away. I held my hand up and smiled. He stopped, squinted his eyes, and smiled, exposing two teeth as he held out the palm of his hand. "Do you have any spare change, sir?" He tilted his head and kept the smile on his face waiting for anything I might be inclined to give.

"What was it you said before?" I asked.

With the smile still on his face he repeated. "Do you have any spare change, sir?"

"No, before that?"

"Any spare change, sir?" He repeated with the smile still plastered on his face.

I gave him a couple of dollars and continued my walk to Ray's.

As I entered the pizzeria, I picked up one of the free newspapers from the stand and pretended to read it. I was really checking out the place to see if any of the people preparing pizzas had demon heads. None. That was good, I did not want to eat a pizza prepared by a demon. Sounds crazy now that I think about it. Everyone in the pizza restaurant had blotches, some faint, others very dark and pronounced. The only one with a demon head was the waiter who spotted me and came up to me.

"You want to sit at a table?" He recognized me from earlier. "Hey, you were in here before with your buddies. Are you OK? What was it you saw when you looked at me? I heard you ask your friends if they noticed anything strange about me?"

It was extremely difficult to look into his demon eyes as his face shifted from demon to human and back to demon, and not react like I had earlier. I smiled and folded my paper. "I'm sorry, had a bit of a panic attack earlier, overdue for an eye exam and kept seeing spots all day. I'm feeling better now, seeing things as they really are."

"Cool man, OK. Say if you ever need anything to help with panic attacks or anything at all. You come see me." He leaned in close to me as thought we were now good buddies. "I've got some good shit. It'll blow your mind." He winked. I saw his demon face drool.

"Thanks, I'll keep that in mind."

"So, you gonna sit at the counter? Joe will take care of you." He pointed to the man taking a pizza out of the oven."

"Thanks." I took my seat at the counter and looked around. Demon waiter buzzed about the place serving patrons at the tables.

Joe came up to the counter. "What can I get you?"

"Two slices of pepperoni please and a coke." I replied.

Joe took the stub of a pencil he kept tucked behind the top of his right ear and wrote my order on a small sheet of green receipt paper. Then he put it on the narrow counter behind him with the other order tickets. Five minutes later, he placed two hot slices of pepperoni pizza and a coke in front of me. "Thanks!" I said.

He nodded and got back to his pizza making.

Half way through my first slice, a man and a women entered the restaurant. The man had a demonic head and the woman both had blotches on their faces. They took their seat at one of the tables. Another customer entered a minute later. She took a seat at the counter next to me. Even with the blotches on her face, I recognized her as the young woman in my dream. Her face with outstretched hand was emblazoned on my memory.

Joe came up to the counter. "What can I get you?"

"A cheese calzone, please." After ordering she fidgeted nervously.

She caught me looking at her. I gave her a smile. She forced a smile and looked the other way. I noticed the scars on her wrist.

"How are the calzones here, any good?" I asked.

She turned her head, surprised by my question. "Yeah, they're pretty good."

"I haven't had a calzone in ages." I said.

She didn't respond.

"Don't I know you from somewhere?" I asked.

Her head whipped around. She looked me over. "Aren't you a priest or something? You're not supposed to be hitting on women are you?"

I blushed a bit. "I'm sorry. But, I'm not hitting on you. I just became a priest today, as a matter of fact."

"Well, fact is 'Don't I know you from somewhere?' is the lamest pick up line in history," she said. "Besides for all I know, you could be some psycho pretending to be a priest."

At that, I couldn't help laughing. It caught her by surprise and she chuckled.

Joe came to the counter with her calzone.

"Thanks." She said.

I extended my hand to her. "My name is Fr. Oliver. I'm not a psycho. I promise."

She shook my hand. "Clare."

"Nice to meet you, Clare."

She blew on her calzone to cool it off a bit. "So, what made you become a priest? She looked me over again. "Kind of a waste if you ask me."

"It's just something I always wanted to do. It's a little hard to explain; became kind of an obsession. I just had to do it."

She took a bite of her calzone. "You're psycho. You gave

up sex." She said as she chewed her food.

"Sometimes you have to give up something to get what you really want. For me, it was to become a priest."

She shook her head. "Whatever. I couldn't do it."

"I know, you couldn't even if you wanted to. They don't allow women to become priests."

"That's bullshit," she said. "Was that a God thing, or did some frustrated old fart make up that stupid rule?"

I laughed again at her response which made her smile. "It's complicated." I said. "But that's the way it is. In my heart, I don't believe it was a God thing. Your old fart theory might merit further investigation."

"I don't believe in God anyway." She said, as she took a sip of her soda. "No offense, I just don't think a God would let so much bad crap happen if he really existed."

"What kind of bad crap are you talking about?" I asked.

She turned to me, her piercing green eyes surrounded by the dark blotch all over her face. "Don't you ever watch the news? People killing each other, idiots running the country, greed, simply trying to survive, men who can't commit to anything except beer. All the good men are taken, the rest are gay, or unavailable because they're priests or some such crap. Then there's the past due rent, stress from all the BS at work, the abortion you live with everyday of your life, the guilt, the feeling of hopelessness and loneliness, the successful sister who has it all and thinks you're a loser. I can go on. It just makes you want to stuff your face with a calzone followed by a gallon of rocky road ice cream, or better yet, to check out all together. Today it's the calzone, tomorrow...who knows."

I paused and gave her my full attention. "Blessed be You, O God, for having created me."

"What the hell is that supposed to mean?" She asked with a mouthful of food.

"One of the reasons I became a priest is because I have always been inspired by Francis of Assisi. If he were alive today, he'd be locked up and labeled crazy. He walked away from a life of riches and luxury and embraced a life of poverty and devotion to God. I think he may have been the happiest man on the planet at the time. There were others with wealth who wanted that kind of joy. Some wound up giving all their stuff away, land, money, you name it and joined Francis."

"Yeah, so, he *was* crazy. So were those rich guys."

There was a woman who decided to follow Francis and left everything including a proposal of marriage from a rich man. Her name was Clare. She was an inspiration to many other women of her time and they joined her. She lived in poverty and did manual labor. I do mean poverty. She had nothing. The last thing she uttered before she died was "Blessed be You, O God, for having created me."

"So, what does that have to do with me? Just because we have the same name doesn't mean squat, and it certainly doesn't make me a saint."

"No, it doesn't. But aren't you the least bit curious how someone with absolutely no possessions, doing manual labor, with no husband, and a bunch of critics could be so happy as to utter those words on her death bed? By comparison, you are wealthy, you can afford the calzone you just ate and a gallon of rocky road ice cream if you want it. You have a phone and other possessions. You probably own some jewelry like the necklace and earrings you are wearing right now."

She shrugged her shoulders. "I guess she was crazy too."

"Yeah, but wouldn't you want a little bit of that crazy? To feel such utter joy, even with nothing...I wanted that kind of crazy. Don't you want just a little bit of that feeling. A feeling no one can take from you."

"Now you sound like a pusher. You're not trying to sell me drugs are you?"

I laughed again and it made her jump. "Sorry, but it sure does sound like that? I never thought of it that way... No, what I'm talking about does not wear off."

"Sorry, Oliver, but there is no way I'm going to go off the deep end like your crazy Francis and Clare. I like my possessions."

I chuckled. "That won't be necessary. A life of self-imposed poverty is not for everyone."

She looked at me and for a split moment I thought I caught a glimpse of hope in her eye. "What then? What are you telling me to do?"

"It's simple, Clare, just two things. It's almost too simple, but I promise, things will get better if you do them."

"I'm listening."

"Here, give me your hand."

Reluctantly, she placed her hand in mine. "Be thankful for what you do have and be open, allow God into your life. That's all."

She said nothing for a few moments. I could see tears pooling in her eyes. "I've done a lot of crazy shit. If there is a God, He might not be interested in the likes of me."

"Oh, He's interested all right. I can promise you that. You and I meeting was no accident."

"What do you mean?"

"It's a long story. I'll have to tell you about it some time. Were you ever baptized as a child?"

She shook her head. "No, my family was not religious."

"It's pretty simple, and it's a sacrament that claims you for Christ. It's an important step in accepting God into your life. When you are ready, I would be happy to do it."

"Yeah, that sounds great." She looked at her watch, got up from her stool and walked over to the cashier. Before heading out she came back and said, "Do it now."

"Do what now?" I asked.

"Baptize me. You said it was simple. Go ahead and do it now."

I wasn't sure how to respond to her request. "Well, typically I would do this at church."

"I don't want to wait that long. Do it now."

"But, I have to…"

"Look, if you don't do it now. I'll probably never get around to asking again."

I sat for a moment then asked her to sit down.

She took her seat again. "Will this hurt?"

I could not suppress a smile. "No, it won't hurt. I'll have to ask you a few questions, and take your confession before I can baptize you. Are you OK with that."

She nodded. Some of the customers were now bending an ear to listen to what the crazy priest was saying to the pretty young woman.

I looked into her eyes and asked. "Clare, are you sorry for

your sins? For things you have done in the past which may have hurt others or otherwise not been acceptable to God?"

She nodded.

"You have to say it with your mouth, Clare."

She nodded again. "Yes, I am sorry for all the awful shit I've done during my wretched life and for everyone I've hurt. For the baby I kil…" She began to weep as she spoke. "For the baby I killed." She continued to sob. "I'm sorry. I'm sorry."

I traced the sign of the cross on her forehead. Then I realized I didn't have water. So I grabbed the glass of water from one of the patrons. "Excuse me." I said to the man at the nearest table.

"Hey!"

I traced the sign of the cross on Clare's forehead. "Your sins are forgiven. In the name of the Father, and of the Son, and of the Holy Spirit, Amen" As I lifted the glass to pour water over her head. I realized, I didn't know her last name.

"What is you last name Clare?"

"McLamb," she whispered.

I lifted the glass and poured the water on her head. "I claim you for our Lord and Savior, Jesus Christ. I baptize you in the name of the Father and of the Son, and of the Holy Spirit, Amen."

I put down the glass just as demon waiter rushed up to me and grabbed my arm. "You can't do that! What do you think this is, a church?"

I remained calm in spite of my desire to slam demon waiter's face against the counter. "I think you are mistaken. Where two or more are gathered in God's name… well, that's a church. So, yes, this is a pizzeria, and for the moment a church. Now, take your hand off my arm."

Demon waiter released my arm. I went to the register to pay for my pizza. Joe stood at the register trying to hold back a smile. He looked at me and did a little wave of his hand. "Not necessary Father, it's on the house."

I returned the smile. "Thank you, but that's not necessary."

Joe continued smiling and doing his little wave. "Si Father, it is on the house. You have a good night."

"I shook the pizza maker's hand. "Thank you, Joe. That's very kind."

Clare was busy drying her hair and clothes with napkins. As she looked at me, I noticed the dark blotches previously all over her face were now gone. She looked different. She looked hopeful. We stepped outside the restaurant together. "Sorry about the water. It's part of the sacrament of baptism. It symbolizes washing away all your sins. If you stick with this and come to church and read the bible, you'll learn all about it."

She pulled my arm down as she leaned in and kissed me on the cheek. "Thanks," she said. "I'm not sure what the future holds, but for the first time in my life I feel like there may be hope for me."

"Let me be the first one to welcome you to your new life as a Christian." I took hold of her hand and shook it. "If you come by the friary tomorrow, I'll have a bible for you as a welcome gift. The Franciscan friary is just three blocks up the street."

"I'll do that. Thanks." She turned, waved, and walked up the street in the opposite direction of the friary.

When I arrived at the friary, I stopped at the storage closet and selected one of the bibles. As I closed the closet door, Fr. Manuel greeted me. "How was your pepperoni pizza?"

"It was great. Maybe next time I'll try a calzone."

"Hmm, that sounds good." He rubbed his stomach. "Maybe, I'll come with you."

"Goodnight, Fr. Manuel"

"Oh, Oliver, with everything going on today, I forgot to congratulate you on your ordination." He reached and shook my hand. "Congratulations, you will make a fine priest. We are lucky to have you." His expression turned serious for a moment. "But you must take extra care with the female members of the congregation, you being such a strapping fellow and all. You must avoid temptation."

"Thank you, Yes, Sir. I'm excited about what lies ahead."

Just then Fr. Wayne stepped into the room. "Oliver, there's a woman downstairs who says you have something for her. She says she's sorry, but she just couldn't wait."

You can follow Fr. Oliver's adventures in *Persistent Evil, The Demon Slayer,* Book 2 of the Praying Mantis series, available on Amazon. And you won't want to miss Book 1, *A Rabbit's Tale, An Easter Story*, the 2015 Global Ebook Gold Medal winner.

Visit the author's website at www.diogenesruiz.com.

A Psalm for Evening –*Fr. Steve Kluge O.F.M.*

At the close of day,
YOU
Raise prayer
Within me:
Thanksgiving
Wraps round my contrite spirit
Since even sensing Your Shadow filled me with dread.
And though I often fled
Throughout this day,
YOU
Matched me step for step
And I could not run away.
From You,
Through You,
I ran and hid
Only to be found within the enclosure of Your embrace.
Graced with unearned and undeserving grace.

Acknowledgements

Thank you to Passage Home, their staff, and the many volunteers who carry out Christ's mission each day, supporting people in their effort to get out of poverty.

A special thank you to all the authors who contributed stories for this anthology, using their gifts of writing to help those in need.

Nancy Stout and Tricia Downs, thank you for your contribution to this project with your editing expertise.

Thank you to you for purchasing a copy of Birds of Passage which helps Passage Home continue its work.

About the Authors
(Alphabetical by Last Name)

Kim Bond lives in Saint Louis with her husband and two children. Her fiction appears in over thirty publications. She has a passion for glorifying God and helping others draw near to Christ through Christian literature. Visit her at www.drawneartochrist.com.

Bobbie Ann Cole is a speaker, writer, ghostwriter, and teacher. As a Jew who's passionate about Jesus and His homeland Israel, where she also lived, she was inspired to write *Love Triangles, Discovering Jesus the Jew in Today's Israel.* She is author of her acclaimed faith memoir *She Does Not Fear the Snow,* an Amazon #1 bestseller, and of the *Disciples Indeed Workbook*, which helps people share their faith experiences compellingly. See www.love-triangles.com, email bobbie.ann.cole@gmail.com.

Parker J. Cole is a diehard Trekkie (TOS), sci-fi lover, fantasy dweller, romance junkie, anime freak, old movie buff, churchgoer, off and on Mountain Dew and marshmallow recovering addict who writes to fill the void the sugar left behind. She is also the author of several Christian fiction romance and speculative fiction novels including *Many Strange Women, The Other Man,* and *Dark Cherub.*

R.S. Crow lives in North Carolina with his wife and four children. Having graduated college with a psychology degree, he currently works full-time as a counselor for mentally ill children, while writing in his free time. He has written two books, *Late Autumn Trees,* and *Haunts of Cruelty.* Having grown up with haunting dreams and visits from the Boogieman, R. S. Crow enjoys writing to unfold his dark perspective through a love of imagination and storytelling, and hopes to continue with further works.

Greg M. Dodd lives in Columbia, South Carolina with his wife, Caroline, and their Anatolian Shepherd, Desmond. His debut novel, "*A Seed for the Harvest*" won a Silver Medal for Christian Fiction in the 2015 Illumination Book Awards. Greg earned both his bachelor's and master's degrees from the University of South Carolina. His other published works include a contribution to the anthology "Precious, Precocious Moments" (compiled by Yvonne Lehman). He is currently writing "*The Last Harvest,*" a sequel to "*A Seed for the Harvest.*" Readers may contact Greg through his website www.gregmdodd.com.

Jarrod L. Edge is the author of the *E7Prophecy*™ Christian sci-fi fantasy series. He loves spending time with his wife, Lisa, and their four children. Jarrod is currently working on several short stories in a series named The Acts of the Dragons, also a part of the *E7Prophecy*™ series. Each of his four children will co-author individual short stories about the "acts" of Rebecca, Matthew, Jacob, and Elizabeth. Jarrod and his family are Christians and love learning about and growing in the Lord.

Kelsey Gillespy is co-author of "*Winning Kids With Sport*", a book that delivers sport psychology techniques to youth coaches. She publishes weekly posts on her personal webpage, Kelsey's Grammar. Her work also appeared in the *Columbia Business Times, Columbia Home Magazine, Columbia Faith & Values,* and *Jefferson City Magazine* on a monthly basis. Her poetry won the 2013 George Herbert Award from Athanatos Christian Ministries and was published in their anthology, *Descant.*

Jeff Hendricks was born in New Orleans, Louisiana in 1974 in the back seat of a Chevrolet. He is the author of "Seeking the Heavens" a fiction, fantasy tale of self-discovery. Jeff is an accomplished musician, an avid tinkerer. He won his first literary award when he was twelve. Jeff currently lives near Thibodaux, Louisiana, and says the food there is second to none.

Helena Kamerra was born and raised in Alabama. She is married with four beautiful daughters and she enjoys spending time with family, hunting, fishing and practicing veterinary medicine at least part of the time. She loves to write edgy Christian fiction that leans toward contemporary romance. It isn't all fluffy but it does deal with real issues that many folks face every day. Happy reading!

Fr. Steve Kluge (pronounced Kloo-gee), originally from New Jersey, is a Franciscan friar currently serving the St. Francis of Assisi parish in Raleigh, NC. He loves holding the door on Sunday mornings greeting the Saints of God. He is a talented and gifted friar and has written numerous poems which appear in the parish bulletin.

Kristine Kohut is a military wife, mother of two adopted preschoolers, and a dog person. She spent her twenties in Washington, DC where her debut novel *Big Toe People* is set. It reads like a Christian season of *Sex and the City*. Kristine grew up in the US Air Force, living in Oregon, Mississippi, The Netherlands, England, and California. After DC, she moved to Okinawa where she met her husband and where her current work in progress is set. Visit Kristine's author page at http://kristinekohut.net.

Ken Kuhlken's stories have appeared in *Esquire* and dozens of other magazines and anthologies, been honorably mentioned in *Best American Short Stories*, and earned a National Endowment for the Arts Fellowship. His novels are *Midheaven*, a finalist for the Ernest Hemingway Award for best first novel, and the often- awarded Tom Hickey California crime novels. With Alan Russell, in *No Cats, No Chocolate*, he has chronicled the madness of book tours. In *Writing and the Spirit* he offers a wealth of advice to everyone looking for inspiration. *Reading Brother* Lawrence follows him on a trip to the Kingdom of Heaven. He resides near the Pacific Ocean and the U.S.- Mexican border with his Zoë and at kenkuhlken.net.

Fr. David McBriar celebrated 50 years as a Franciscan friar of Holy Name Province in 2008. David was the first Franciscan pastor of St. Francis of Assisi in Raleigh, NC, and when his term as pastor was complete, he became pastor of Immaculate Conception in Durham. He has returned to St. Francis as a senior friar. Fr. David. He has published three books of homilies. David McBriar is a champion for social justice and was instrumental in the formation of Passage Home.

Wendy Stenzel Oleston is a Bestselling Author who currently lives in Janesville, WI with her husband, Ryan, and their two children. She is a very proud recovering alcoholic who thanks God everyday for the freedom she has found through Him. After taking an eight year hiatus from writing fiction, a new vision for her writing began in January 2014. That new vision was "Very Edgy" Christian fiction with a specific goal: to give something of value to the world instead of taking something valuable away.

Deb Palmer is a Christian story teller who'll slap your heart then make you laugh. Her current book in progress, "In Spite of Us – Stalked by a Loving God," is a scandalous true story of a love triangle with God at the tip, herself and husband grasping at the base. Forever the storyteller, she has dabbled in journalism and written two award winning children's educational videos for the Department of Ecology. Wife, Mother, Nana to five boys, and the owner of an antiques business.

Peggy Payne is a New York Times Notable novelist. She is the author of *Cobalt Blue, Sister India* and *Revelation,* among others. Peggy lives near Chapel Hill, North Carolina, and is married to a psychologist who specializes in clinical hypnosis. She is a gardener, kayaker, traveler, and of course: reader. Her novels and nonfiction books have been published in ten countries, and she has written for many national magazines and major American newspapers. She is a consultant to other writers.

Danyele Read writes inspirational fantasy and science fiction, with historical and romantic themes. Originally a New Yorklahoman, she resides in Texas.

Diogenes Ruiz writes suspenseful Christian fiction thrillers, books you want to read twice. His debut novel, *A Rabbit's Tale, An Easter Story* climbed to No 1 on Amazon two years in a row. It also received the 2015 Global Ebook Award Gold Medal in the category of Christian fiction, and earned a prestigious 5 stars from Reader's Favorite. You can follow Fr. Oliver's adventures in Book 2 of the series, *Persistent Evil, The Demon Slayer.* The third book in the Praying Mantis series, will be out in 2016. Look for *The Francis Conspiracy* on Amazon.com.
Visit www.diogenesruiz.com.

John Shaver was born and raised in western Colorado. He and his wife are avid travelers, proud parents, and the owners of an impressive selection of souvenir glasses from The Hard Rock Café John currently lives in South Korea and is working on a paranormal thriller.

For more great books from today's leading Christian fiction authors, visit www.edgychristianfiction.com.